A HIGH TIDE MURDER

Also by Emily George:

Cannabis Café mystery series

A Half-Baked Murder

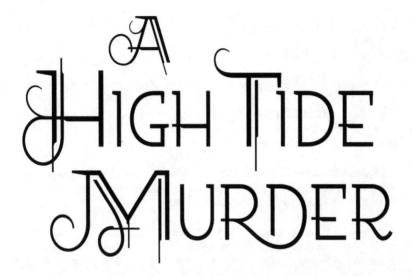

A HIGH TIDE MURDER

EMILY GEORGE

Kensington Publishing Corp.
www.kensingtonbooks.com

Content Warning: Suicide

KENSINGTON BOOKS are published by

Kensington Publishing Corp.
119 West 40th Street
New York, NY 10018

All Kensington titles, imprints, and distributed lines are available at special quantity discounts for bulk purchases for sales promotion, premiums, fund-raising, educational, or institutional use.

This book is a work of fiction. Names, characters, businesses, organizations, places, events, and incidents either are the product of the author's imagination or are used fictitiously. Any resemblance to actual persons, living or dead, events, or locales is entirely coincidental.

To the extent that the image or images on the cover of this book depict a person or persons, such person or persons are merely models, and are not intended to portray any character or characters featured in the book.

Special book excerpts or customized printings can also be created to fit specific needs. For details, write or phone the office of the Kensington Sales Manager: Kensington Publishing Corp., 119 West 40th Street, New York, NY 10018. Attn. Sales Department. Phone: 1-800-221-2647.

The K and Teapot logo is a trademark of Kensington Publishing Corp.

ISBN: 978-1-4967-4051-9 (ebook)

ISBN: 978-1-4967-4050-2

First Kensington Trade Paperback Printing: March 2024

10 9 8 7 6 5 4 3 2 1

Printed in the United States of America

To my husband, we are stronger together.

CHAPTER 1

I never thought I would say this, but I really relate to the scene in *The Little Mermaid* where Ariel washes up on the shore, with her shiny newfangled human legs, and is all, *How the heck did I end up here? This is rad.*

I get it. One day you're living your normal life, going to work, thinking your fiancé is the best thing since sliced brioche, and then one thing leads to another and . . . boom! You're single and running a weed café. Oh, and you get a write-up in the local paper because you solved a homicide and now people are calling you Murder She Baked.

But maybe that's just me.

Isn't life wild?

That question circled in my head all day long as I stood behind the counter of my very own business, Baked by Chloe, on the first day of opening. My baked goods had been selling out quicker than I could restock the shelves, and now I was serving my last macaron with weed-infused buttercream. With less than three minutes to closing, there were customers lingering at the tables my aunt and I had lovingly sourced from charity shops up and down the coast for the perfect Parisian café meets whimsical cottagecore aesthetic.

"Chloe, this has been marvelous." Local real estate agent extraordinaire, Diane, sat at the corner table with her twin sister, Lucinda. Both women had a shock of frizzy brown hair and a knack for colorful style, with Diane wearing a bold magenta pantsuit and Lucinda wearing a sunflower-yellow dress with gold buttons down the front. "I knew from the moment your aunt mentioned the cannabis café that it would be a hit. You don't seem to have stopped all day."

"I don't think we have," I admitted, pushing a few loose strands of my blond hair away from my sweaty forehead. It was one thing to be in the kitchen baking all shift, but quite another to juggle that *and* serving customers. "It's been . . ."

I couldn't help the giant grin that spread over my face, nor the surge of satisfaction that flowed through my veins when I thought about how opening day had gone. Customer after customer had praised my baking. Some were completely new to edibles while others had tried the more traditional style gummies or basic cookie bites. A few had even attempted baking with weed at home, but none had made anything as luxurious as my Valrhona chocolate and gold-leaf brownies, which were made with a specially sourced strain of cannabis that had a naturally fruity flavor. All the while, I'd been working to educate my customers about safe and responsible consumption, as well as helping to destigmatize cannabis use.

There was nothing like adding pastry and chocolate to make something mass appealing.

"It's been a wild ride," I finished with a laugh.

"And we couldn't be prouder." Aunt Dawn came up beside me and slipped an arm around my shoulders, her patchouli rose perfume dancing in my nostrils and her wild dark purple curls tickling my cheek. "Baked by Chloe has started with a bang."

"I, for one, am feeling *very* mellow," Lucinda chimed in with an easy smile. She was slouched back into her chair, her eyes drooping a little. "You know, this is exactly what I needed. With all the stress of moving house and my daughter going off to college and my husband suddenly losing his job . . . I don't think I've taken a moment to relax in weeks."

I pressed a hand to my chest. "That is a *lot* to deal with."

"She's barely been sleeping." Diane looked at her twin with a furrowed brow. "So I knew I needed to bring her here today, no matter how long we had to queue for a table."

"I'm glad the CBD chai latte helped." I clasped my hands together. "It's been my personal go-to in managing the stress of getting the café ready to open."

Lucinda had a dreamy look on her face. "My tension headache is *finally* gone."

This was exactly what I'd hoped to achieve with Baked by Chloe—helping people to take a moment out of the humdrum and stress of the everyday, and give them a joyful chillout experience. Food and flavor had always been my passion and my own personal escape. Now, I could share that with the people in Azalea Bay.

I was quickly drawn to another table of customers, who wanted a moment to tell me how much they enjoyed the café and my creations. Pastel-pink and pistachio-green crumbs littered one plate, the only remnants of the macarons that remained. A pink-and-white–striped bag was filled with the goodies they purchased to take home.

Over the next few minutes I bid everyone goodbye, and when the last customer left, I flicked the lock on the front door and sagged back against it. I'd officially survived day one of being a business owner. Looking over the space—taking in the soft pink wallpapered room and painted white furniture, the vintage chandelier and the Parisian-themed art, including a beautiful watercolor painting of the Arc de Triomphe—I almost couldn't believe I'd done it.

Well, *we* had done it.

Aunt Dawn was my business partner in crime and she had worked every bit as hard as I had to make today a success. And what a success it was!

A bubble of excitement rose up and I pressed my hand over my mouth to trap a giddy laugh inside. Mere months ago, I'd arrived back in my hometown with my tail between my legs. Heartbroken, humiliated and stressed, I'd abandoned my career as a pastry chef with dreams of Michelin stardom and left my cheating fiancé in Paris where he belonged. I'd come home to care for my beloved Grandma Rose after she'd received a devastating breast cancer diagnosis. In that moment, I truly thought my life was falling apart.

But sometimes things needed to break so that one could see which pieces were worth keeping.

Starting afresh wasn't easy—I'd given up so much. All the training I'd hoped would make me a world-famous head pastry chef at a fine-dining restaurant felt like it had gone to waste. The happily ever after I'd hoped for as a Disney-obsessed little girl was nothing but a sham. And a renowned food critic had shredded my work in a very public and humiliating way, calling it "amateurish" and "a bitter disappointment better suited to a supermarket bakery than a five-star restaurant." There were days where I wondered if I should get "failure" tattooed on my forehead. Not to mention, worrying about my grandmother twenty-four seven had taken its toll.

Yet here I was—still standing, still striving, still trying.

My troubles hadn't beaten me down. I'd pivoted. Taken a new path. Chosen to support my family by fighting for a new dream instead of clinging to old ones that didn't suit my life anymore.

And that made me feel pretty damn proud.

"Aunt Dawn?"

The shop front was empty and all the tables had been cleared of plates and cups. She was excited to get her hands dirty as much as I was, and we'd already put together a rotating schedule for the closing procedure. Tonight was her night. But I was too wound up and excited to go home just yet.

I glanced at the empty pastry cabinet which had been filled with all manner of cannabis-infused treats that morning—everything from handmade chocolate truffles, to my "everything but the kitchen sink" cookies, buttery cheese and herb scones, macarons in every color of the rainbow, and, of course, three different types of brownies.

Rule number one of weed baking: you can never have enough brownies.

All that remained in the cabinet were some crumb-scattered plates and my handwritten signs. By the cash register, there were several pamphlets about how to consume cannabis safely, a dosage suggestion guide, and information on effects and benefits that my customers might find useful, including the differences between THC and CBD. Not only was I passionate about creating the best treats possible, but I was also passionate about education.

I realized that Aunt Dawn hadn't responded when I'd called out and a flash of worry went through me. Recently, things had gotten a little tense in the usually calm and serene Californian seaside town of Azalea Bay. A murder had shocked us all and worse, my aunt had been the number one suspect! In the pursuit of trying to clear her name, I'd thrown myself into the path of the killer, who'd snuck into my shop and attacked me.

Murder investigation was not for the faint of heart or the soft of head, let me tell you. And, if I was being honest, there were moments now when I jumped extra high if I heard a noise in the shop while I was working.

I let out a breath. The killer was in custody and I had no need to worry. Azalea Bay was still the same charming little town I'd loved since I was a child, and the murder was thankfully behind us. It was probably one of those freak things that would only happen once in a lifetime in a place like this.

At least, that's what I hoped.

"Aunt Dawn?" I called out again and headed behind the counter so I could get into the back of the shop, where the kitchen and storeroom were housed. "Where are—"

"Surprise!"

I almost leaped out of my skin at the sound of more than half a dozen people crammed into the kitchen shouting at the top of their lungs. The cry was punctuated by popping—both of a champagne cork and some of those things that shoot curly colored streamers into the air. With my heart almost thumping its way out of my chest, I let out a breathless laugh and shook my head at the group standing in front of me: my closest family and friends.

Grandma Rose was there, wearing her signature pink from head to toe, including a silk scarf over her thinning hair. My best friend, Sabrina, was pouring champagne into plastic flutes lined up on my preparation table. My grandmother's closest friends, Ida, Luisa, and Betty, also known as my "other grand-mas," were standing there, all smiles. Plus my newfound friends from the local Dungeons and Dragons group—Sabrina's boyfriend, Cal Kallis; Ben Wong and Matt Wilson, the most adorable couple ever; Archie Schwartz, the moral compass of the group; and the pint-sized, pixie-faced Erica Simms—were all covered in curly streamers from the poppers they'd set off.

There was also one person standing to the side. My next-door neighbor, Jake. I wasn't sure quite how to classify him. Friend? Crush? Something more? We'd left things on uncertain terms recently, after he came clean about lying to me. But he'd also possibly saved Grandma Rose and me from a killer . . .

If I still regularly used Facebook, our relationship status would absolutely be "it's complicated."

"We wanted to get everyone together to celebrate your first

day," Grandma Rose said. She shuffled forward and wrapped her arms around me in a big hug, planting a pink lipstick kiss on my cheek. I was so happy I didn't bother to wipe it away. "We're so proud of you, my dear. Both of you."

"Let's toast." Aunt Dawn passed around the champagne flutes with Sabrina's help, and everyone raised their glasses into the air. "Wishing Baked by Chloe many years of happy baking. May our success grow like weeds."

"Hear, hear!" The group cheered and laughed.

"Very funny," I said, giggling before I took a sip of my drink. Being surrounded by all these wonderful and supportive people was truly more than I could have hoped for when I came home to Azalea Bay. "But in all seriousness, keep the puns coming. I love it."

"I don't think I've seen this town quite so excited about a new business in a *long* time." Betty, who seemed to exist in a permanent cloud of Chanel No. 5, came over for a hug. Her coiffed silver hair was perfectly in place, as always. "You had a line down the block!"

"I'd say it was almost down *two* blocks," Ida chimed in, her natural black hair and dark skin complemented by a vibrant red and yellow handknit shawl draped around her shoulders.

I'm sure some of the people who'd lined up were only there out of curiosity—after all, our little town wasn't exactly the kind of place people had expected to be home to a cannabis café. There were some people strongly opposed to the idea, in fact. People who thought that I was going to bring the town into disrepute or be a bad influence on our younger residents. I'd even had a few nasty emails through the contact form on my website once it went live, people anonymously yelling at me because they didn't agree with legalization and who thought I was nothing more than a lowlife drug dealer.

Those emails had stung, of course, and I'd taken great pleasure in hitting the delete button.

Their ire was misplaced. I'd seen firsthand how cannabis had helped my grandmother battle the nausea from her chemo treatments and sleeplessness from the stress of being ill. I'd developed relationships with local cannabis farmers who'd told me all about their own reasons for getting into the industry, including one woman who'd suffered severe seizures after a head injury sustained in a car accident and another who'd been able to support his family after needing to quit his office job to take care of his little boy who had a disability.

And if I could help people in this town to be less judgmental about those who used cannabis, whatever their reason, then I would be happy. As I always said, the way to a person's heart was through their stomach and I specialized in happy stomachs!

"You've done *such* a fabulous job with the decorating." Ben Wong took a sip of his champagne and smiled up at his boyfriend, Matt Wilson, who slipped an arm around his shoulders. "We were just saying the whole cozy Parisian vibe is chef's kiss. So classy."

"Too right," Matt said, his Aussie accent loud and clear. "You've done a bang-up job."

"Thanks, guys." I grinned. "We really took our time selecting every piece with care."

"Did we ever." Aunt Dawn snorted. "I swear I drove back and forth between the same three antique stores to decide on the hutch for all the gift items."

We'd come up with the idea to have a section of the store feature cannabis-themed gift products from local artisans, including some gorgeous hand-poured CBD candles, greeting cards on luxury cardstock featuring vintage botanical-style paintings of cannabis leaves and seeds, and even some stunning silver necklaces with a pendant fashioned to look like the molecular structure of THC. Chic, but subtle.

And, of course, I'd wanted the *perfect* place to display all these amazing items.

"It was worth the effort, right? That cabinet looks incredible." We'd sanded it back and painted it white, using a dry brush technique to allow some of the wood to still peek through. Then we'd changed out the handles on the drawers for cute porcelain vintage knobs and lined the shelves and drawers with pink and white paper.

"It looks really amazing, Chloe. I knew you'd create something special." Jake raised his glass and I flushed from the praise. I caught Grandma Rose nudging Aunt Dawn in the ribs and grinning.

"I sold at least four of the candles today *and* one necklace," I said proudly. "I think the gift items are going to be popular."

"Oh, did you say candles?" Sabrina's eyes widened. "Put me down for one of those. I love candles!"

She came up beside me and hooked her arm into mine, squeezing me as I answered questions and shared my plans and generally basked in the spotlight and love from those closest to me. The champagne tasted even sweeter knowing I was sharing it with people who had my back and who wanted me to succeed.

Despite the winding and rocky path that had led me to this moment, I couldn't imagine turning back now. I was at home in Azalea Bay and with every day that passed, I set more roots down, and created more bonds and friendships than I'd ever known possible.

It was probably the reason that I never saw disaster lurking right around the corner.

CHAPTER 2

One week later . . .

Remember that thing I said about my hometown being "peaceful" and "calm" and "serene" and all that jazz? Yeah. Well, there's one time of year where none of that applies and Azalea Bay essentially turns into a theme park, with business owners scrambling to capitalize on the influx of tourists and many locals getting the heck out of Dodge.

This is known as: surfing season.

Or, more specifically, the period of time when a pro surfing competition descended on our tiny town, packing the streets and every single café and restaurant with shell-necklace-wearing, shaggy-and-sun-bleached-haired folks who smelled like surfboard wax and ocean salt.

Love it or hate it—and there were definitely people on both sides—the Azalea Bay Pro Challenger Surf Competition was a mainstay for local businesses. It had gone through several names over the years, changing sponsors and branding, but for as long as I could remember, when it came to town our population swelled in size until it felt like a throbbing mass that was both terrifying and exhilarating. I never learned much about surfing myself, despite having lived with a glorious beach on my doorstep since I was a baby. But I enjoyed watching the people glide across the water like they were flying.

This year, however, I went from being a mere observer of the surf competition to being one of those local businesses hoping to fill seats and make myself a nice financial cushion that would last through the down season later in the year. So far, so good.

"That's six THC-infused macarons in total—two passion-fruit and chocolate, two strawberry and basil, and two lavender," I confirmed with my customer as I showed him the colorful lineup nestled in a pink-and-white–striped box. "Plus one cheese and herb cannabutter scone, and a slice of 'extra special' brownie."

"Right on." The guy in front of me nodded as he tapped his credit card to my point-of-sale unit. He had thick chestnut-brown hair that hung down past his shoulders and deeply tanned skin which featured several tattoos on his right arm, including an image of a sun setting over a large wave. "I never thought I'd find a place like this in such a small town."

I grinned. "You're here for the surfing competition, I take it."

"Yeah, me and my bro are hoping to make it to the Challenger level next year. I'm here supporting a friend who's competing."

"Make sure you tell your friends to pop in while they're here." I bagged his items and handed them to him over the counter. "And good luck to your friend."

"Thanks." The guy motioned with a friendly wave and headed toward the door.

As I glanced around the café, every table was full and yet I didn't recognize a single face. It was Tuesday, which normally would be one of our closed days (my "weekends" were going to be Monday and Tuesday), but we'd decided to open every day this week to capitalize on the extra business of people being in town for the surf competition *and* to get some momentum for Baked by Chloe in these early days. Being busy enough to turn people away would mean a more sustained interest over the summer.

Although Aunt Dawn *had* insisted that we hire a part-time server to help out, which I agreed was a good idea. Luckily, I knew just the right person.

"You should take your break soon," Erica said, as she walked out of the kitchen carrying a tray of fresh cheese and herb cannabutter scones that I'd stuck into the oven earlier. Her pixie-cut blond hair was slicked back away from her face, making her large brown eyes look even bigger than normal. "It's almost two and you haven't had lunch."

Hiring Erica Simms was a no-brainer. She had been looking for work after being fired from her previous job when a vengeful colleague falsely accused her of theft. Which worked out perfectly for me! Erica was brilliant with customers and was the kind of person who always went above and beyond. She was part of the Dungeons and Dragons group, and we'd become fast friends. Bringing her on to support Aunt Dawn and me had seemed like a natural progression.

"You're right. My stomach has been growling for the last forty-five minutes," I admitted. "I might duck out and grab a sandwich from Casa Italiano's."

Really, I could easily make something for myself out in the kitchen. But I'd been baking up a storm from the wee hours this morning and I was starting to feel like a battery about to run out of charge. I needed fuel, stat.

"I grabbed some paninis on the way in," Erica replied with a smile. "There's a prosciutto and brie one with arugula that's still wrapped up. I thought you might like that flavor."

My shoulders sagged in relief. "You're a godsend."

"I stuck a few bottles of water into the fridge as well, so you can grab one of those if you need it." She smiled. "Gotta stay hydrated in this weather!"

I wanted to hug her, but instead I headed right out the back, suddenly ravenous now that I'd stopped. I grabbed the sandwich and a bottle of water, and headed outside into the balmy, early-summer air. My café wasn't on the main strip—the rent of *those* spots was a little too steep for my budget—but we were situated right off the main street, and still got loads of foot traffic. Nearby was a small patch of green space, with a few benches dotted around the base of a big cypress tree.

I dropped down onto one of the empty benches and sucked in a whiff of tangy ocean air mixed with the fresh, slightly resinous and sweetly balsamic scent of the many cypress trees around our town. Lord, how I'd missed that smell when I lived in Paris for five years. As great as it had been living in such a cool city—everything they say about Paris is true, the people *are* all effortlessly stylish and the food *is* amazing—there was nothing like the comforting smell of home.

Feeling content, I bit into my panini and chewed. The bread had a great texture, and the prosciutto was perfectly salty and chewy, which paired excellently with the rich, creamy cheese and slightly bitter taste of fresh arugula. As I sat there, enjoying the lunch Erica had kindly bought me, the sun beat down on the top of my head, melting my bones and softening my muscles. If I wasn't careful, I would drift off for a nap. Given that I'd taken a few months off work when I returned to America while setting up the business, the super-early starts would take some getting used to.

I'd forgotten how hard it was getting up well before dawn.

"Chloe!"

My head snapped up at the sound of my name. Walking toward me were Matt and another man, who looked like he was in his early twenties. They both waved and I returned the gesture, sitting up a little straighter as they approached.

"G'day." Matt grinned. "You having a lunch break?"

"Sure am." I took another bite of my panini. "Want to join?"

"Love to. This is my brother, Ethan." Matt gestured to the younger guy, whose grin mirrored his own.

"I can see the resemblance." I shuffled along the bench to make space for them and they both sat. "Nice to meet you."

"You too," Ethan replied.

Matt had told me previously that he and his brother had different dads and were about ten years apart in age, but the half brothers still shared a number of traits. Both were tall and lanky, with sandy hair and freckles scattered across their noses, and had stunning green eyes. While Matt's features were a little sharper, like his square jaw and aquiline nose for example, Ethan had slightly softer features and a rounder face. Both men, however, had impish smiles and I expected they probably had well-matched cheeky senses of humor.

"You're a surfer, right? Matt told me you're quite the pro."

"On my way to being one." Ethan nodded. "The Qualifying Series is a really big deal, because that's how they determine who makes it up to the Challenger Series, which is the step before you make it to the Championship Tour."

"Aka, the Kelly Slater level," Matt quipped.

"Don't even joke about comparing any of us to the king," Ethan replied. "I'm not realistically in the running for one of the top spots this year, I don't think. There are a couple guys really duking it out. But it's great experience and it should put me in good shape to attack next year when I've got another year under my belt."

I listened to Ethan speak with curiosity. He had quite an unusual accent, as though it was a mix of Australian and American sounds. Some soft R's, while others were hard. A little bit of an upward lilt at the end of his sentences.

"Doesn't sound like me, does he?" Matt asked, as if reading my mind.

"Not quite."

"I moved to America with my dad when I was ten," Ethan explained. "But I would go home and spend summers with my mother in Australia, so my accent is a weird mash-up. Best of both worlds, I say."

"Though he leans on the Aussie accent when he wants to pick up girls." Matt rolled his eyes affectionately.

"Works like a charm." Ethan winked.

I laughed. "I'll bet."

I could see Ethan being *very* popular with the young surfer girls who crowded our shores in summertime. He was handsome and athletic, and seemed to have a great personality. His family was likely delightful too, if Matt was a good representation.

"Ethan's actually one of the reasons I ended up moving over to this side of the world," Matt said, planting a hand on his brother's shoulder. "It was hard being away from him all those years while I stayed in Australia after he moved. So I packed up when I was twenty-five and came over here."

"It was good for your career, too," Ethan pointed out. "Not as much video game work in Australia."

"True." Matt nodded. He was a music composer for a video game company. Sometimes it meant making dark and moody music to heighten the player's tension for a survival horror game, and other times it was about creating a sense of victory for a battle won or a treasure found. "And I met Ben. So it was definitely worth it."

"Aww!" I pressed a hand to my chest while it was Ethan's turn to roll his eyes.

"You guys are so in love it's sickening," he said with a laugh.

"When you find the right someone, you'll be just the same."

Matt ruffled Ethan's hair in a way I suspected he'd been doing for many years. "Trust me."

"As much as I would love to stay and keep chatting, I have to get back to work," I said, as I popped the last bit of panini into my mouth and wadded up the paper wrapping in my fist. "Business calls."

Ethan glanced down at my uniform top, which had the Baked by Chloe logo embroidered at my chest. "Oh, you run the weed café! That's so cool. Matt was telling me all about it. My roommate—he's also in the surf competition—said we should stop by."

"I hope to see you both soon." I stood and brushed the crumbs from my pants. "I know Matt's been super excited that you were coming to town. He's been talking about it for weeks."

"What are you up to this evening?" Matt asked. "A few of us were going to head down to the water and watch the guys practice at sunset. Ben and I are going to have everyone back to ours for drinks and food after. You should come."

I was already cringing at the thought of being out late with such an early start ahead of me. But I didn't have to stay out all night. I could meet everyone at the beach and then head home when they went off to grab food. I was business-minded and wanted to succeed, of course, but I also wanted to have a life and spend time with my friends.

Wasn't that the eternal push-pull of the self-employed?

"I'd love to join for a bit," I said, nodding and feeling good about my decision to find balance in my life. "I'll see you all down there after I close up shop."

We ended up closing Baked by Chloe ten minutes early because we, once again, had completely run out of stock. Since the business was new it had been hard to figure out exactly how much to make and I was trying to avoid excess wastage.

But the customers were ravenous. While I knew this was partly due to the influx of tourists for the surf competition, I hoped the demand would continue after they all cleared out in a week or so.

Tomorrow, however, I would bake a little more than I had today.

Closing early meant I had a pinch of extra time to head home, shower the smell of cannabutter—butter infused with cannabis flowers—from my skin, and change into something cuter than my chef-standard uniform. I threw on a red sundress with a tie at the back and a pair of flip-flops. The weather had warmed up significantly in the last week and even though it was getting later in the evening, I didn't need any kind of outer layer.

After drying off my hair—which was back to a light golden-blond shade thanks to the strong Californian sun—I slicked on some lip gloss and tucked my wallet and phone into a straw bag. Comfy but cute, that was my general approach to fashion. I checked my appearance once more in the full-length mirror and, deciding I didn't look quite as bedraggled as I felt, I headed downstairs to say goodbye to Grandma Rose *and* pick up my furry best friend, Antonio.

"I'm heading to the beach to watch the surfers," I announced as I came down the stairs and into the lounge room.

Grandma Rose sat on the couch, not wearing the silk headscarf that had been ever present in recent weeks. Her fluffy silver hair was considerably thinner than it had been before her chemo treatment, and her scalp showed through in several spots. I knew she was self-conscious about it—hence the recent affinity for scarves—but I still thought she was the most beautiful grandma in all the world. She wore fluffy slippers the color of cotton candy on her feet and had a tiny dog snuggled up on her lap, his small body folded into a kidney bean shape and his buggy little eyes closed in contentment.

Antonio was a three-year-old Chihuahua we'd recently adopted. He was mostly black, though part of his chest, underbelly and three of his four paws were white, making it look like he'd lost a sock. His tail curved into an adorable question mark shape, and he had the sweetest set of satellite dish ears that trembled when he was excited. Tan patches ringed his snout and circled the black markings around his eyes, giving the distinct impression he had a bandit mask on.

And yes, he was totally named after Antonio Banderas for his role playing Zorro, the charming, masked vigilante.

"Did you hear that, Antonio?" Grandma Rose said, putting her book down and running her hand along the little dog's back. "Chloe is going to take you for a . . ."

She paused right before the W word and Antonio's head snapped up in anticipation.

"Walk," she finished.

The word was barely out of her mouth before the dog took a flying leap right off her lap and landed soundlessly on the carpet, his little tail wagging back and forth so hard it created a blur behind him. He did an excited little dance—which we called "tippy taps"—while looking up at me with big, luminous brown eyes.

"Come here, little fella." I bent down and he raced toward me. Scooping him up, I walked to the wall by the front door where we'd made a hanging area for his walking gear—which included a leash, harness and a little jacket for days when there was a chill in the air. Today, however, he wouldn't be needing the extra layer. "Yes, I know you're excited."

"Who's heading down to the beach?" Grandma Rose asked as she pushed herself off the couch. It was clear she had no plans to leave the house again today, since she'd already changed into a pair of pajamas with a silky pink robe.

"Sabrina and Cal will be there," I said, placing Antonio on the ground and slipping the harness over his head. I slid it into place and gently eased his paws through the shoulder openings. "Ben and Matt, too. Matt's younger brother is one of the competitors this year, which is exciting. I've never had someone to cheer for before. Did you want to head down one day on the weekend and watch a bit?"

"Actually, Lawrence is taking me to dinner on Saturday. We've got a table at Foam."

I looked up, my hand still hooked into Antonio's harness to keep him still. "Fancy."

Foam was the closest thing Azalea Bay had to a fine dining restaurant. They had a great wine menu, super fresh seafood and incredible views of the ocean from their al fresco dining section. It was a favorite spot for locals celebrating something special—wedding anniversaries, milestone birthdays, and other such occasions.

Put it this way, Foam was *not* somewhere people went for a casual meal.

"Lawrence has good taste," Grandma Rose said, flushing.

Lawrence St. James was the older brother of one of my grandmother's dearest friends and had been my grandmother's certified crush for some time now. My grandfather—bless his soul—passed away almost twenty years ago, and Grandma Rose had remained single ever since. But lately she and Lawrence had been spending more time together.

And now, a fancy dinner at Foam.

"If he wants to spend time with you, then I would say he has *impeccable* taste," I replied, clipping Antonio's leash into the hook on his harness, and standing.

"It's not a date," she said sternly, as though anticipating that I would tease her about it.

She was right.

"*Sure* it isn't," I replied with a wink. "You're going to wear boring old jeans and a ratty T-shirt, right? No makeup or perfume?"

"Oh hush. Now go on before I chase you out with a broom," she muttered. But then something flashed across her face. "Is Jake going to be at the beach tonight?"

"How is it okay for you to talk about my love life when I can't ask about yours?" I quickly realized my error. "Not that Jake is part of my love life. Not at all."

She looked amused. "Must be why you're wearing boring old jeans and a ratty T-shirt, then, instead of a dress."

I looked down at my cute outfit. "I wore this for me."

"*Sure* you did," she said, mimicking me.

I rolled my eyes, but I couldn't help but allow myself an amused smile. My grandmother loved to tease me and there was nothing that made me happier than seeing the mischievous twinkle in her eye. For a while when I'd first come home, I felt like that twinkle had disappeared. Between the stress of her cancer treatments and Aunt Dawn being questioned for murder, life had felt pretty darn serious.

I would put up with her teasing if it meant things were getting back to normal. In fact, I would relish it.

"Jake isn't going," I clarified, opening up my straw bag and shoving in a foldable water bowl so I could give Antonio a drink if he got thirsty later.

"Are you still mad at him?" she asked.

Jake and I had gotten off to *such* a good start. He was so kind and charming I'd been ready to admit that maybe happily ever afters *weren't* a sham meant to sell princess costumes to little girls. Only it turned out that Jake had committed the one cardinal sin in my book: he'd lied to me. Given I'd fled Paris after finding out my fiancé had cheated on me and gotten a junior kitchen hand pregnant, I had a *thing* about lying.

And by thing, I meant that I hated it with the fire of a thousand suns.

Jake had told me his brother had done a stint in a juvenile detention center after falling in with a bad crowd and getting temporarily blamed for something he didn't do. In reality, *Jake* was the one who'd been sent to juvie. He didn't even have a brother. He'd been afraid the truth would pop the bubble of attraction we had and the budding *something* between us. Maybe he was right. But I hated being lied to more than anything.

In Jake's defense, however, he'd come clean of his own accord. That had to count for something, right?

"I understand why he did it. But I'm taking things slow when it comes to relationships. No point rushing things, right?"

I could see my grandmother trying not to wrinkle her nose. She thought "taking it slow" was a risk for me, at twenty-eight. We'd had numerous conversations about it since I'd been back home, and it was hard to make her see that being single in your late twenties was hardly something to worry about.

As far as I was concerned, I still had my whole life ahead of me.

"How are *you* feeling, anyway?" I asked.

"Pretty good. But we'll see how I go when the next cycle starts."

Grandma Rose's chemotherapy was being done in cycles, which consisted of a small number of infusions followed by a rest period to give her body time to recover.

"My nails have gotten quite brittle," she continued, looking down at one hand where her pointer fingernail was broken, making it much shorter than the others. Grandma Rose had always had beautiful nails and loved having them painted. "I might have to get a fake one put on because I feel silly with one short nail and nine long ones."

"Why don't we have a girls' day at the salon when I have a day off?" I suggested. "We could get our nails done and go for lunch."

"I would love that." Her face lit up. "I'm so glad you enjoy spending time with your old gran, even though you're all grown up now."

"I'll always be your granddaughter, no matter how old I get." I kissed her on the cheek. "I'll book us in."

Antonio sniffed around the floor, impatient for us to get going. But his attention was momentarily captured by a toy sitting by the front door. It was a stuffed hamburger that was bigger than his head, but he snatched it up in his mouth and tugged on his leash, his question mark tail pointed up in the air.

"Nope, that stays at home." I coaxed the toy out of his mouth. "We don't want you getting sand all over it."

I opened the front door, waving as Grandma Rose blew me a kiss. My grandmother was my favorite person in the whole wide world, and it was so good to be home and spending more time with her.

Although I could do without her sassing me over my pseudo love life.

In fact, I'd been hoping to avoid thinking about Jake all together. But then who did I see the second I walked down the driveway? The very man in question, of course.

"Chloe, hi." He was walking toward his house, which was situated right next to my grandmother's. As he got closer, I could see the reddish gleam in his thick brown hair, the warmth of which always looked more pronounced later in the day. He was tall and muscular from the work he did restoring his grandfather's vintage Chevy Camaro, and he wore a pair of light blue denim jeans, a gray T-shirt and a pair of Converse sneakers.

"Hey." I waved my hand in greeting and tried not to look affected.

"What a cute little guy." Jake crouched down and reached a hand out to Antonio, whose tail wagged energetically. The dog pressed the top of his head into Jake's palm, ready and willing to receive all the attention he could get. The dog lived for being the center of attention. "He must barely weigh more than a bag of sugar."

"I have bags of sugar that would crush him." I looked down at the dog indulgently. "But don't be fooled, he's got enough fight in him for a dog five times his size. Just ask the teddy bear I bought him last week."

Poor old Mr. Bear hadn't even lasted twenty-four hours before his eyes were plucked off and the stuffing was pulled out through his nose. It was a gruesome end to Mr. Bear's life.

Jake gave Antonio a good scratch behind the ear and then stood, his gaze meeting mine. His green-flecked hazel eyes looked extra warm, like rich maple syrup, in the early evening light. It was quite unfair that I found him *so* attractive. Honestly, when I'd returned home to Azalea Bay, romance had been the last thing on my mind.

Maybe it should stay that way . . . like until the year 2075.

"So, uh . . ." He raked a hand through his hair. "I was wondering if you wanted to grab a coffee sometime. Or would that feel too much like work, being in a café? I wanted to ask you to dinner, but I thought maybe that was a step too far, you know? Well, I guess that might feel like work, too, since you used to work in a restaurant."

He was babbling, and it was adorable.

Jake swore under his breath. "You'd think at this age I'd have a little more game than this."

"I'm not a fan of game," I replied with a smile.

"Me, either," he admitted.

An awkward silence settled and I bit down on my lip. Antonio's head swung between us like he was watching a tennis match, only in this game the volleys were us beating around the bush and neither one of us could seem to hit an ace.

If you hate game so much, then why don't you extend an olive branch, huh? Even if romance isn't on the table yet, you can still be friends.

Yet. I wasn't sure how I felt about that word.

"I'm going to the beach on Saturday after work to watch the surf competition," I said, biting .the bullet and speaking up first. "Maybe we could grab an ice cream and watch the action together?"

"That sounds great." His shoulders dropped a little in relief. For a moment, he looked like he was about to open his mouth to say something serious, like to talk about what had happened recently.

But I wasn't quite ready for that.

"I have to get going," I said briskly. "I'll see you around."

"See you around, Chloe." He nodded and stepped out of my way so I could walk Antonio down the street.

I felt Jake's eyes on my back as I walked and a tingle of excitement started low in my belly. I might not be ready to leap into another relationship, but ice cream on the beach with a cute guy sounded pretty darn good to me.

If only I'd known what shocking news the next twenty-four hours would bring.

CHAPTER 3

One of the things I loved most about my hometown was the view of the ocean from the high points of town, especially late in the day. As I walked over a gently cresting hill, the view revealed itself in all its picture postcard glory.

The sky was a gradient of bright azure blue through to a rich, red-toned gold where the sun was dipping down, the fat orb descending for another night. Pink clouds streaked the sky like splashes of watercolor paint and the ocean was a vibrant jewel blue with a hint of green. Silver foam capped the arcing waves. At least a dozen surfers dotted on the water, arms outstretched and boards gliding as they balanced with ease.

Clusters of people watched the surfing activity while kids played at the shoreline, scattering seagulls into the air, and music floated from a speaker somewhere. Antonio and I headed along the boardwalk. The little dog trotted ahead of me, happy to be out in the fresh, tangy air. He loved the beach. Scanning as we walked, I eventually spotted our friends and we took the nearest set of stairs down to the beach. Grains of sand were dispersed along the wooden slatted steps, and when we got to the bottom, I removed my flip-flops and let the sand bunch beneath my toes.

Ahead, Matt's tall figure stood sentinel at the edge of the water, his pants rolled up to just below his knees. Beside him was Ben, as well as Sabrina, Cal and a few other folks I didn't immediately recognize. The scent of cypress trees mingled with sweet vanilla ice cream and remnants of coconut sunscreen applied through the day, all sharpened by the salty ocean air. I filled my lungs and practically floated down the sand.

This is home, I thought to myself. *The best place in the world.*

But as I got to the water's edge, I noticed that not all was well. What I hadn't noticed from the boardwalk was the crackling tension—it was thicker than overworked cupcake batter. The people I hadn't recognized appeared to be young surfers and I spotted Ethan standing between two men around his age. His hands were up, as if ready to stop a fight. All three were shirtless, with water dotting their skin, and wearing board shorts.

"Guys, calm down," Ethan pleaded. His curly blond hair rustled in the wind and a few strands blew across his green eyes. He huffed them clear with a sharp breath. "We're all here trying to achieve the same thing."

"I'm not sure that we are." The man to Ethan's right had deeply tanned olive skin, thick shoulder-length black hair that was shampoo commercial–worthy, wide-set dark brown eyes and an attractive face. He was shorter in stature.

"Makani, stop—"

"I think your *mate* here has some ulterior motives."

The way he leaned on the word "mate" seemed to mock Ethan's unusual accent. Either that, or he was implying that Ethan and the other guy weren't really friends. It was hard to tell.

"Like you're just here for the waves and nothing else? Have they nominated you for sainthood yet?" The other surfer had the opposite appearance to Makani—rather than being compact and sculpted, he was bean-pole tall and rail thin, with corded muscles in his arms, long straggly red hair, fair skin and freckles.

"Cut it out, Aaron." Ethan shot the redheaded guy a look.

"I'm not here to screw up anyone's life, that's for damn sure." Makani almost spat the words out. "So how about you get out of my face?"

"How about *you* get out of *my* face, kook."

Makani lunged past Ethan, hands grabbing out for the guy who'd insulted him by calling him a kook—whatever the heck that meant. Matt stepped in and grabbed Aaron by the shoulder, yanking him away from the fight.

"Enough," he bellowed, in a more commanding voice than I'd ever heard him use before. "This isn't the place for a fight. There are children here."

Aaron brushed Matt's hands away, glaring at him. "Stay out of it. This is old business."

Matt looked at the young men and rolled his eyes. I'd never ever seen him get annoyed over *anything* before. He was as chill as a Popsicle most of the time. But now . . .

"Old business? You only became bloody old enough to drink a year ago and you think you have "old" business? Give me a break." Matt tossed his hands in the air. "You've got so much ahead of you, so many great opportunities, and you're wasting the experience fighting about petty crap."

"Him dumping my sister publicly is not petty crap," Makani retorted. Ethan had an arm out, stopping him from coming forward. "Him borrowing money and not paying people back isn't petty crap, either. He's happy to step on anyone to get what he wants, doesn't matter who he hurts."

"And you're so perfect, aren't you?" Aaron spat. "Doing your yoga at six a.m. for the 'gram every day and putting your face all over TikTok, because you think that's what this sport is about."

"You wouldn't know discipline if it smacked you in the face. And I use social media to raise my profile because I'm a professional athlete, unlike you." Makani glared, hatred radiating from him like a shimmer in the air. "Probably why I've got more sponsorships than you and mine actually stick around."

For a moment, I was sure Aaron was going to throw a punch, but then he swore under his breath and stalked off, stopping only to snatch a surfboard from the ground. Then he headed back up the beach toward the boardwalk. I noticed a crowd had gathered, but since it became clear that a fight wasn't going to break out after all, people began to disperse. This included Makani, who'd been joined by a friend, and the two of them headed off away from the water, in the opposite direction from Aaron.

"Too much testosterone for me," Sabrina said under her breath as she came up beside me and looped her arm through mine. "Thank goodness Matt and Ethan have their heads screwed on properly. I thought those guys were about to come to blows."

Cal, who was standing on the other side of Sabrina, looked at us and shook his head. "This is why I never got into sports. Can't stomach the competitiveness."

I had to laugh. Cal was well over six feet and built like he could snap a tree in half with his bare hands, and yet he had the gentle, happy and affectionate nature of a puppy. I could never picture him fighting with anyone and I knew Sabrina really appreciated his happy-go-lucky personality. They were a good fit, like that—she inspired him and he brought her down to earth when stress got the better of her.

Ethan looked up at Matt, eyes brimming with worry. Something told me this wasn't the first time he'd gotten stuck playing peacemaker between the other two men. "I thought they'd patched things up last time."

"It's okay, mate. It's not your job to babysit them," Matt said, shaking his head. "They'll grow up eventually."

Ben reached for Matt's hand and gave it a squeeze, silently showing his support. Since the argument was over, people turned their attention back to the waves, where several surfers remained out on the water.

"Come on, everyone," Matt said, his smile looking a little forced. "Let's all get comfy and settle in for a show, eh?"

I was always inspired by watching people execute skills I would never personally possess. Like the time I'd gone to the ballet in Paris. My ex had taken me for a romantic night out and I'd sat there, wearing a fancy dress, absolutely mesmerized by the dancers' stunning display of physicality and grace. The way they balanced on their toes and held their body in beautiful shapes awed me, and I felt something similar watching the surfers.

I couldn't even stand in tree pose during yoga class without wobbling more than a pile of Jell-O, yet these folks balanced on their boards so steadily the ocean may as well have been solid ground. It almost looked as if they were suspended by invisible strings. There was something so serene about it, and yet so powerful and magnetic.

"Wow," I breathed, leaning back on the beach towel I was sharing with Sabrina. Antonio was sitting next to me and I stroked one of his dark, velvety ears. "Don't they look magnificent?"

"Right?" She glanced at me, a smirk making her cheekbones pop out as the wind ruffled her dark, curly hair. She might have hated her hair ever since we were kids, but I'd always envied her curls, especially when compared with my fine—read, limp—ponytail. "You'd think we might have picked up some kind of ocean-related skills living here our whole lives."

I snorted. "Remember that time I panicked because I thought

a shark was in the water and it turned out that someone had just lost their black T-shirt."

"It made a deceptive shadow," she said supportively, patting my leg. "And it wasn't too long after that shark attack. We were all a little jumpy."

Our school had brought a marine expert in to educate us about sharks after that poor person had died, since we all had it in our little heads that if we so much as dipped a toe into the ocean that we would be immediately snapped up by Jaws. The teaching staff had wanted to strike a balance between encouraging children to be safe at the beach without stigmatizing the large animals that cruised the blue depths, since they had already been villainized so much by the media.

One way they had done this was a perhaps ill-advised activity called "what is more likely to kill you than a shark?" The list included such things as vending machines, jellyfish, falling coconuts, roller coasters and lightning. Unfortunately, the next time Azalea Bay had a thunderstorm the school received a record number of complaints from the parents whose kids thought that they were going to be zapped to death.

But the funny little tidbits of information had stayed with me, along with a strange concern about being conked on the head with a coconut.

Ethan rode a wave down to the shore and hopped nimbly off his board, before bending down to scoop it up under one arm as he jogged up the sand. His curly blond hair was wet, and he flicked it back with a shake of his head, looking every bit the surfing heartthrob. A group of girls huddled together and squealed as he jogged on by. They were all dressed in skimpy bikini tops and denim shorts cut high enough to have their butt cheeks hanging out. One young woman stood apart from the group, long black hair trailing down her back as she looked out over the water, almost melancholy. She had a small dolphin tattooed onto her ankle, around which a dainty silver anklet hung, catching the dying light.

It was getting darker now, with only a band of fiery orange left on the horizon. Overhead, the sky was rapidly turning inky and stars had begun to peek out and wink at us. We'd all been lounging around and snacking on fruit and chips and other light food. But I was getting hungry for something more substantial. No wonder, I thought as I checked my phone, it was a hair before eight thirty p.m.

"Who's coming back to ours for drinks and food?" Ben asked. He was sitting on a towel with Matt, dressed in his usual preppy attire of shorts with a crease pressed into the front, boat shoes and a pink polo top. His black hair was neatly styled, and he didn't appear to have a grain of sand on him. How did he do that? "We're going to throw a few shrimp on the barbie."

Matt rolled his eyes. "They're prawns. Not shrimp."

"We've also got burgers, salads and beers *and* I picked up a few delightful treats from the hottest new business in town: Baked by Chloe!" Ben looked at me and winked. "Tell me I'm not the only one who's desperate to try out her fancy-pants weed brownie with the gold leaf on it."

"Oh, I love brownies." Archie grinned. He was wearing his signature wire-rimmed glasses that made his eyes look owlish. "And Elena's mom and dad have taken the kids this week, so I have zero responsibilities."

"Hold up, I don't think I've ever seen Archie the Family Man without responsibilities," Cal teased.

"I don't think I have, either." Archie jabbed at his glasses, looking positively giddy.

"You're coming, right?" Ben looked at me, smiling. Ever since I'd joined the Dungeons and Dragons group since returning home, all the members had made me feel incredibly welcome. They treated me like I'd been part of the group all along and I never had to fish for an invite.

"It's an early start for work tomorrow," I said, shaking my head. Antonio looked at me imploringly, like he really wanted to go to the party. *Please, Mom, can we go?* "I have to be in the kitchen at the butt crack of dawn."

Sabrina snorted at my joke. "Sounds shitty."

"Oh, come on." Ben reached over and grabbed my arm, giving me a playful little shake. "Just one drink. Doesn't even have to be an adult beverage! Just a soda. One teensy little soda never hurt anyone, right?"

"I really can't," I said, but already my resolve was breaking down. Antonio wagged his tail and did his little tippy-tap dance as if he knew I was on the verge of caving.

Would it be *so* bad to be tired in the morning? I could stay for one drink, right? I wasn't usually the kind of person to be swayed by a case of FOMO (in reality, my introverted self was more of a JOMO kind of gal—Joy of Missing Out). But I was becoming very attached to my new group of friends and they had been so incredibly supportive of my business.

Ben turned his puppy dog eyes on me, as if mirroring Antonio. "Pretty please."

I felt my adult sensibilities snap like a rubber band pulled too tight.

"Fine," I said with a laugh. "One non-adult beverage. But that's it. I can't be cranky for my customers tomorrow."

"We won't let you turn into a pumpkin, I promise," Matt said with a smile.

We gathered the towels and bags, and headed toward the beach's parking area. There was a line for the showers, with people washing the sand and saltwater from their bodies, and the parking lot itself was still pretty full, despite the later hour. There were several vans and SUVs with surfboard racks clogging the space, and people standing around talking, some of them with boards still tucked under their arms. I thought I heard some people gossiping about the argument between Aaron and Makani.

. . . they've always fought like cat and dog . . .

. . . he's a troublemaker, that one . . .

. . . it's over a girl. It's always *over a girl . . .*

"I've got to take Ethan back to his hotel room so he can get some proper clothes and dump his surf gear," Matt said. "Ben, why don't you go on ahead and get everything started?"

"You can come in our car, Ben," Sabrina offered. "We're already taking Archie, though. So it might be too squishy in the back with Chloe and Antonio as well."

"You can ride with us if you don't mind a little detour," Matt said, looking at me. "That way Ben and the others can get the food started. Dogs are totally welcome, too."

"Sure," I replied with a nod. "That sounds great."

"You can see my fancy accommodation," Ethan offered with a wink.

Matt, Ethan, Antonio and I bundled into Matt's car, with Ethan insisting I sit in the front. He was just like his older brother—charming, friendly, kind, a bit of a joker. The three of us were almost crying with laughter as Ethan told a story about a time he had a smack-talk battle with some crusty old surfer who loved trading insults on the waves.

We drove to the edge of town, where a small, old hotel of about four or five stories sat high up on a hill with a great view of the beach. But now I understood why he winked after using the word "fancy" to describe it. The hotel was run-down, with discoloration on the façade and several of the lights not working in the glowing roadside sign. So, instead of saying OCEAN VIEW HOTEL it said OCEAN VIEW HO_E_, which gave it an entirely different meaning.

"You *have* to come inside," Ethan said, as Matt pulled the car into one of the guest spots. A sign indicated that it was a pet-friendly hotel. "Seriously, if you think the outside looks bad, just *wait* until you see inside."

I laughed. "I'm game."

The three of us plus Antonio got out of the car and trooped

into the hotel foyer. I carried my furry little friend and he swung his head this way and that, excited to see the world at such a high altitude.

Ethan wasn't wrong. This place was . . . well, it looked like it hadn't been updated since some time in the mid-'70s. There was a peach shag rug underneath a cluster of chairs covered in a hideous floral velvet featuring fifty shades of poop brown which had gone bald in the high-use areas. Behind the front desk, a woman was cracking gum so loudly the pops echoed through the empty foyer. The walls were a strange mix of beige paint, dark wood paneling and a faux stone. The theme also seemed a bit confused, containing elements of vintage hunting lodges (think creepy wall-hung taxidermy), the beach (strands of seashells making a fringe to cover the door behind the reception desk) and sporty stripes (painted along the wall in blue, yellow and acid green).

"I am so confused right now." My mouth hung open as we walked toward the elevator.

"It's like the world's ugliest time capsule," Matt joked.

"The room is even better. Or would that be worse?" Ethan cringed. "The bedspread is . . . well, I won't ruin the surprise for you. Oh, and we should take the stairs. The elevator is a little dicey and we're only one floor up."

We followed him to the stairwell and began making our way up single file. I continued to carry Antonio, because his tiny legs would have struggled with the high concrete steps. Maybe I needed to think about getting one of those little carrier things people used for babies. What were they called? A BabyBjörn? Or maybe I could find a backpack with a little cutout for his head.

"Why are you even staying at this dump?" Matt asked as our footsteps echoed in the stairwell. "I would have loaned you some cash if you needed it. Or you could have crashed with Ben and me."

"It's Aaron," Ethan said with a sigh. "We've roomed together since we were grommets."

"Grommets?" I wrinkled my nose in confusion.

"Young surfers," Matt clarified.

"Aaron's been having money trouble for a while but when I offered to pay so we could stay in a better place, he got upset. Said he didn't want to take advantage of me after I'd stuck with him through all the drama." Ethan huffed. "But this was the best he could afford, even going halves."

"And my brother is too much of a kind soul to tell his friend to find a new roommate," Matt added, although I couldn't tell from the tone of his voice whether he thought that was a positive or a negative.

"Aaron's a good guy. He's made a few bad decisions here and there, but I know he'll get back on his feet. He's got big plans for the future and if he can keep on the straight and narrow, the sponsors will come back."

We reached the landing and Ethan pushed the door open, revealing a hallway that was just as gloriously ugly as the foyer. More peach carpet, more stripes on the wall, and more hunting-lodge-inspired wall hangings.

"Ocean View Hoe, indeed," I said and beside me, Matt snorted.

"I could be mad at Aaron for making me stay in such a shithole, but honestly the story makes it totally worth it," Ethan said, grinning. "I put a video up on my TikTok and people loved it."

He unlocked the door to his hotel room with an old-fashioned key, rather than one of the more common electric keycards, and the door swung open. "Get a load of . . ."

As Ethan's voice died down, his words leaving an eerie trail in the air, I peered past him into the room. There, sprawled out on the most hideous quilt I'd ever seen, was the sleeping form of his roommate, Aaron. Weird. It was early and the blinds weren't closed.

"Aaron?" Ethan stepped into the room, and Matt and I hovered at the threshold.

Aaron lay face down on the bed closest to the balcony door, which was ajar. His red hair was scattered messily and he wore a black T-shirt and jeans, clearly having changed at some point. The room was in a bit of disarray and smelled like man—sweat, cologne, dirty socks, several of which I could see discarded on the floor. On the bedside table there were an array of random items—a book with a cracked spine, sunscreen, an empty bottle of grapefruit juice, and an open packet of salt-and-vinegar chips. An open suitcase sat on the floor, clothes spilling out of it, and two drawers from the little table between the beds hung open.

Aaron was on top of the covers and he still hadn't moved. That's when I noticed something strange: he had a note in his hand. And there was an orange pill bottle on the floor, empty, the lid sitting face up a few inches away.

"Oh my god." I clamped a hand on my mouth as it dawned on me that Aaron wasn't taking a nap.

He was dead.

CHAPTER 4

How was I in this position again?

Matt, Ethan and I all sat in an unoccupied hotel room. Antonio was curled up on my lap fast asleep and totally oblivious to what was going on around him. This room only had one bed, a queen-size, and we were lined up in front of Detective Alvarez and Chief Gladwell. I could confirm the bed quilt was as ugly as the two in Ethan and Aaron's room—a color palette of faded orange, lime green and a sickly yellow doing absolutely nothing to help the room's overall appearance.

Why was I focusing on the quilt, you ask?

Because I would do anything to avoid remembering the look on Ethan's face as he rolled his best friend's body over to discover that he was dead. If that meant I had to fixate on ugly quilts, so be it.

Detective Alvarez stood in front of us, while the chief was in the doorway, quietly talking to one of the EMTs who'd shown up when we called 911. The detective was dressed in black pants, a tan shirt and her long, dark hair was slicked back into a high ponytail. Every time I saw the detective she wore a different pair of glasses—this time it was a vintage aviator style with a thin gold frame.

"Can you walk me through what happened when you entered the hotel room?" she asked, holding a small tablet and stylus in her hands, ready to take notes.

"Nothing much happened," Ethan said, hanging his head. His curly blond hair was shielding his face, but I could hear the tears, even if I couldn't see them. "We came back to my room so I could get changed. I wanted to show my brother and Chloe how ugly the room was . . . it was meant to be funny. When I opened the door, he was there. Dead."

"He was facedown on the bed," Matt clarified. He sounded calm but his hands were knotted tightly in his lap. "At first we assumed he was sleeping. But he didn't rouse when we entered the room."

"Did anyone touch the body?" she asked.

"I did." Ethan nodded. "I thought something was wrong when he didn't move, so I turned him over. I was ready to perform CPR, because we're all trained in first aid and lifesaving techniques through our surf clubs."

"But you never began CPR?" The detective's stylus swished over the screen of the tablet.

"No, ma'am."

"Why is that?"

"I could tell he was dead." Ethan's voice cracked. "One of his eyes was partially open and I couldn't feel a pulse. There was foam at his mouth as well and . . ."

Matt had stopped him from administering CPR in case there was a risk of him ingesting whatever had killed his friend.

Matt put an arm around Ethan's shoulders. "You did the right thing."

Detective Alvarez nodded. "And there was a note in his hand when you found him?"

"Yes." Ethan raked a hand through his hair and looked up. His green eyes were red-rimmed and his mouth was downturned. "It fell to the ground when I moved him. I'm sorry, I don't know if I should have moved him or not, but I thought if I could help . . ."

"It's okay, Ethan," the detective said in a calm and reassuring voice. "I'm not asking you questions because you've done anything wrong. I just want to understand what happened."

He blew out a breath and nodded.

"The note appears to be a suicide note," she continued. "I'd like you to take a look at it to confirm the handwriting, but if you don't feel that you can—"

"Show me."

I glanced at Ethan, my heart aching for him. He was being strong for his friend and stepping up in a big moment. I was glad that his brother was here for him. Detective Alvarez produced the note, which had been secured in a plastic pocket, and Ethan took it from her. His lip trembled as he read, his eyes flicking back and forth.

"I'm not sure," he said eventually, looking up. "To be honest, there haven't been too many times when Aaron and I have seen each other's handwriting. It could be his, but I'm not one hundred percent certain."

"You were close friends?" the detective asked.

"Yeah, we've been on the competition circuit a long time and we always share a room, ever since we started traveling on our own. But he lives in Florida . . ." Ethan's head dropped again. "*Lived* in Florida."

"And you're based where?"

"California. Santa Cruz."

"You never sent letters to each other, did you?" the detective asked, though her expression said she didn't hope for much. "I suppose people your age probably don't have pen pals."

Ethan shook his head. "We texted, mainly. Or used Snapchat."

"Did you know that Aaron was taking antidepressants?"

Ethan looked up sharply. "No."

"He'd never talked to you about having any feelings of depression or mentioned anything about ending his life?"

"Never." Ethan shook his head vehemently. "He was a happy guy."

I raised an eyebrow. It certainly hadn't seemed that way down on the beach earlier that evening. Aaron seemed to have a lot of pent-up anger—both men did.

"Did he display any behavior that was out of the ordinary lately? Did he do or say anything that seemed unusual?" The detective looked at Ethan with a neutral expression. I wondered how many times she'd asked these questions in the course of her career. "Anything catch your attention or sit funny with you?"

"I don't think so." Ethan scrubbed a hand over his face. "We met up in town yesterday morning. I drove up and he flew in. Everything seemed normal. He was excited for the competition, although I could tell he was a little nervous, too. None of that was out of the ordinary."

"Do you know if anything was on his mind in particular? Anything that had him worried?"

For a moment Ethan didn't say anything and it was almost like he was contemplating whether to share a secret. I caught Matt frowning and watching his brother intently.

"He's been in some money trouble," Ethan admitted. "Aaron had issues with gambling in the past. But he's been trying to mend his ways. I know he went to a support group for a while and he had a plan to get himself out of debt. It's why we were staying in *this* place."

He gestured to the room around them with a wrinkled nose. Detective Alvarez nodded emphatically like she shared our opinion of the run-down hotel.

"Did you know him to take any other kinds of drugs?" she asked.

"He . . ." Ethan swallowed. "Aaron liked to party. I don't know what he did exactly, because that's never been my scene. We're athletes, right? We have to take care of our bodies. But Aaron liked to blow off steam, especially if he didn't do as well in a comp as he wanted. I know he drank a bit. But I never went with him to clubs or anything like that."

The detective nodded.

"Did any of you notice anything strange when you went into the room?" Detective Alvarez asked. "Anything that appeared missing or out of place?"

We all shook our heads.

"Well, that's everything for now." She closed the cover on her tablet and tucked the stylus into a little slot on the side. She retrieved some business cards and handed one to each of us— although I still had her number in my phone from last time. "If you think of anything else, please call me. We'll need to keep the room secured for now, so you'll have to find somewhere else to stay. I'm sure the hotel will be able to give you access to another room."

"He can stay with me," Matt said protectively. "It's impor-tant to be around family right now."

"I agree," the detective said, offering an empathetic smile.

She bid us good night and exited through the door, taking the chief with her. Their hushed voices were indecipherable as they disappeared into the hallway. For a moment, neither one of us moved. I cradled Antonio to my chest and his tail wagged happily. If only I could be as oblivious as my furry best friend. My gaze fixed on a crack in the wall, a hollow feeling expand-ing in my chest.

That poor man. What pain he must have been in.

"He wouldn't have killed himself," Ethan said quietly, al-most as though he wasn't speaking to anyone in particular. "I know he wouldn't."

"Come on." Matt patted him gently on the back. "Let's get

you back to my place. Chloe, I'll drop you home on the way. I don't think we're going to be having much of a party after all tonight."

I nodded and cuddled Antonio tightly to my chest. All I wanted right then was to get home to my own family. Tonight I would be hugging everyone a little harder.

The following day I felt like roadkill.

I hadn't slept a wink because every time I closed my eyes, all I could see was the frozen face of Aaron as Ethan turned him over. When my alarm had gone off at an ungodly hour, it had almost been a relief to give up on trying to sleep. But now I was three coffees in, had more bags under my eyes than a Louis Vuitton store and my head was pounding like a nightclub. Thank goodness I could hide all my hair under my chef cap, because I hadn't even found the energy to brush it this morning.

"Good call on getting Erica to come in today," I said to Aunt Dawn as I stood at the preparation table, working on a batch of macarons. "I don't think I could have faced trying to be cheerful with customers all day."

I held a piping bag tightly in my hand and piped perfect two-inch circles of macaron batter onto three large baking sheets. I could practically do the squeeze-swirl-release motion in my sleep because macarons had been a staple in my baking repertoire for a *long* time. I'd been perfecting my technique since I was a teenager.

"Are you okay?" My aunt looked on with concern.

"Just tired." Squeeze, swirl, release. Squeeze, swirl, release.

"Chloe." She laid a hand gently on my wrist, making me stop what I was doing. "I know you think it's a good thing that baking is both your job and your favorite form of avoidance, but I'm still going to check in with you and I want you to be honest with me."

I sighed, letting my bag hover in midair, while a little bit of batter oozed from the tip. Today I was making a batch of "do all" shells. These shells were made from uncolored batter that I could use for experimental flavors, differentiating them from one another by using something sprinkled or dusted on top without having to make multiple batches of batter in different colors. My plan was to try three new flavors and see how the customers liked them, with the hope of adding one of the flavors to the permanent rotation.

First, I was going to make an apricot and cardamom macaron with a little gold dust on the shell. Second, I'd wanted to try my hand at making a black sesame dessert ever since Sabrina and I had gone to an incredible Japanese dessert bar one time when we took a trip to Seattle. These ones would have a few seeds sprinkled on the center of the shell. And third, I was going to try something out-there by not flavoring the buttercream in the macaron at all, in order to let the natural cannabis flavor shine through. I'd chosen a specific strain for this version, so there would be some natural fruitiness and I would leave the shells completely plain.

"Chloe." My aunt snapped me out of my foodie thoughts and back to the present, where the image of Aaron's dead face floated back to my consciousness. She was right—baking *was* my favorite form of avoidance. "Please talk to me."

"I had a terrible night after seeing the second ever dead body of my life," I admitted. "I feel bad for Ethan. They were close friends and losing someone so young is . . . I can only imagine how devastating it must be. And poor Aaron . . . what a dark place he must have been in."

"Come here, girlie." My aunt pulled me in for a hug.

I let myself sag into her embrace, even though one of her earrings was digging into my forehead and her perfume was tickling my nose. My aunt and my grandmother had been the people who'd comforted me my whole life. They were my lifelines. My support. When I was eleven years old, my mother had announced that motherhood "didn't suit her" and "wasn't her calling in life." She moved away with a boyfriend and after a few half-hearted attempts at phone calls for birthdays and Christmases, she'd all but disappeared from my life. Without her, Grandma Rose and Aunt Dawn were all I'd ever had. As for my father? Well, I didn't even know his name since he was a one-night stand. I doubted that he even knew I existed.

So, knowing I could always have a hug from my grandma or aunt when I needed it was reassuring.

"That's a lot," she said, squeezing me.

"I'm okay," I promised. "Just a bit shaken up."

"Understandable." She pulled back and I noticed the worry hadn't eased from her blue eyes. We all had the same eyes in my family—light as a morning sky and clear, expressive. Hers told me that this wasn't going to be the last time she would probe me to see how I was doing. "Promise me if you need to talk about it that you'll say something, okay?"

"I will."

"Okay." She reached for an apron hanging from the hook on the wall inside our office.

Calling the space an office was being generous, admittedly. It was little more than a supply cupboard with a tiny desk jammed against one side with a filing cabinet stashed underneath. You had to straddle one of the legs if you wanted to put your feet forward and I'd rolled back into the shelves behind trying to get out more than once. But hey, we were a baby business and sacrifices had to be made for the sake of our budget.

"How's Maisey doing?" I asked.

My aunt flushed as she slipped the apron over her head. "Good."

Recently, my aunt had told us that she was gay—something I had suspected for many years and was thrilled she finally felt comfortable enough to be open about—and that her friend had expressed romantic feelings for her. At the time Maisey was married, but she'd recently separated from her husband of more than fifteen years, and she and Aunt Dawn had been spending a lot more time together.

"She's coming over tonight with Annabel," Dawn said. "We're going to practice our routines for the meet next month."

Dawn and Maisey had started hanging out while doing their favorite hobby—canine freestyle dancing. Yes . . . dancing with dogs. It was a dog sport that involved lots of creativity, well-trained dogs, tricks and showmanship. My aunt's border collie, Moxie, was a fierce competitor and they'd won several awards since they'd started competing. Maisey was newer to the sport and her papillon, Annabel, was still learning the ropes.

"That sounds fun." I smiled and went back to piping macaron shells while we talked.

"Moxie and I have been working on a new routine," she said, her eyes sparkling. My aunt loved nothing more than an opportunity to shine and taking the stage with Moxie gave her that in spades. "We're doing a *Labyrinth* theme to the song "Magic Dance." I'm going to dress Moxie as baby Toby in the red-and-white–striped pajamas."

"And let me guess, you're going to dress up as the goblin king Jareth?" I laughed.

"How could I not?" She grinned. "David Bowie is an *icon* in that movie."

Of course my aunt would want to be the goblin king instead of Sarah in her white princess dress. Before we could continue singing David Bowie's praises, Erica poked her head out the back. Her cheeks were pink as though she'd been run off her feet serving customers. Or maybe that was just Erica. She seemed to move at the speed of light even on her bad days.

"Hey," she said. "Do we have any more of those peanut butter brownies? We're all out. I'm down to two squares of the plain chocolate and three of the extra special, as well."

I glanced at the ovens. "There's two about to come out any moment, but they need time to cool. We've got one regular flavor and one of the caramel swirl. No peanut butter, unfortunately. I'll make a note to do the peanut butter again tomorrow."

"Okay. There's a girl here asking if we do special orders." Erica grinned. "She wants to buy a whole tray to take up to her boyfriend's vacation house."

"So long as she knows not to cross state lines," I replied. Cannabis might be legal in California as well as several other states, but the rest of the country and the federal regulations were still catching up. "And I haven't set up a process for special orders yet, but take her details down and I'll figure out a price."

I hadn't even thought that people might want to buy a *whole* tray of brownies.

Aunt Dawn nudged me in the ribs with her elbow. "Special orders already rolling in? That's a good sign."

"It is," I agreed.

Erica disappeared back through the doors and my aunt followed her out to help with managing the front area. Smiling at the din of happy customers and the sound of sales being processed floating into the kitchen, I got back to my work piping the macaron shells. After the last shell was done, I banged the tray against the preparation table a few times to pop any bubbles in the mixture and to help the shells spread and flatten a little.

Then the timer for the brownies went off and I retrieved them and set them down in the area we'd designated for cooling. Brownies always needed longer to cool than people realized, and I didn't want to end up with messy slices from cutting them too soon. There was also a tray of the "everything but the kitchen sink" cookies ready to go, so I carried them out to the front and refilled the cookie area.

A quick glance around the café showed that every single seat was taken *and* a line snaked out the door. I noticed a familiar face from the beach last night—a girl with dark hair who had a dolphin tattoo and a fine silver chain around her ankle. She was sitting alone, tapping away at her phone, a half-eaten cookie in front of her.

Just as I was about to turn around and head back into the kitchen to whip up a batch of scones, someone caught my attention by waving. It was Matt. He looked even worse than I felt after a night of dismal sleep, his usually clean-shaven jaw dusted with golden stubble and his long hair scraped back into a messy man bun.

He was the only living man I'd ever seen who made that hairstyle look good.

"Chloe, have you got a sec?" He glanced around the restaurant and cringed. "Let me rephrase that. I know you don't have a sec, but would you give me one anyway?"

I really didn't have the time. But the look of desperation on his face stopped me from saying so. I liked Matt a lot. He was a kind person, had quickly become a good friend and it was clear he needed someone to talk to.

"Sure," I said, nodding. "Come around the back and I'll meet you there."

I headed back through the kitchen and out the rear door to the alleyway that ran behind my café and the rest of the businesses on this block. It was the entrance we used for our deliveries and for staff to come and go. A few seconds later, Matt rounded the corner.

"I'm sorry to drop in on you at work like this," he said, smoothing a hand over his hair. He wore his usual attire of a band T-shirt under a vest, a pair of jeans with a rip in one knee, and black combat boots, despite the heat. On one wrist was a leather cuff with some studs and around his neck he wore a strip of thin leather with a shark tooth hanging from it. "I just . . .

I wanted to talk and I've been driving Ben nuts all morning. I bet he's regretting his decision to work from home today."

"I'm sure he's not," I replied gently. "But how can I help?"

Matt sagged back against the wall of my café and sighed. "I honestly don't know. But since you were there last night and this isn't your first time dealing with a murder—"

"Murder?" I blinked. "I thought it was a suicide. There was a note . . ."

"Ethan doesn't believe Aaron ended his own life." Matt looked at me.

"What makes him say that?"

"He said the whole thing feels off. He and Aaron were talking just yesterday about the next competition coming up and where they were going to room together. It sounded like Aaron had gotten himself a new girlfriend and he was trying to pay off all his debts. Why would someone care about debts if they weren't planning to be around?"

"To protect their family?" I suggested.

"But family was the exact reason he'd never kill himself." Matt shook his head. "Aaron had a little brother in Florida, who lives with their aunt. He'd do *anything* for him. That's why he was trying to get on the straight and narrow, so one day his brother could come live with him. Aaron had a rough childhood and his dad wasn't the best guy, so he wanted to make sure his brother had more stability and love than he did growing up."

"But the letter . . ."

"Ethan thinks it doesn't sound like him. He only got to read it quickly, because the detective took it back, but he said the wording was strange. Almost like Aaron didn't write it. He couldn't vouch for the handwriting, either."

I bit down on my lip. I wasn't sure what to make of all this, because it could very well be that Ethan was struggling with grief and looking for someone to blame. None of what Matt had shared sounded like solid evidence to me. The plans Aaron had made weren't concrete, the clearing of debt could be an olive branch to his family and the unfamiliar written words might be as a result of the gravity of the situation. Death often changed people's perspectives on things. This much I knew.

"I know it sounds like nothing and if he wasn't my brother, I'd write it off too," Matt said as if reading my mind. "But Ethan's a sharp guy. He's sensitive, too. He's the kind of friend who learns all your favorite things and pays attention to the details and really knows you. He *knew* Aaron well. They were as close as brothers."

"I'm not sure what you want me to say." I pressed my hand to his arm. "Or what I can do to help."

"I guess I just . . ." He blew out a breath. "Maybe this is stupid, but I know *you* were the reason Brendan Chalmers's murder got solved. The police missed critical evidence and they would have arrested the wrong person if it wasn't for your hard work."

"You mean my snooping." I still wasn't sure how I felt about the whole thing—I did what I thought was right to protect my family, but it made me nervous to think the police missed something so important in their investigation. But maybe they would have found what I did eventually. But what if they hadn't? "I'm no detective."

"That could be why you figured it out, though. You have a fresh outlook! You're not jaded by years of being on the force and being bogged down with rules and regulations," he said passionately. "I believe my brother. The detective didn't when he went to the station this morning, however."

I frowned. "What happened?"

"Ethan remembered something else." Matt looked over his shoulder as if to check that nobody was listening in, but we were alone in the alley. "Aaron's backpack wasn't in the room."

"He's sure about that?"

The time we'd been in the hotel room was a blur. As soon as Ethan had discovered Aaron wasn't waking up, we called 911. The EMTs and police arrived quickly, and I honestly don't remember what Ethan had done in that time. I certainly don't remember him looking for a backpack.

"Yeah. He said Aaron was ridiculously precious about his backpack—it was the only possession he really cared about in life. Apparently, he kept his journals in there. He loved to draw and he had some superstition about having to sketch the beach he was at before the surfing competition. It was part of his process for getting to know the waves, apparently," Matt said. "He always kept the backpack right next to his bed, at easy reach. He'd flip out if anyone touched it and he never left it in the room alone, either. It went with him everywhere."

That was an interesting detail, but one missing backpack did not a murder make.

"And the detective didn't believe Ethan's suspicions of foul play?" I asked.

"The detective said they were looking into it, but Ethan made out like she thought he was just grieving."

I wasn't sure I blamed Detective Alvarez there, because I was having the same thoughts. I couldn't see anything pointing to murder, other than a few "gut feelings" from someone struggling to come to grips with what had happened.

"I believe him," Matt said, sincerity radiating from his face. "I believe Ethan when he says that something seems fishy."

"Then you have to press the police," I said, squeezing his hand. "Take Ethan back and stand your ground. I'm not the right person to help you with this. Last time . . . last time was a fluke."

I'd bumbled my way through finding a killer and saving my aunt from false arrest, and it was lucky I didn't get *myself* killed in the process. I couldn't do that a second time.

"I understand." Matt nodded and I pulled him in for a hug. It was so hard seeing him in pain like this and I could only imagine the state Ethan must be in.

"If I hear anything at all, I promise you'll be the first to know," I said, thinking the chances of me turning up anything at all were thinner than a single sheet of filo pastry.

How wrong I would turn out to be.

CHAPTER 5

Baked by Chloe closed on another successful day. Even with having extra wages to factor in for Erica, we were still way ahead. Not only had we sold out of almost everything I'd baked fresh that day, but we'd moved almost half the stock of our candles, as well as a good chunk of the greeting cards and necklaces.

During the last hour of business, I'd emailed all three of the artisans to request another order for the shop, and had started thinking about what else we could sell. One idea was cannabis bath and body products. I'd found a woman down the coast who made all kinds of lovely things like goat milk soaps infused with organic hemp oil and whipped hemp oil body butters in enticing scents like Sicilian lemon, spiced chai and lavender cake. In fact, I was thinking of making up some gift baskets containing one of the body butters and a small pack of macarons or chocolate truffles with flavors to match the scents.

My creativity was at an all-time high. Every day I worked I thought of more ways to grow the business. As I swept the floor and wiped down all the tables and stacked the chairs, I felt a deep sense of accomplishment wash over me. I'd taken a risk and I was feeling increasingly confident that it would pay off. Running a small-town café might not have the glamour and prestige of fine dining in a large city like Paris or New York, but I was on my own path now. I was building something for me. For my family. For the future.

After cleaning and preparing the front of the store for the following day's trade, I felt strangely wired as if I hadn't spent the entire day running on no sleep and copious amounts of caffeine. It was still relatively early, since we closed the café at four thirty. Partially this was because I could only make so much product as a single baker, and with the hype we'd received, keeping the café open when there was nothing to sell wasn't a good look. But I wanted to wait a while to gauge how well we were doing before hiring another baker to help out.

For now, I was doing the best with what I had . . . which was my own two hands.

I double-checked the lock on the front door and went to change out of my uniform and into a pair of black Lululemon leggings and a vintage Disneyland T-shirt that I'd stolen out of Grandma Rose's closet one day. It was pink and had a picture of Minnie Mouse on the front with a bow on her head and polka dots on her skirt. Then I changed out of my work shoes— a hideous pair of chef clogs that were as practical as they were ugly—and into my white sneakers.

I'd sent both Erica and Aunt Dawn home as soon as we concluded trade for the day, preferring to do the close-up procedure on my own because my mind was churning like a storm. I couldn't get the idea that Aaron had been murdered out of my head.

I headed to where I'd parked my car that morning, down a small side street. I'd been too tired to walk after such a late and sleepless night. But after I slipped into the driver's seat and started the engine, I felt a jittery curiosity swell inside me. Instead of driving toward home, I went in the opposite direction.

The opposite direction being toward one run-down, cheesy '70s-style hotel.

My grandmother's car, which she'd recently decided to gift

to me permanently, was a powder-blue Fiat 500. We lovingly called it the Jellybean for its cartoonishly small size and cheerful color. Its pros included good gas milage and being so small you could throw it sideways into a parking spot with room to spare. The cons, however, were that it required a gentle touch when getting it started in cooler temperatures and would sometimes make weird noises.

I navigated the Jellybean into the hotel's small guest parking lot out front and was struck with a sense of déjà vu. Nobody appeared to be coming or going from the hotel. I got the impression from Ethan that this wasn't standard accommodation for the surfers and even though most other places would be booked up in Azalea Bay this week, perhaps people preferred to stay one town over and drive in for the action rather than sleep on a bed with an ugly quilt and a stuffed squirrel staring down at you.

I got out of my car and looked around.

"What the heck are you doing?" I asked myself. "Are you looking for trouble?"

Maybe. But I figured trouble seemed to find me anyway, even when I wasn't looking, so what was the harm in poking around? I walked around the side of the building to where Ethan and Aaron's room was situated on the second floor. There was nothing much on this side of the hotel. Yes, it might have a nice partial glimpse of the ocean, but it overlooked a crummy pathway that led toward the dumpsters *and* it had a prime view of the gas station next door. Not exactly a postcard-worthy view.

A wire fence separated the hotel from the gas station and the rooms on the ground floor each had a tiny courtyard—although they were so small, I hesitated to even call them such—with some barely alive potted plants and sad-looking plastic tables and chairs. The courtyards were separated with wooden slatted fencing for privacy.

I inspected the courtyard directly below Ethan and Aaron's room. A large potted plant had been overturned and cracked, with dirt scattered across the tile pavers. One of the chairs was also broken, I noticed, with a huge crack running through both the seat and one of the legs. The shades were open, allowing me to easily see inside the room. The twin beds were neatly made, and there weren't any signs that the room was currently occupied—no luggage or clothes or any other personal debris littered around.

I took a step back and glanced up at the balcony attached to Ethan and Aaron's room. The balcony was barely bigger than a postage stamp and I'm sure if the men had been standing there with another friend it would have been a tight squeeze. The door was ajar—not much, just enough that someone could slip an arm through.

I frowned. I wonder why it hadn't been closed by whoever secured the scene. Or perhaps the police hadn't done a thorough collection of evidence or anything more than simply taping the door off. Maybe they didn't go through the scene until it was determined that there was cause to suspect foul play.

At that moment, just as I was about to turn away and head back to my car, the blinds in the window rustled. I gasped. Someone was in the room! I stepped back, my eyes glued to the balcony and the windows. Was it a member of the police force doing their job? Or had the killer returned to the scene of the crime?

I knew I should hightail it out of there, but the door to the balcony slid open before I had a chance to get my legs moving. If I ran back to my car now, whoever was in the room would see me. My only option was to hide and hope I could stay out of sight. I caught a glimpse of a figure dressed in black before I ducked underneath the balcony into the tiny courtyard of the room below and tried to open the sliding glass door. It was locked.

And there was nothing to hide behind.

Crap on a cracker!

Silently freaking out and with my heart pounding like a bass drum, I scooted over to the wooden slatted wall that divided this courtyard from the one next to it and flattened myself back. I was not hidden. Like, at all. But I had nowhere else to go. Sliding down, I tried to scrunch myself into as small a position as possible in the hopes the one potted plant that remained upright would at least partially conceal me.

Above, I heard the sound of a sliding door being closed. Then footsteps. I held my breath and pressed back against the wall, praying that whoever was up there wouldn't look down. For a moment, all went quiet and I thought I might have gotten lucky. What I didn't anticipate, however, is that whoever was in the room, wasn't planning on exiting via traditional means—like the front door. Because a second later, I heard the sound of something hitting metal, a dull clang that made me clamp my hand over my mouth.

They were climbing over the railing.

Now it was definitely too late to run and the second they dropped down, if they were facing the building, they'd see me. Another dull clang sounded overhead and then a figure dropped to the floor, letting out a soft *oof* when they landed. Something told me the way they'd jumped was practiced, skilled. No fear. Solid landing. They didn't appear injured and I wondered if this wasn't the first time they'd jumped down from that balcony . . . maybe they'd done it on the night Aaron died?

Mercifully, the person was facing the other way. I tried to capture all the details—black baggy sweatpants, sneakers, a black oversize hoodie with the hood pulled up, black leather gloves. Not exactly a regular summer outfit.

And there was only one reason to be wearing gloves on an eighty-something-degree day: concealing fingerprints.

I gulped as the figure got up and dusted themselves off, mercifully not bothering to look behind them. The person was holding something—an empty bottle of juice. But why would someone sneak into a crime scene to steal an empty bottle of juice? Or were they so dehydrated that they needed to take a drink with them?

The person quickly jogged along the path toward the front of the hotel, tucking the empty juice bottle under one arm and taking their gloves off as they ran. But they were moving too fast for me to catch any further details—like if they were wearing any rings or if the hands looked like a woman's or a man's hands, or even what exact color their skin was.

In my heart, I wanted to go after the person and yank their hood back like they did in Scooby Doo. But I was frozen to the spot, the memory of being attacked by a killer still fresh in my mind. I'd been snuck up on in my store and hit over the head with a cast-iron skillet. Some days I wonder what might have happened if they'd been more serious about hurting me—like if they'd pulled a knife or a gun—or if my aunt hadn't showed up at the exact right moment.

I could have died.

My breathing came hard and fast and sweat beaded along my hairline, and I cursed myself for being afraid. For not being braver. Yet as I sat there, trying to steady my breath, I knew one thing for sure: Ethan had every right to suspect that something fishy was going on.

I drove straight to Matt and Ben's place.

Ben's car was parked out front and he stepped out of the vehicle holding two shopping bags as I pulled up behind him. Matt had mentioned he was working from home, which explained why he was here at this early evening hour. Usually, Ben commuted to San Jose where he worked for a video game company as a quality assurance manager. When I'd first met him, he said he "tested for bugs" during video game production, but I'd come to understand that his job was much more involved than that, including managing all the people who actually did the testing, helping to scope testing work for individual projects, scheduling and much more.

I got out of the car and held my hand up in a wave. "Hi Ben."

"Hey Chloe!" He looked genuinely happy to see me. "What brings you to our humble abode?"

"I was hoping to chat with Ethan, actually," I replied. Ben nodded and motioned for me to follow him to the front door. "How's he been doing? Was he competing today?"

"No, his first heat is tomorrow." Ben sighed. "He's doing as well as can be. But he spoke with the detective again this afternoon and it was a bit of a blow."

"How come?"

Ben unlocked the front door. He and Matt lived in a sweet bungalow with a well-maintained garden and a small concrete kangaroo by the front door. I wasn't sure if that was something Australians did back home—maybe they did kangaroos instead of garden gnomes?—or if it was a bit of a private joke between the two of them.

"The detective told him that they're certain Aaron's death is a suicide and that they would be opening the hotel room back up tomorrow. I believe they're still doing an autopsy, but she gave the impression it was standard procedure to determine the exact cause and manner of death. Not because they think he was murdered."

My stomach churned. Given what I'd seen this afternoon, I wasn't sure I agreed with them. "What makes them so certain?"

Ben pushed the door open and held it for me as we went inside.

"They managed to get in contact with Aaron's aunt, who

confirmed that the handwriting on the note was his," he said. "The aunt also said there was a history of mental illness in the family and that she was under the impression Aaron had been seeing either a therapist or psychiatrist of late. Obviously that by itself doesn't mean his death was a suicide, but coupled with the letter and some of the information about his gambling debts . . . it certainly looks like he may have ended his life."

"Ben? That you?" Matt's voice floated in from another room.

"Yep," he called back. "We have a guest."

I bent down to untie my sneakers and set them neatly to one side, where several other pairs of shoes sat—including a pair of Doc Martens, a pair of scuffed black combat boots, and some high-top Converse sneakers. Hanging on the wall in the entry was a large red tassel dangling from an intricate knot, which Ben had once told me was a gift from his aunt in Shanghai on Chinese New Year and was meant to ward away evil spirits, as well as bringing luck and fortune into the home.

I hoped the knot tassel would do its work, because my gut told me trouble was brewing in Azalea Bay. Again.

Matt came around the corner. "Hey Chloe. Nice to see you."

If I thought his face had looked drawn earlier, now he seemed even more worn out. But he still managed a genuine smile, which said everything there was to say about him as a person.

"Hey Matt. Is your brother around?" I asked. "I was hoping to chat with him."

"Yeah, come on in. We're just having a beer out back." Matt still wore his faded Iron Maiden T-shirt but had changed into a pair of shorts and flip-flops—which Matt insisted on calling *thongs*, much to my amusement. "If you want to stay for dinner, we're going to fire the barbie up in an hour or so. We've got plenty of food since . . . well, since our plans were cactus last night."

"Cactus?" I looked to Ben.

"Ruined," he clarified. "And yes, please stay. We've got a whole lot of lovely food that I would hate to waste."

"That would be great. Thank you."

I followed Matt out to the back of the house, where they had a great wooden deck built and a big picnic-style outdoor setting. Ethan was there, curly blond hair in disarray, staring sadly into a pint glass with the dregs of a beer wallowing in the bottom. Strands of white foam made a pattern on the glass, showing that he'd nursed the drink for a while.

"We've got a visitor," Matt announced as they walked outside. "What can I get for you, Chloe? We've got a couple of different craft beers, including a great pale ale from up the coast. Or I can get you a glass of wine or a soda?"

"Just a soda would be great, thanks." I took a seat next to Ethan, who held his glass up to his brother, signaling that he was ready for another drink. Matt disappeared back into the house. "I heard you had a tough chat with the detective this afternoon."

If he was annoyed that I jumped straight into things, he didn't show it. "Yeah. They did a video call with Aaron's aunt and she identified his handwriting and showed some card he'd written her that looked pretty damn close. The detective said they couldn't call it an exact match without a handwriting expert to confirm it, but . . . I guess it was enough for them in combination with everything else."

"I'm really sorry."

"So am I." He looked at me, and I could see his eyes were red and puffy. "Aaron might not have been perfect—far from it—but he was my best friend. I knew him as well as I know my own brother. He didn't kill himself."

The raw conviction in his voice made my heart clench. "I believe you."

"Too bad the police don't." He sighed. "They just think I'm being emotional. Like I'm saying these things to avoid accepting the fact that he's gone. But that's not it at all. If I thought he did it, then I would try to make peace with it. I would try to deal with it rather than looking for alternatives."

I believed *that*, too. For a guy in his early twenties, Ethan struck me as mature and levelheaded. Responsible. Just like his big brother.

"If only I had something to prove my suspicions," Ethan said sadly.

"Well, I don't have proof," I said. "But I did see something that indicates you might be right. A person was sneaking around in your hotel room this afternoon . . . and they could be the killer."

CHAPTER 6

A few minutes later, Matt and Ben had joined us around the table, everyone with drinks in hand, and I relayed what I saw. The men stared at me, open-mouthed. Ben, most of all. I suspect he may have wondered, like the police, if Ethan was simply struggling to cope with the loss of his friend.

"You didn't see their face? Skin color? Tattoos? Anything?" Matt asked.

I shook my head. "They were dressed head to toe in black, including gloves, and they never turned toward me. By the time they took their gloves off, they were too far away for me to see anything much. It could have been a taller woman or a slightly shorter guy. The clothing was baggy too, so it was hard to determine build."

"But why would someone be rifling around in there? And why the heck would they take an empty juice bottle?" Ethan asked, taking a long draw on his freshly filled beer. I got the impression he didn't usually drink while competing, but these were exceptional circumstances. Summer air warmed my skin as the late afternoon sun beat down and I scooted along the bench a few inches to keep in the shade. "It doesn't make sense."

"Maybe they took something else as well?" I offered. "It's possible they could have shoved something small into a pocket."

"But what? Aaron didn't have any money or expensive jewelry. He's worn the same surf bracelet since he was a teenager, which was just a cheap thing. What could be small and valuable enough to steal?"

"A phone?" I suggested.

"He had a crappy old phone which he put prepaid minutes onto because he doesn't have a credit card," Ethan replied. When I raised an eyebrow, he continued, "Because of the gambling trouble he got into, the bank closed his credit card account and had debt collectors come after him. Now his credit score is ruined, so he can't get a credit card. He has to pay for everything with cash or debit."

Aaron was so young to be in such financial trouble. It made me wonder if there were people looking for money from him. "Do you think he might have an outstanding debt that would cause someone to go looking through his things . . . or worse?"

"Honestly, I don't think so," Ethan said. "He'd been working hard to clear everything up and save for a place where his brother could come live with him. But it was tough after the sponsors dropped him. So he'd been doing some odd jobs and running surf workshops for extra cash, plus he did well in the last competition. Came in second, which has some decent prize money. Ten thousand, all up. Winners get about twenty grand, give or take."

"Wow." My eyes widened.

"It sounds good, but being on the Challenger circuit isn't cheap," Matt said. "The surfers have to pay for membership to the league, plus an entry fee of a couple hundred bucks per event. Then there's insurance, flights, accommodation, equipment like boards and wetsuits, plus training, physio, massage, coaching . . . we're talking tens of thousands of dollars each year simply for the chance to compete."

"The real money comes when you make it to the Championship Tour," Ethan added. "That's what we're all hoping for, that we score enough points to get to the next level. But I've seen people sink all their money into this level and then crash and burn. You can dig a deep hole if you're not careful, or if you don't have some kind of backing."

"Like sponsors?" I asked.

"Or family connections. Makani—the guy you saw on the beach last night—comes from surfing royalty. His dad was one of the best, so Makani has a huge amount of backing both from his family but also from all the sponsors who want to capitalize on the family name."

I nodded. "Was that frustrating to someone like Aaron, who had nothing?"

"Uh yeah, just a bit." Ethan let out a dark chuckle. "Those two . . . They've been rivals since we were teenagers. They both got banned for a season back when we were in high school, because a fight broke out at one tournament. Aaron thought Makani used his name to get ahead, and Makani thought Aaron was weak and undisciplined."

"Do you think *he* could have done it?"

Ethan shook his head. "No way. Makani's too concerned with his golden boy image to do something like that."

But I remember watching the two men fight—Makani *could* have been the person I saw coming out of the hotel room. He was about the right height, on the shorter side for a guy, but plenty athletic enough to jump over a railing. It was also clear he had beef with Aaron. Maybe Makani followed him back to the hotel room after their spat and things got even more heated.

Yeah, but what about the suicide note in Aaron's handwriting and the pills? How does a fight explain that?

"What did the note say?" I asked. "You read it, right? Do you remember?"

"It's burned into my brain," Ethan replied in a voice that sounded haunted. "It said, 'I can't do this anymore. Whatever I thought this life would be, it's not this. I need to be released.'"

It certainly sounded like someone who was at the end of their rope, although it was light on details. But I'd had no experience with suicide. I wasn't sure if this kind of wording was typical . . . or even if there *was* a typical kind of wording. Maybe it was different for every person.

"The weird thing was that it was written in bullet points, which seems odd for a suicide note." Ethan wrinkled his nose. "But Aaron wasn't the best writer. His texts were always full of errors and weird formatting."

"Why were you at the hotel, anyway?" Ben asked me all of a sudden. There was no judgment in his tone, only curiosity.

"I . . ." I looked at Matt, hoping I wasn't about to put my foot into it. "Matt came to see me at work today. He was upset because the police weren't considering Ethan's opinion and . . . well, it made me curious. I guess I'm a glutton for punishment with this stuff."

Or maybe I was simply a nosy small-town cliché. As much as I didn't want to think that about myself, there were certainly some signs pointing to it being true.

"I'm glad you did," Ethan said, nodding so that his curly hair bounced around his face. "Because someone snooping around his room is a big deal! I wonder how they got in."

"The woman we saw behind the counter last night didn't exactly seem like a stellar security person," I replied. "She barely even looked at us as we walked in."

"I noticed that, too," Matt chimed in. "Anyone could bypass her and sneak up the stairs or use the elevator."

"But how would they get into the room if it's locked?" Ben asked, scratching his head. "Even if they could duck under the security tape the police put up, they would still need to get the door open."

"I noticed that they used old-fashioned keys rather than those electric card type locks. Maybe they picked it. It probably wouldn't be hard to do."

"The locks were pretty shoddy, anyway," Ethan said. "I forgot my key the other day when I ducked downstairs to ask for new towels, and when I came back I managed to jig it open with my bank card."

"So anyone could have gotten in." I sighed. "That doesn't help us narrow it down."

We sat in silence for a moment, minds individually churning over what might have happened to Aaron. Maybe he was forced to write the note? Maybe he was interrupted while writing a letter to someone? Maybe it was a creative piece rather than a suicide note?

"Who do you think might have reason to kill him?" I asked. "Maybe that's a good place to start thinking about this whole thing."

"There's a guy in the industry, Fisk Clemmens. He's one of the competition judges and I think something happened between him and Aaron. He told me to stay away from Fisk one time, said he was a bad egg." Ethan shrugged. "Aaron was having some trouble with his girlfriend, too. Her name is Celina. They were fighting a lot. She's down here for the competition but she's staying somewhere else."

I raised an eyebrow. "Is that normal that Aaron and his girlfriend wouldn't stay in the same accommodation?"

"Yeah, kinda." Ethan pushed his curly hair back away from his face. "Aaron needs to get into the zone before a competition and he was also more than a little superstitious. He used to call me his lucky charm. The few times he roomed with Celina instead of me, he didn't do too well. But I'd put that down more to him being distracted from fighting with her than anything luck related."

"Do you really think she'd have reason to kill him?" Matt asked. "I met Celina a few times. She seemed sweet."

"Sweet?" Ethan snorted. "That girl has a temper hotter than the molten core of the sun. She and Aaron were a fireworks show ninety percent of the time. They were always breaking up and getting back together and breaking up again."

"So why kill him this time?" I asked.

"Who knows. Why don't we talk to her?" Ethan's eyes lit up. "There's a huge party going on tonight. It's at some mansion owned by one of the sponsorship reps and all the industry people are invited. I was going to skip it, but it could be the perfect opportunity to get information."

"And you can bring a group of people along?" I asked, dubious.

"Well, no," he admitted. "But I *can* bring a plus-one."

When Ethan said the party was taking place at a mansion he was not kidding. The large home sat on a hill like a gargoyle perched atop a castle's walls. It was expansive and white, sleekly modern and without any of the personable charm embodied by the smaller, more modest homes on the street where I lived.

I hated it on sight.

"Looks like this is it." Ethan pulled his car into a free spot sandwiched between two luxury sport cars, neither of which had names I could correctly pronounce. I was *so* out of my element. "I always wonder what people are compensating for when I see a house like this."

I snorted.

"That was mean, wasn't it?" Ethan flashed me a cheeky grin, his green eyes twinkling. Gone was the redness and the downturn of his mouth. He seemed energized again, like the first day I'd met him. Poor guy. All he wanted was someone to take his concerns seriously. "Although I'm sure they don't care what *I* think. Not exactly like they'll be crying into their piles of money over the opinions of a lowly surfer."

"You're not a lowly surfer," I said. "You're a surfer on the rise. A rising star, one might say."

He chuckled. "And how do you know that? Are you a surfing expert?"

"Your brother told me how good you are."

"He has to say that. Come on, let's go."

Outside we followed a small cluster of people heading up a sweeping path that circled a fishpond filled with vibrant koi and ended at an impressive and imposing set of double doors. One was open, giving a glimpse inside. As we approached, I could see there was a woman standing with a tablet who appeared to be checking the guests in. She was absolutely gorgeous with long black hair swept up into a glossy ribbon of a ponytail, deep olive skin, dark eyes fringed by heavy lashes and a heart-shaped face. She struck me as vaguely familiar and then I remembered that I'd seen her standing at the water's edge last night, watching the surfers, and then again in my café.

"Kaila, what are you doing working the door?" Ethan asked as we approached.

She returned his friendly tone with an attempt at a smile. "Trying to keep myself distracted."

There was a slight wobble in her voice and Ethan immediately reached out to hug her. They stood there for a moment and I saw tears sparkling in her eyes, but she quickly released him to brush them away.

"How are *you* doing?" she asked.

"Not great and also seeking a distraction," he admitted.

"Aaron always loved a party. He'd want us to have a good time." She nodded as if convincing herself while she scrolled through a list on the tablet. "There you are. And you've got a plus-one?"

"That's right," he said. "This is Chloe Barnes. You may know her from such incredible business ventures as the Baked by Chloe cannabis café."

"Oh, I was there today." Kaila's eyes lit up. "It was wonderful. I'll definitely be coming back again before I head home."

I smiled. "I'm happy to hear that."

We entered and walked through the house, moving slowly as Ethan seemed to know most of the people there and stopped every few feet to say hello to someone. He introduced me around and all the faces and names immediately blurred together. Eventually we found ourselves outside, where a ton of beautiful people were dotted around an expansive outdoor eating area surrounded by lush greenery and exotic-looking flowers. An in-ground pool stretched out, glittering like a giant piece of aquamarine from all the lights under the water. The tiles had an iridescence to them and there was a subtle pattern across the sides made of mother-of-pearl pieces, all of which created a magical atmosphere.

Oh, and there was a mermaid in the water.

I blinked, wondered if I'd done a little too much taste-testing at work today. Nope, it wasn't the weed baking and the mermaid was still there. She had long blond hair that floated behind her like a sheet of glossy gold silk and a tail made of shades of purple, blue and green that shifted and shimmered in the light. Her fins fluttered in the water as she swam, graceful as a ballerina, with long arm strokes and sensual undulation to her body. Several people stood and watched.

As she broke the surface, I could see that her extravagant makeup was perfectly intact, including the iridescent particles on the tops of her cheekbones and the rich blue eyeshadow on her eyes. She waved. Her nails were long, likely fake, and they also shimmered and caught the light. I got the impression that every single part of her appearance was well thought out and tailored to bring the fantasy of a mermaid to life. No aspect was too small to warrant careful consideration.

I stood, mesmerized as she splashed her tail in the water.

"Wow," I breathed. "She looks amazing. If I was a child, I'd totally buy that she was a real mermaid."

You couldn't even see any seams or zips or closures on her tail. Nothing that might break the illusion.

"That's Mariah," Ethan said. "I've known her a long time. She used to be on the competition circuit back in the day. But now she's a full-time professional mermaid."

"I had no idea there *was* such a thing."

"Me either. But apparently it's a real job, because she's always posting pictures on her socials from events she's done around the country and even overseas. Last year she went to a convention specifically for professional mermaids and she was one of their big speakers."

"Color me impressed." I followed Ethan around the pool, my eyes stuck on Mariah as she chatted with someone at the water's edge. "Did she give up surfing to become a mermaid?"

"Not specifically to become a mermaid." He shook his head. "She uh . . . she got attacked by a shark."

I gasped. "Really?"

"Yeah, it was pretty bad. Tiger shark bit her on the thigh while she was surfing somewhere in Hawaii. She lost a lot of blood and was rushed to the hospital. Thankfully, there was an off-duty EMT surfing that same beach and he helped her before the ambulance arrived. The doctors said he saved her life. Scary stuff."

"And she couldn't surf after that?" I asked.

"After extensive rehab she *could* surf, but she was never the same as before. Her balance was off and she had pretty serious muscle deterioration in her injured leg. Ultimately, I think she decided that it was time to retire from the competition scene." Ethan nodded. "I know some people speculated for a while that it was because she was scared of getting bitten again, but it's not true. Mariah is tough as nails. Now she's studying marine biology at college and she wants to work with sharks, and help to educate people about how important they are to our ecosystem."

I shook my head in wonder. "That's super impressive."

"Right?" He chuckled. "I have mad respect for her."

We wandered to the far corner of the pool and a waiter in a traditional black-and-white uniform offered us a drink. I took a glass of champagne, but Ethan opted for a Coke since he was driving. Now that we were away from the crowd a bit, we could talk.

"Fisk is over there," he said, taking a sip of his soda. "White pants and the blue shirt."

I glanced in the direction Ethan was looking until I found the man who matched the description. He had a thick head of dark hair, deeply tanned skin and the kind of lines and wrinkles that came from years spent in the sun. A heavy gold watch sat on one wrist and it matched a thick chain peeking out where the top button of his shirt was open. He wore linen pants with the hems rolled up and a pair of loafers that gave Hugh Hefner vibes.

I bet he was the kind of guy who had a velvet robe with his initials monogrammed onto it.

"Is this his house?" I asked.

"No, this house belongs to a sponsor." Ethan shook his head. "Fisk is a competition judge. He used to be a surfer back in the day and, at one time, I really looked up to him. He was the kind of guy who went to marches about saving the ocean and he donated his time and money to beach cleanup activities."

I raised an eyebrow. The guy looked significantly more bougie than someone who walked along the beach collecting trash. "But?"

"He changed." Ethan wrinkled his nose. "He married a rich

socialite and became obsessed with money and status. The plans he had to start his own charity fell through and now he doesn't seem to give a crap about the environment. Too busy driving his Ferrari all over the place."

"And Aaron didn't like him?"

"Nah, they *definitely* had some kind of beef. But I have no idea what."

Money seemed to be a theme surrounding Aaron, from what I'd heard so far. The issues with his gambling debts, the cost associated with competing as a surfer, and him having beef with someone who married into money. Then there was the comment that Makani made when he was fighting with Aaron on the beach.

Him borrowing money and not paying people back is not petty crap, either. He's happy to step on anyone to get what he wants, doesn't matter who he hurts.

"Do you think Aaron borrowed money from Fisk?" I asked, taking a sip of my champagne. It was the good stuff. I'd experienced my share of it during my time in Paris, and I could recognize a quality glass of bubbles. Someone was spending big for this party.

See, there was the topic of money again.

"I'd like to say that I don't think so, but who the heck knows." Ethan shrugged. "Aaron was desperate there for a time. I helped him out when I could, but I'm not exactly rolling in it either and I don't want to go to my dad or my brother for a handout."

I nodded. "Fair enough. Although I'm sure Matt would never say no."

"Exactly why I don't ask for his help unless it's absolutely necessary," Ethan replied. "Family doesn't take advantage of one another."

The response made me smile. It was clear Ethan and Matt had the same core values in life, values I happened to share myself.

Another surfer came by to say hello to Ethan and I watched Fisk from a distance. He was holding court with a group of younger people, mostly women, though there were two guys as well. He seemed to enjoy having an audience and it looked like he was telling a salacious story. I noticed the group was standing by a table where some food was set up.

"I'm going to grab a bite," I said to Ethan. "Be back in a minute."

I walked around the side of the pool and made my way toward the food table and got a closer look at the people standing with Fisk. One of the young women stood out to me. She had a camera slung around her neck, and black hair that was so long it brushed against the back pockets on her jeans. She was taller than me by a good few inches, slender in build and had small, upturned eyes in a rich dark brown. A canvas tote bag was slung over one shoulder that had *Celina Sato Photography* printed on it along with a cute logo of a camera poking out of some waves.

I wondered if this was the same Celina that Ethan had mentioned as being Aaron's on-again, off-again girlfriend.

But it was her expression that caught my attention more than anything else—the way she almost looked like she was glaring at Fisk as he talked, totally unapologetic in her reaction. The other people were so enraptured by his story they didn't seem to notice.

"They're going to have me out on set, you know. I'm the film's top consultant." Fisk puffed out his chest. "I heard they signed Brad Pitt on to be the top-billing star. That's the actor who gets paid the most."

Celina rolled her eyes.

"I'll probably stay in Hollywood while we're shooting, since they need my input for basically the whole thing." He nodded with a serious, thoughtful expression on his face. "They want the movie to be super realistic, not like some of those other trash ones that stick a few girls in bikinis and call it a day. Although I'm sure there *will* be lots of girls in bikinis."

Fisk looked to the two young men and winked. Ugh, gross. I couldn't really judge Celina for glaring at the guy. He seemed like a douchebag.

"Do you think they'll be looking for extras?" one of the young women asked. She was pretty with green eyes and chestnut brown hair. Her earrings were tiny yellow surfboards and she had a skirt slung low on her hips, exposing a flat stomach of suntanned skin. "I've done some modeling and I would *love* to get some film work."

"I'm sure they'll come to me for recommendations on such things," Fisk said, though I didn't believe a word of what he was saying. No doubt the guy would use his position to his advantage, though. "Why don't you send me an email and we'll keep in touch. That way when the director and I start talking about such things, I can keep you in mind."

I moved out of earshot before anyone noticed me eavesdropping and stopped by the food table. To say Fisk thought highly of himself was greatly understating things, but I'm sure Aaron had more reason to hate the guy than him inflating his involvement with a movie for the sake of ego.

I grabbed myself a plate and used a set of mini tongs to select a few pieces of sushi and a delicious-looking miniature roast vegetable tart. As I was dishing myself up, someone appeared next to me to do the same thing. It was Celina Sato.

I glanced at her as she reached for a pair of tongs sitting on a platter beside the savory pinwheel pastries. "The guy is full of hot air, isn't he?"

She looked at me as if I'd snapped her out of a deep thought. "Sorry?"

"That guy." I inclined my head back toward Fisk and offered her a friendly smile. "I walked past and heard him talking about a movie. Sounds like he's full of hot air."

"Most men are." It didn't sound like a joke.

Her expression was difficult to read. Through my life I'd found that people warmed to me quickly, because I tended to be chatty and I smiled readily. But Celina struck me as guarded. Not rude, but I could sense that she was the kind of person who didn't let others in quickly or easily.

I wondered how Aaron won her over.

"They're more trouble than they're worth," she muttered.

It struck me as an odd thing to say merely days after her boyfriend was potentially killed. Or perhaps they'd broken up before Aaron's death. Unless I'd got it wrong and she was a completely different Celina altogether.

"Tell me about it," I said, not having to fake my agreement too much. "I was engaged not too long ago."

Celina raised an eyebrow. "What happened?"

"He couldn't keep it in his pants and now he's going to be a father." I could finally say the words without wanting to hurl something at a wall. My ex, Jules, had called frequently after I first left Paris, thinking he could win me back. But trust was like crystal, once it was broken only an expert could repair it.

And Jules was no expert.

It seemed he'd finally gotten the hint, however. I hadn't heard from him in over a month.

"Brutal." Celina shook her head. "My ex had the same problem. Are some guys biologically wired to screw around? Makes me not want to bother with any of them."

Interesting. That might explain why she didn't seem too cut up about Aaron's death, if they'd split up because he was cheating on her. Would I feel the same way if I found out that Jules had died? Part of me thought I'd still be sad, even if I knew I would never have gone back to him. But I didn't detect any emotion in Celina at all.

Curiosity got the better of me and I decided to push a little.

"Is he here, your ex?" I asked. "Like, is he part of the surf scene?"

"Nah, he's not here." Her eyes dropped to the floor for a moment, and I caught a flash of something raw. "He died, actually."

"I'm so sorry for your loss." I felt terrible for pressing on something painful, but at least I could confirm that I was talking with the right person. That would be way too much of a coincidence for her to be another Celina. "It must be tough to grieve when you have complicated feelings about him."

"Yeah." She nodded. "It is. But he clearly wanted to go, so . . ."

I resisted the urge to ask anything further. I wanted to help Ethan, but I wasn't monster enough to use someone's grief to get information.

"Sometimes you can't help people no matter how much you want to." She looked back up and her eyes were sparkling with tears. "Excuse me."

Celina walked away before I had the chance to say anything else and I stood there, feeling slightly ashamed of myself for making assumptions and for poking at a sore point. But at least I knew her name now and I could look up her business.

What are you doing, *Chloe? Remember last time when you said you would never get involved in anything like this ever again, huh? What happened to that?*

I popped another piece of sushi into my mouth and chewed, feeling conflicted. The police were the correct people to be looking into this. I knew that. But I also knew they'd made mistakes before. Not to mention they seemed convinced that Aaron's death wasn't suspicious, when the person closest to him believed otherwise. Plus, I'd seen a figure rifling around in the dead man's hotel room . . .

Part of me knew I should tell the detective what I'd seen. But how could I explain *why* I was there to the police when they'd gotten mad at me last time for meddling?

I decided to give myself until the end of the party to see if anything suspicious at all turned up. If after chatting to people here and asking questions it seemed like there was no reason for anyone to have killed Aaron, then I would tell the police what I saw when I went to the hotel and leave it in their hands, come what may.

CHAPTER 7

Two hours later I was itching to go home. Other than the entertainment of Mariah the mermaid putting on quite the show in the swimming pool, the party was dull. I was also starting to question whether I'd jumped to conclusions about the person who'd snuck into Aaron and Ethan's hotel room. Maybe it was theft—a crime of opportunity—and nothing more.

Because right now, all I had was the suspicion of a grieving best friend and a very weak set of potential suspects. One, there was a girlfriend who'd been cheated on and was done with men. Being that I was one of those myself and still had zero desire to commit murder, I couldn't rule it likely that Celina was a killer unless we found something else to indicate it. Two, there was a slimy judge Aaron didn't like for some unknown reason which could mean literally anything. And three, there was someone he borrowed money from whom he may or may not have paid back.

Not exactly the makings of a great investigation.

Maybe Ethan really *was* clutching at straws and I'd been pulled in by his genuine grief and the possibly unrelated incident of someone opportunistically breaking into his hotel room.

It was certainly possible there was no foul play at all.

I stewed on my lack of progress as I watched the crowd. Waiters effortlessly balanced trays of cocktails—dirty martinis and margaritas—as they serviced the guests. Celina was taking photos, staying mostly back in the shadows as an observer and I'd realized quickly that this party was meant to be a networking event between young surfers and potential sponsors, as well as other people in the industry like agents.

I hadn't even known that surfers *had* agents.

Not all of them did, but Ethan and Aaron had both been signed with one—a guy named Bryce Whitten who was an aging surfer type, with a brown ponytail, weathered skin and teeth so artificially white they practically came with their own *ping* sound effect.

"They're going to have a minute of silence for Aaron on the day of the competition," Bryce said. He plucked an olive out of his martini and popped it into his mouth. Despite the upmarket drink, he had the kind of accent that reminded me vaguely of Keanu Reeves in *Bill & Ted's Excellent Adventure*, even when he was speaking about a serious topic.

"The show must go on, I suppose," Ethan muttered.

"Right on." Bryce clamped a hand on his shoulder. "Aaron would want everyone to be in the water. You know that. The water was where he was his best, most awesome self."

Ethan nodded. "You're right."

"Did you represent Aaron for a long time, Bryce?" I asked. It was hard to tell how old he was—I could have guessed anywhere between mid-forties to mid-fifties. He had a full sleeve of tattoos on one arm, which encompassed a lot of surfing and ocean-themed elements like orcas, waves, tropical flowers, suns, shells and surfboards. It was an impressive collection of artwork.

Bryce nodded. "Since he was eighteen. He's had some troubles over the years, but his talent was undeniable. I knew he was going to go pro the first time I saw him."

If Ethan was jealous of the praise his agent was showering on Aaron, he didn't say anything. I wondered if it had been tough for them to be friends and also be represented by the same agent—although maybe that was totally normal in the surfing world. I had no idea.

"It's a huge loss to the community," Bryce added, nodding slowly.

"Do you really think he did it?" Ethan asked, almost as if he were speaking to no one in particular.

Bryce sighed. "I wish I could say no, but . . ."

I glanced over with interest.

"Aaron had a rough life for a young guy," Bryce explained, meeting my gaze. "Over the years he told me about his family. He had a fractured relationship with his dad, who'd been verbally and emotionally abusive toward him. He died when Aaron was twelve and his mom took off not long after that, and the boys went to live with their mom's sister. It left Aaron with a lot of baggage on those young shoulders. Plenty of people hide more pain than we could ever know."

I nodded. That rang true for a lot of people, myself included. I was stressed about my grandmother's cancer, about how I was going to manage my business long term, about whether I would ever trust anyone enough to fall in love again. But I kept it all inside. In that moment, I had a sinking feeling that maybe I'd egged Ethan on by coming with him to the party tonight and supporting his insistence that Aaron was murdered.

It felt like I couldn't see the forest for the trees. Or, in this case, the ocean for the waves.

"How are *you* doing, Bryce?" Ethan asked. "I'm sure you're going around checking on everyone, but you were close to Aaron, too."

I wanted to hug Ethan. Even in his darkest hour, he still cared about how other people were feeling. He had a good soul.

Bryce sighed. "I'm still processing it, to be honest. I got in from Croatia two days ago and the time difference is messing me up. You know I don't sleep well in the best of circumstances and I didn't get a wink after you texted about Aaron last night, even with some assistance. I couldn't stop thinking about him."

What a horrible text to receive in the middle of the night. I could only imagine how upsetting it must have been for Aaron's brother and aunt over in Florida.

"How was the trip?" Ethan asked, as though trying to move the conversation on to something less sad. "I know you were scouting a young guy out there."

Bryce's eyes lit up. "I was! He was totally rad. Super talented. I think he might have the chops to make it big."

As the conversation turned to business, I excused myself to go to the restroom so I could have a moment to think. I wove through the crowd toward the house. The party was getting a little messy, with some people swaying on their feet and the champagne and beer and spirits still flowing freely. Mariah the Mermaid appeared to have ended her shift in the pool and was nowhere to be seen, and now there were a few bodies wading in the water. A couple kissed up against one wall.

The music pulsed through unseen speakers, so loud I felt the bass of it resonating in my chest as I entered the house. There were people draped all over the couches in an opulent lounge room—with white leather and chrome everything. One girl drunkenly danced on a coffee table, and two older men were standing by a bar, drinking something amber-colored as they talked with heads bowed. It was a strange mix of people—old and young, some, like Ethan, totally on the straight and narrow because it was a work thing, while others were not.

I searched for the bathroom and, to my shock, found two stalls with a shared basin area separated with a heavy door. What kind of house had toilets like a fancy hotel? They must have *a lot* of parties here. So far, I hadn't met the host personally but Ethan had pointed him out when he talked with Fisk.

Neither one of the toilets were occupied, so I slipped inside one of the stalls and pulled the door closed. As I sat there, letting my mind whir, there was a sudden blast of music and then it was muted again, likely when the big door to the bathroom area was opened and closed.

"I can't believe you did that." The woman's voice sounded strained. I heard heels clicking as someone, presumably the woman talking, walked around the bathroom. There was a sigh and running water for a moment, but I could still hear over it. "You could have gotten in big trouble!"

She was clearly looking for the same peace and quiet I was, and the brief moment of silence told me that she was on the phone.

"I don't know how many times I've told you to stay out of my business. It's not your job to protect me." She huffed. "What if the police had seen you going to the hotel?"

My entire body went still. Was she talking to the person I saw leaping off the balcony earlier today?

"Did you do it?" There was a distinct wobble, the telltale sign of tears, and more than a hint of accusation. "Did you kill him?"

Holy meatballs. I held my breath, waiting to see what would come next.

"I heard there was a *huge* fight the day he died. Someone heard him yelling in his room." Desperation dripped from her voice. "Don't lie to me, okay? I'm not an idiot."

Whoa. The only fight I knew about was the one I witnessed at the beach. But he'd fought with someone at the hotel, as well? Had Makani followed him back there to finish what they started? Or was it someone else?

"Look, I *know* he didn't kill himself, okay? I would bet every last cent in my bank account that he was murdered." She huffed. "Don't give me that crap. I already told the police what I think. If I find out it was you, so help me God . . ."

I pressed myself to the door, trying to see if I could spot any details through the gap between it and the frame. But the woman must have been standing to the side of the sink and I couldn't catch a glimpse of her. The voice didn't sound familiar, but that could have been because she was so emotional it was distorting the way she spoke. Not that I knew anyone here well enough to recognize their voice in an echoing bathroom, anyway.

I went to grab the handle, ready to turn it and push it open so I could see who else suspected that Aaron was murdered. But at that exact moment the music flared to life again and the sound of a group of women pouring into the shared basin area cut off the phone call. A loud high-pitched giggle was followed by a shriek and more laughter.

"Oh my *god*, Cindy! You're so freaking drunk." This new voice was like nails on a chalkboard. "You were hitting on that guy and he's old enough to be your dad."

"What?" the girl I assumed was Cindy responded in a slightly slurred tone. "This is *networking*, okay? I'm doing it for my career. There's no need to be such a Karen."

"You did *not* just call her a Karen!" a third voice chimed in.

I pressed the button to flush the toilet, even though I hadn't used it. And when I pushed the stall open, I saw the door to the basin area swing shut. Three women in their early twenties crowded around the mirror, drunkenly applying lipstick and lip gloss and checking their teeth while they discussed what officially defined being a Karen.

Not one of them sounded like the woman talking on the phone.

By the time I got home, my head was all over the place. The party hadn't yielded any concrete evidence that Aaron had been murdered, nor had it illuminated any strong motives as to why someone would want to kill him. But Ethan wasn't alone in suspecting foul play *and* it sounded as though there had been a second altercation involving Aaron the day he died.

It wasn't enough to cry murder . . . but it was enough to leave a funny feeling in my gut that maybe not all was what it seemed.

Ethan drove me home from the party and we spent the entire ride dissecting what I'd overheard in the bathroom, although to no end. We couldn't identify the woman, nor had she given any details that might point to the person she was speaking to *or* who had the fight with Aaron in his hotel room. I'd promised that I would keep my ear to the ground. But beyond that, I wasn't sure how much more I could help.

After Ethan dropped me off, I trudged up the driveway feeling a little like I'd let him down. A bubble of anxiousness lodged itself behind my breastbone. The surfing competition was only in town for a few days. Come Sunday evening, everyone would be clearing out. If there *was* a murder here, then it would need to be solved quickly or all the suspects and evidence would be scattered to the wind.

My somber mood was instantly lightened the second I walked into the house and spotted Aunt Dawn in the living room. "That outfit is *amazing!*"

My aunt's halo of frizzy dark purple curls had been neatly tucked away under a pale blond mullet wig that was totally, as they say, business in the front and party in the back. She wore a tight pair of black leggings tucked into long black riding boots, a pale silver silk shirt with voluminous ruffles down the front and a cropped royal-blue jacket adorned with all manner of jewels and sequins on the lapels, shoulders and frilly sleeves. The outfit was capped off with some outrageously '80s make-up, including sweeping white eyeshadow bracketed by thick black eyeliner that winged out from my aunt's eyes, all the way to her temples.

"Jareth the goblin king." She slowly twirled around so I could see the costume from all angles. "In all his glory."

"From the ballroom scene, no less." I nodded my appreciation. "It's a great replication."

Although the movie *Labyrinth* was a bit before my time since I was a nineties baby, it was one of Aunt Dawn's all-time favorites and we'd done a yearly rewatch together for as long as I could remember. I could practically recite it word for word.

On the floor, Moxie stared up at me balefully. The border collie had been stuffed into a white-and-red–striped onesie that was a size too small and made all her fur poof out the neck and leg holes in the most comical way. If the dog could tele-pathically communicate, I could only imagine her saying, *Send help. She's gone mad.*

"I still think we could take the waist in a little." Grandma Rose stared critically at the jacket, a small pincushion affixed to her wrist and a measuring tape draped around her neck. When I was a kid, she'd made all my Halloween costumes from scratch and people had stopped me in the street to take photos of her handiwork. "It would help to emphasize the broadness in the shoulders from the pads we put in, give it a slightly more masculine shape."

"The canine freestyle community won't know what hit 'em." I grinned as my grandmother fussed over my aunt, pinning the fabric and muttering to herself about other possible altera-tions. "Your concepts are always so good."

"It's important to stand out," Dawn said, nodding as she slipped out of her jacket and handed it to Grandma Rose, who set it aside with the pins still in it. "The judges have seen the same themes over and over and over. There are only so many fairies and ballerinas and rock and roll things you can watch before you feel like you've seen it all before."

"I bet they've never seen *this* before," I replied. "Although Moxie seems . . . less than thrilled."

We all turned toward the dog, who flopped dramatically onto her back and let out a long mournful sigh. I smothered a giggle behind my hand. Lord love that dog, but she was dramatic. Although I had to admit, her drama queen antics made her the perfect dog for my aunt. Antonio, on the other hand, trotted over to me, tail wagging and satellite dish ears pricked up, his eyes begging for cuddles. I bent down to scoop him up.

"How did your practice session with Maisey go?" I asked as I sank down onto the couch, setting Antonio onto my lap where he promptly curled up and went to sleep. "Or did you abandon all that and spend the whole time making out?"

"We're not teenagers." Dawn narrowed her eyes at my teasing. "And it went well—she's got a lot of potential, she just needs to have a better command over her dog. Annabel can be a little . . ."

I raised an eyebrow.

"A little bit of a princess," she finished. "She's not as well-trained as Moxie."

As if to demonstrate her point, my aunt snapped her fingers and Moxie leaped up to all fours, standing at attention. Her body almost seemed to vibrate with energy while she awaited her next command—she'd been like that ever since she was a puppy, eager to do things, to be useful and active. Antics aside, she was exceptionally smart and trainable.

"But I think with a bit firmer discipline Annabel will be a

great competitor. Not as good as my baby, of course." She crouched down and helped Moxie out of her white-and-red–striped prison and the dog shook herself, happy to be free. "But still very good."

"Sounds like a successful practice session, then." I grinned. "So, are you two officially . . . together? When do we do the whole 'meet the family' thing?"

I'd met Maisey before, of course. But only briefly, and I was eager to get to know the woman who'd helped my aunt to fully embrace her most authentic self. I wanted her to feel welcomed into our little family. I also felt like I had a little apologizing to do, since I'd been snooping around Maisey's private life while trying to solve a murder mystery not too long ago.

A delicate shade of pink rose up into my aunt's cheeks. For someone who was very open-minded, independent and forward-thinking, my aunt almost *never* blushed. That's how I could tell she liked Maisey a lot.

"I'm not ready to put a label on it and neither is she." Aunt Dawn shook her head, making the mullet wig slide slightly out of place. "The divorce is going to be an ugly one, she thinks. I want to give her time to deal with that before we worry about us. I'm in no rush."

"That's very patient of you," I said with a teasing smile. "Most out of character."

"How was the party?" Grandma Rose asked. She'd retired to the other end of the couch and was sewing some more beads onto my aunt's costume. If she added any more, astronauts would see Aunt Dawn from outer space.

"It was okay," I replied.

My lukewarm response immediately got the attention of both my aunt and my grandmother and I could feel their concern radiating toward me.

"Ethan is convinced that Aaron was murdered," I said, leaning back against the couch and letting my fingertips play with the comforting velvet smoothness of Antonio's ears. "I went to the party tonight to see if we could find anything that might back him up. The police believe it was a suicide, even though Ethan has raised his concerns with them twice now."

"And did you find anything?" My aunt sat on the floor, next to Moxie, who was gnawing at a dog chew.

I relayed everything that Ethan had told me and what had occurred at the party. "So, all in all . . . I have nothing but the suspicions of two people who are clearly very sad that Aaron is gone. I can't exactly blame the police for not suspecting foul play if that's all the evidence there is."

"True." My aunt nodded. "But it should be pretty easy to confirm who came and went from the hotel room the day he died, right?"

"Of course, security cameras!" My declaration startled Antonio, who'd been fast asleep in my arms. But within a few seconds, he melted back against me with a contented sigh.

The hotel would surely have security cameras in the foyer, covering the entrance to the hotel. They may even have them in the hallways on each floor, as well. It occurred to me that the police had probably already gone through this activity. Although perhaps not.

If they really believed that Aaron had ended his own life, then perhaps they skipped over that altogether.

"I don't want you getting wound up in anything dangerous," Grandma Rose said, her silvery eyebrows knitting together and her wrinkles deepening on her forehead. "Last time there was a murder around here . . ."

Her voice shook as she trailed off, her eyes growing distant for a moment. I swallowed back a surge of guilt. It wasn't only me who'd gotten in the crosshairs of a murderer. Grandma Rose had been a victim, too.

"Anything I come across will go straight to the police," I said, nodding. "I promise."

If there was even an inkling that Aaron had been murdered, then they would *have* to investigate, right? If we found something in the security footage from the hotel, then it might be enough to convince them to take a closer look and, at least, put Ethan's mind at ease.

CHAPTER 8

The next morning I felt . . . *rough.*

I'd tossed and turned all night, having strange dreams about masked baddies, mermaids and endless blue. At one point I'd been pulled underwater by some unseen force, my throat and nose and ears being filled with salty ocean water as I struggled to break free. There were shadows lurking, great slithering beasts that brushed by me as I sank and sank and sank. When I woke up, sweat was beaded along my brow and running down my back, and I gasped for breath.

Outside my bedroom door, there was a whine and a scratching sound. I forced myself to get up and flick on the lamp. It was still dark as sunrise wasn't due for another hour or so. When I pushed open my bedroom door, I found Antonio sitting in the hallway, staring up at me.

"Why are you awake so early?" I asked as I bent down to pick him up. He trembled in my arms.

Man, I had no idea how much Chihuahuas trembled when we adopted him. Excited to receive a snack? Trembling. Scared of a noise outside? Trembling. Air has a slight chill to it? Trembling intensifies. They were basically the Tickle Me Elmo of dog breeds.

"You can't possibly be cold," I said, cuddling him to my chest. He pushed the top of his head against the crook of my neck and snuggled in. "Did something scare you, bud? Bad dreams? I know that feeling."

I carried him into my room and I sat on the edge of the bed to snuggle for a few minutes while I tried to get my head straight.

"How am I going to get through a whole day of work with all this stuff going on, huh?" I said to Antonio, who let out a little doggy snore in response. "You're no help."

I let him stay on my bed while I got ready for work by showering, changing into my work clothes and slicking back my hair into a bun that would fit under my chef's cap. When I turned to say goodbye, I found that Antonio had "nested" by pushing the blankets around until he'd created a cozy pile of material to burrow down into. This was another Chihuahua idiosyncrasy I'd learned since adopting him—coziness was king.

Before I headed off to work, I fed Antonio, put a pot of coffee on to brew so it would be ready for when Grandma Rose woke up, and pulled out a quiche I'd made and frozen the previous week to thaw out. Then I headed outside, jumped in the Jellybean and drove to work.

The time before the café opened was usually a peaceful and creative time. I knew lots of bakers and chefs who *hated* the early starts, but after I acclimated to waking up before the sun, I tended to enjoy starting my day alone, with plenty of time to think and problem-solve before the doors opened. The challenge I was currently working on was finding the balance between what I needed to make fresh each day and what I could prepare ahead of time to ensure we had consistently stocked shelves without burning me out. It was becoming increasingly apparent that if we continued to fill seats like we were, I would absolutely need to hire extra staff if I wanted any semblance of a life.

Aunt Dawn was a fantastic help with most things—and she'd taken over perfecting our infusion methods for the cannabis butter, oil and honey that we used in our products—but a professional baker she was not. Which meant I still had to be here every day we were open to prepare our freshly baked products.

This morning that included: vintage cheddar and rosemary savory scones, salted caramel sweet scones, our "feature" macaron of the day (black sesame, with the shells I had made yesterday), the "everything but the kitchen sink" cookies, plus the dessert special, which was an apple and blackberry galette.

A galette is essentially an open-faced pie, which is made with a simple pastry base topped with either a sweet or savory filling. The edges are folded in, leaving the center of the pie open, to create a delicious, yet rustic dessert. A lot of people assume that all French desserts are tricky, temperamental and finnicky (and really, I can't blame them! Choux pastries, any-one?) but the humble galette is the antithesis of all that. I'd made my share of them on my days off, because they're perfect for using up produce, like any leek or mushrooms languishing in the back of the fridge.

Today, however, I was using the freshest ingredients—blackberries from a local farm and apples from a nearby or-chard. I started by making the dough. Aunt Dawn had made a fresh batch of cannabutter butter yesterday, so I portioned that out along with flour, sugar and salt, and set about com-bining the ingredients.

One of the things that had been a fun topic of conversation lately between myself and customers was how the term "weed baking" was kind of a misnomer. In many cases, you don't bake directly with the cannabis. Rather, it was infused into a carrier ingredient like butter, oil, honey, cream or milk (among other things) after being decarboxylated, which was the process of physically altering the chemical structure of the cannabis through heating, so that it became psychoactive. This was the most important part of the process, because it both allowed people to experience a high as well as turned the cannabis into a powerful anti-inflammatory and pain-relief treatment.

But before I got started with any of my baking there was one thing every good kitchen needed: music.

I grabbed my phone and popped it on the docking station in the office, where it connected to a portable Bose speaker.

"Hey Siri," I said and my phone's screen lit up in response. "Play Throwback playlist."

Britney Spears's "Toxic" blasted out of the speaker.

"Perfect." I shimmied to the music and danced back into the kitchen.

Now it was time to get to work.

I started by making the pastry dough and rolling the dough balls out into the required number to make individually portioned galettes. Yes, it would have been easier to make a few large galettes and sell them by the slice. Possibly more cost effective, too. However, when it came to weed baking, it was always easier to ensure the correct dosing per dish if things were individually portioned. This was because I could calculate the exact dose by dividing the total milligrams of cannabis used in the recipe by the percentage of THC in the strain, divided again by the number of portions.

When you sliced a larger item up, it was almost impossible to ensure the slices were exactly the same size, which would affect the dose a person was receiving. A larger slice would result in a bigger dose, and vice versa. Why was it important to get this correct? A, because I took my responsibility as a cannabis business owner seriously; and B, I believed that people deserved to know what they were putting into their bodies.

After making the pastry, I moved to the stove to make a simple syrup using sugar, water and a few cinnamon sticks. Then I peeled, cored and sliced the apples, washed and dried the blackberries and placed all the fruit in a bowl along with a scraped vanilla bean, lemon juice, sugar, cinnamon and a sprinkle of flour, and mixed to combine. Now that I had all my components, I could begin the time-consuming process of assembling the galettes. I covered my entire preparation bench with the rolled pastry, then I circled and spooned filling into the center of each one, leaving room to fold the edges. Once they were all folded, I brushed the pastry with a little cinnamon syrup to give them extra flavor and to help the galette brown nicely in the oven.

The rest of my preparation time flew by. Aunt Dawn was coming in late that morning because she'd promised to take Grandma Rose to her oncology appointment. So I was by myself until we opened at ten. At a quarter past nine, however, there was a knock on the back door. I almost didn't hear it over the Lady Gaga song pumping through my portable speaker, but then a shadow moving caught my attention through the small square window on the door. At first, a shot of adrenaline rushed through me and I almost dropped the tray of scones I was carrying toward the oven, thinking that someone was trying to break in.

But I recognized the friendly face. It was Jake.

I popped the scones in the oven and went to open the door.

"Caffeine delivery." He grinned and held out a cup of coffee from my favorite café, Bean and Gone. "You've been doing a lot of early starts lately, so I figured you could use a pick-me-up."

I brightened at the kind gesture. "Thanks."

With my scones in the oven and everything else pretty much ready to go for the day, I could afford to pause for a few minutes and enjoy a coffee with him, so I stepped outside.

"How's it all going?" he asked. "I've come past a few times and you've either had a line out the door or, at the very least, every table has been full. You must be thrilled."

"I am." I sipped my coffee and almost sighed with happiness. I hadn't even known I was craving one until that first sip, but Jake had delivered me exactly what I hadn't even realized I wanted.

A little bit like the man himself, huh?

Not quite. Being a Disney fanatic and a romantic at heart, I'd always known that falling in love was on my list of life goals. It was simply a matter of timing. Right now, my life felt too full to even consider dating anyone. But here was Jake, being sweet and thoughtful and cute.

So, *so* cute.

He looked extra beachy today in a pair of light blue shorts with a pattern of tiny palm trees on them, a white shirt with the sleeves rolled back and white sneakers. A pair of sunglasses dangled from the neck of his shirt and he had a thin, braided leather bracelet on one wrist.

"It's been a wild ride," I said, dragging my eyes away from him and focusing on the ground. "I feel like the whole thing was a whirlwind, but now we're open and the seats are being filled. I'm not sure what I was so scared of."

"Our imaginations are almost always harsher than reality," he said, his voice faraway.

For a moment, I wondered if he was telling himself that.

I respected that Jake made amends and faced up to lying to me. As Grandma Rose always said, *Being a good person isn't about never making a mistake. It's about taking responsibility and doing the right thing after you make one.* I believed that was true.

"I always thought having an active imagination was a good thing," I said with a laugh. "But as an adult, I'm not so sure."

Jake nodded. "Everything seems easy when you're a kid. We only learn to overthink things when we grow up."

"That is some truth right there." I took a sip of my coffee and we fell into contemplative silence for a moment.

"I know I already said this once," he said, leaning back against the wall of my shop and glancing sideways at me. "But I'm sorry I lied to you, Chloe. It's uh . . . it's been a long time since I met a woman who stopped me in my tracks."

Heat rose up into my cheeks and I looked down at the coffee cup cradled in my hands. The Bean and Gone logo—which had two coffee beans positioned to look like a heart—was stamped onto the side.

"I spent a good chunk of my life trying to hide those rough years from people," he admitted. "I knew my family was ashamed that I'd fallen in with such a bad crowd. And when I made it to college, I vowed that I would do everything I could to keep that part of my past a secret from everyone I met. On Wall Street, most people I worked with came from money. I knew they would never understand the past I had. So for a long time I just . . . hid that part of my life away and hoped nobody would ever find out."

Sincerity rang true in his voice and I could understand why he'd been so desperate to put the bad times behind him. "It's like muscle memory."

"It is." He nodded. "But I also believe, now, that *all* our life experiences help to shape who we are, even the bad ones. Maybe I wouldn't have been so motivated to make something of myself without hitting rock bottom like that."

"That's a very positive way of looking at it." I nodded. "And maybe I wouldn't have opened my own business here without first finding out that my fiancé had cheated on me."

In another dimension, where my ex might have been a stand-up guy, perhaps I would have come home to help Grandma Rose through her chemo treatments and then gone back to Paris after. Maybe it would have been harder for me to cut ties with my life in France without Jules giving me a metaphorical shove out the door.

"I don't want to say something awfully cliché like 'everything happens for a reason,' but . . ." He shrugged. "Maybe the crappy parts of life are just us figuring out which direction we're supposed to be taking."

"That is definitely food for thought."

I looked at Jake and he let out a self-conscious laugh. Then he raked his hand through his brown hair, the thick strands springing stubbornly back into place. "Sorry, I didn't mean to barge in on you at work and pose a bunch of existential questions."

"I like a guy who thinks about the deeper things in life." I flushed. "Especially if they also bring coffee."

"At least I know I can get that right." He nudged me with his elbow and I smiled. There was something about Jake that made me feel comfortable and safe. One little lie didn't erase that feeling.

"I appreciate that you told me the truth in the end," I said. "Especially since you did it off your own back. I won't judge someone for the things they did in the past so long as they're honest about it and trying to do better now. We've all made mistakes."

He swallowed. "It was one hell of a mistake."

"But look at you now. You're running your own financial consulting business, working for yourself and restoring your grandfather's vintage car. And you live in one of the most beautiful places in the country, if I do say so myself. You're living the dream."

"It's almost the dream." Jake's voice had that faraway quality again and I wondered what part of a perfect life he thought was missing, but before I could ask he said, "You took me by surprise, you know. I thought you were the cute girl-next-door type and then the first time we hung out you asked me to research the weed industry and solve a murder mystery. That's not your average first date."

I snorted. "Technically we weren't on a date. But I see your point."

"I'd like to do it again."

"Solve a murder mystery?" I looked at him and he shook his head, laughing.

"No. I mean, I'd like to hang out again and go on whatever crazy adventure you have cooked up. Whatever it is, I'm up for it."

My face was growing warmer by the second and my stomach was fluttering. Despite the fact that Jake and I had gotten off to a rocky start, I was still attracted to him. I still liked his personality and the brave way he'd stepped up to help Grandma Rose and me when our safety was threatened. He'd followed that up by sending flowers to my grandmother and a chili plant for me, which was still flourishing in the backyard. Not to mention, his crooked smile still made my heart beat a little faster.

Everyone deserves a second chance, right?

"Well, we have a date for ice cream and watching the surfing competition on Saturday," I said. "I don't know if that's much of an adventure, but I'm looking forward to it."

"So this one *is* a date, then?" He looked at me hopefully.

This was it—time to figure out whether I was jumping back into the dating arena or not. No more dancing around things. Was I ready to try again? Jules's betrayal was feeling further away by the day, even though it had only been a few months.

But what was I going to do, stay hurt and angry forever? Life went on. Jules had stopped calling and the relief I felt about that told me everything I needed to know: I never wanted to go back to him.

It was time to move on.

"Yeah," I said, too bashful to meet Jake's eye. "It's a date."

CHAPTER 9

Today Erica had been scheduled to work the afternoon shift alongside Aunt Dawn, so I could leave the café at one p.m. to head off to a meeting with a local cannabis grower. I was thrilled with how Erica had fit into our small team—the customers loved her and I trusted her to do an excellent job, even when I wasn't around.

"One CBD chai latte, a cheddar and rosemary savory scone and a black sesame macaron, coming right up." Erica pulled the scone and macaron from the front counter with a pair of tongs and put them on a plate for the customer. Then she handed over a number for her table so I would know where to deliver the drink. "That's table five, Chloe."

"Got it!"

Being on drinks duty was a nice break from working in the kitchen and I really enjoyed making the chai lattes. We called them our "hug in a mug" and the calming effects of CBD had proven to be a popular choice, especially for first timers. Many of our customers were curious about the differences between CBD and THC, which were two of the major chemical compounds found in cannabis. Essentially, THC was the stuff that got you high. CBD, on the other hand, wouldn't.

I'd wanted Baked by Chloe to offer both products, even though THC was what was more commonly associated with edibles. But the great thing about CBD was that it didn't give you the munchies and you could still legally drive after consuming it (great if you had somewhere to go after visiting the café). Yet it provided a very relaxing effect, which combined with the soothing spices in the chai latte was a match made in heaven.

As I heated up the milk, using the wand to create a little foam for the top, I looked out over the café to see which table I needed to take the drink to. I spotted the sign with the number five in the back corner, where a blond woman sat by herself. She looked familiar but no name sprang to my mind. Where had I seen her before? She flicked her hair over one shoulder, revealing a tanned décolletage and a T-shirt with a mermaid on the front.

That was it! She was Mariah the Mermaid from the party last night.

I might not have figured it out if it wasn't for the hint on her T-shirt, because without the extravagant makeup, body glitter and costume, she looked like any other beach-loving tourist.

At that moment, I saw Aunt Dawn come through from the kitchen, her apron on. "You're good to finish up, girlie. I just pulled that last batch of scones and cookies out of the oven— you outdid yourself. They smell amazing."

"Thanks! I'll head off as soon as I finish this drink order," I replied.

I held the silver jug up to the foaming wand, watching the milk swirl around and become thick and foamy. When it was done, I turned off the air and pulled the jug away. Giving the milk a little swirl, I checked the consistency and then banged the jug against the countertop three times to remove any bubbles.

Our chai lattes were served in cute, mismatched mugs that Aunt Dawn and I had sourced from all over the place. This one was a robin's egg blue with a delicate gold rim and handle. Holding the mug and saucer steady, I headed through the swing door that separated the customer space from the working space and walked over to the table in the back corner.

"One soothing CBD chai latte," I said with a smile as I set the drink down on the table.

"Thank you." Mariah looked up at me with a friendly smile. Then her brows creased. "Do we know each other?"

Good. If she recognized me as well, then it wouldn't be so awkward for me to point out that I'd seen her at the party.

"I happened to see you in action last night," I said. "You're a professional mermaid, right?"

"That's right." She snapped her fingers. "You were at the party with Ethan."

"Good eye." I was surprised she'd taken notice of Ethan and me when she was working.

"I spend a lot of my evening events sitting and splashing at the edge of a pool, so I always have a look around and see who's there," she replied, as if reading my mind. "Are you a friend of Ethan's?"

"Technically I'm a friend of Ethan's older brother, Matt," I explained. "He lives here in town. I only met Ethan very recently."

"Oh, okay." She nodded.

"I've never heard of professional mermaid as a job before. I would have *loved* to have a birthday party with someone like you there when I was a little girl. Ariel was always my favorite Disney princess."

"Mine, too." She nodded enthusiastically. "And I do a lot of kids' birthday parties. About half of my bookings, I'd guess."

"What's the other half? Parties in rich people's mansions?"

She laughed and lifted one dainty shoulder into a shrug. "Yeah, there's the occasional rich guy who wants to impress his guests with a mermaid. But I also do a lot of corporate events and educational activities for schools, as well. I work with several aquariums to help educate kids about how important it is to protect the ocean and all the creatures and plant life within it."

I could see how passionate she was about the topic, because it shined out of her face and eyes. Her whole being seemed to light up. I imagined that's how I looked when I talked about baking.

"What a cool job." I shook my head in wonder. "Maybe this is a silly question but . . . what is your tail made from?"

"I have a whole collection of tails. The ones I swim in are made from silicone—they're super hard to get on and off but they look very realistic. Then I have some 'land tails' for parties where I'm just taking photos and not going into the water that are made from fabric and foam. Those ones I decorate with beads and biodegradable sequins. I even have a tail with LED lights for special night events." She grinned. "And then add to that a whole collection of different mermaid bra tops, crowns, all my makeup and hair stuff, plus other accessories. It becomes a bit of an obsession."

"Wow! You must need an entire other wardrobe for your mermaid stuff."

"Thank goodness I have a spare bedroom." She laughed. "Being a mermaid means having a lot of accessories. Here, if you ever need something to spice up a party, I've got a booking form on my website."

Mariah slipped a business card out of a little pocket on her phone case and handed it to me. The card was a soft pink and in shiny blue-foiled writing it said: *Mermaid Dreams, Mariah Howard.* It had her website, a phone number and her social media handles.

"Thanks." I pocketed the card. "You might have the coolest job ever."

"It's certainly fun and it's helping to pay for college. I'm funding it all on my own." She nodded. For a moment, I saw her sunny demeanor slip and caught a glimpse of the serious, worrisome look behind it. "Every penny helps."

I knew as well as anyone that paying for college was no joke, and if she was funding it all by herself . . . that was a lot of pressure to book jobs.

"You're studying marine biology, right? Ethan mentioned that you want to work in that field."

"I never knew he kept such close tabs on what I was doing." She cocked her head, narrowing her eyes slightly. "Especially not since the thing with Aaron."

I wasn't sure what to say about that. Ethan seemed to have a lot of respect for Mariah, so I had assumed they were friends. But perhaps there had been some kind of beef in the past. What had happened between Mariah and Aaron?

"I'm sure he must be a mess given . . ." Her eyes dropped down to her chai latte. "If you see him around, tell him I'm sorry for his loss, yeah?"

"I'm sure he'd be happy to hear it directly from you," I said gently.

She chewed on the inside of her lip. "I don't know about that."

After a few heartbeats of awkward silence, I told her I hoped she enjoyed her treats and headed out the back to get changed and finish my workday. It sure sounded like there was some history between Mariah and Ethan, or Mariah and Aaron . . . or maybe between all three of them together. A love triangle, perhaps?

It could be nothing, but I figured I'd ask Ethan and see if he knew what she was talking about. Chances were that it wasn't anything important. But I'd learned that sometimes all it took to bring a whole load of ugly truths to light was a small, seemingly inconsequential detail.

And this could absolutely be one of those details.

I headed home to shower and change for my meeting with a local cannabis grower. Getting to meet other people in the industry had certainly been an interesting part of the job. What I'd learned, principally, was that there was no real "type" of person who ended up working with weed.

I'd met people of all ages, from all over the world, with all kinds of motives and desires. Some were in the business because they liked to get high and they'd taken an interest in creating the best experience possible. Other people, like me, were more interested in the medicinal and holistic side of things. Some were in it for the money and thought it was a good financial move.

I'd made it a personal mission to support other small, local businesses. Rather than sourcing my ingredients solely from the larger commercial cannabis growing businesses, I'd taken time to find solopreneurs or small family-run operations not only for my cannabis but for my dairy, flour, fruits and vegetables, too.

Today I was meeting with a grower who ran a very small farm. In fact, the first time I'd driven out to meet him I'd gotten lost among some fields containing a few scattered cows and some overgrown bramble bushes. This time I made sure to keep my eyes peeled for the small handmade sign—which was little more than scrap wood nailed to a tree displaying a haphazardly painted cannabis leaf in white paint—so I didn't miss the turnoff.

The Jellybean protested as I swerved to narrowly avoid a pothole in the packed dirt road that led up to North Pole Organics. The owner, Nikolai—who'd asked me to call him Niki the first time we met—was a big barrel of a man with a prominent belly, a long white beard and warmly crinkled blue eyes. He'd been growing weed for almost twenty years and had earned himself the nickname "Weed Santa" for both his appearance and generous personality. Nikolai, it turned out, wasn't really his name, but I appreciated his commitment to the theme.

I leaned forward, squinting as I drove, to look for the gate that served as entrance to the organic farm. In addition to cannabis, Niki also grew organic strawberries and tomatoes, and sold the eggs from his small brood of chickens. Spotting the open gate, I slowed and turned. The road was dustier here and, in the rearview mirror, I could see the small cloudy trail behind the Jellybean that would no doubt mean I'd need to give it a wash soon.

Niki was waiting by the front door of the homestead where he lived and worked, clutching a regal-looking white Silkie chicken. The bird was covered in downy feathers, even on its legs and feet, and sported a rather comical-looking cluster of feathers atop its head, making it almost look as though the chicken was wearing a fluffy hat.

"Hello there," he bellowed as I got out of my car, a smile revealing slightly yellowed teeth through a small opening in his abundant white beard. The chicken appeared disinterested in my arrival. "Good to see you, Chloe. What a fine day it is!"

"Hi Niki. Great to see you again."

"Come, come." He motioned for me to follow him around the side of the house and down a path that led to the cannabis-growing operation. We walked past the chicken coop and about twenty chickens pottered around the large, fenced-in space, pecking at the ground and chasing one another. He had a few different types, mostly Rhode Island Reds but he favored his Silkies.

"I got some new seeds in that I'm very excited about," Niki said to me as we headed into one of several polytunnels that were dotted across the property.

These structures worked in the same way as a greenhouse, but rather than having glass walls, the polytunnels were framed with steel and covered with plastic sheeting. While certainly not as aesthetically pleasing as a pretty glass greenhouse, Niki had told me that the polytunnels provided smaller farms more planting space for a lower financial outlay.

Cost was often a barrier to entry if one wanted to grow weed on a larger scale.

"A buddy of mine who runs a bigger farm up north hooked me up. These little guys are still germinating but he also gave me a mature plant to try." Niki placed the Silkie chicken on the ground and gestured to a row of plates covered with damp paper towels. Peeling back the top layer of the soaked paper towel, he revealed a small collection of seeds that had started to sprout taproots. "Hmm, this needs some more water."

He reached for a spray bottle and gave each of the plates a few mists. Most of the other farms I'd visited, even the smaller ones, tended to work with clones rather than seeds. A clone was a cutting from a live cannabis plant that was planted into a small container and fed to encourage root growth, so that it would develop into a full plant itself. Growers tended to like this method because seeds could be fickle and it made for slower production. Using clones could shave a month off the growing process which, to a small business, really impacted the bottom line. Niki, however, said that working with the seeds made him feel more connected to the plants because he got to nurture them from being "babies" all the way to adulthood.

I found his whole attitude toward the plants really wholesome.

"I thought of you as soon as I tried it," he continued, walking farther into the polytunnel away from his germinating area to a large workstation, which was scattered with dirt and humble-looking tools. Bags of soil were stacked to the side and an uneven tower of empty pots was next to that. There were also a few young plants in pots which looked as though they had just been transplanted. Their distinctive elongated leaves bobbed as a warm breeze rolled through, gently rattling the plastic siding of the polytunnel.

I felt something brush by my leg as the Silkie chicken scuttled past me, heading straight for the soil bags. It pecked enthusiastically at one.

"Esmerelda, stop that!" Niki admonished. The chicken continued to potter around our feet, its fluffy body looking like a giant cotton ball. Niki reached for a plant that was still in a medium-sized pot. "Now, this here is called Christmas Morning. So can you see why my buddy was so keen for me to try it."

I laughed. "How could you *not* grow something with such a perfectly fitting name?"

"Exactly." He nodded. "It's one of the sweetest strains I've ever tried. It has an almost candy-like flavor as well as some natural fruitiness. Blueberry-like if you ask me."

"Oh!" My eyes lit up. "That does sound like something I could work with."

"Be warned, though, she packs a punch. The THC content could be upwards of twenty percent, so it's not necessarily for new players, you see."

"Hmm." I nodded. "I might have to use it in a smaller dose, then."

"I would think so," he agreed. "But the flavor is worth a little fiddling to get the dosage right. It's got that sweet terpene, linalool. I thought it would be right up your alley."

Terpenes were naturally occurring chemical compounds found in plants which were responsible for aroma and flavor. I was familiar with linalool, specifically, since it was also found in citrus, lavender and mint. Knowing more about the terpenes—something that Niki was helping me learn more about—made for a great starting point when trying to figure out what to pair the cannabis strain with to really make it shine, since you could choose to add other things that naturally had the same terpenes for a more harmonious flavor pairing. Blueberry, lavender and lemon was a winning combination because of the shared linalool.

So this new strain might make for an excellent scone or macaron recipe . . . although I had been wanting to try cannabis pancakes, too.

Linalool was also known for its relaxation-boosting effects, which was exactly the kind of experience I loved to provide my customers. In fact, I tended to gravitate to those kinds of cannabis strains across the board. That was the benefit of building business relationships with growers—once they knew what you were looking for, they could make excellent recommendations.

"Here, I set some flowers aside from the samples my buddy sent." Niki unscrewed the lid on a small jar filled with cannabis buds. He dug one thick forefinger into the jar to jostle the flowers around. "Have a whiff of that."

Buds didn't look like typical flowers, since they were devoid of petals. They almost looked like small clumps of moss in a way, but with a totally different texture. The buds were where the terpenes and cannabinoids lived, which was what would produce a high and provide pain-soothing, anti-inflammatory benefits once they had been through the decarboxylation process.

Fun fact: I'd also learned recently that only the female plants produced buds. The more you know!

"Oh wow," I said after inhaling the scent of the flowers. "The blueberry note is beautiful."

Anybody expecting a pure blueberry smell would be disappointed, because the cannabis still smelled like . . . well, cannabis. But this strain didn't have anywhere near as much of the earthy, funky (or skunky) scent that some people found off-putting. Instead there was a gentle grassiness, along with a touch of citrus and a sweet, almost blueberry jam note. I could already tell how amazing it would be in pancakes.

As if on cue, my stomach rumbled.

"Got the munchies and you haven't even tried it yet." Niki chuckled. "Should I put you down for some of this?"

"Yes, please." I handed the jar back to him and he screwed the lid back on.

"Wonderful." He beamed. "It's good to have a reliable customer like you on the books. Since some of those bigger operations started springing up in the area, it's been hard to compete."

And *that* was exactly why I wanted my business to support people like Niki.

"Now, shall we do the rest of your order over coffee? Henrietta put some fresh biscuits in the oven a while ago and they should be just about done."

My tummy rumbled again.

"I'll take that as a yes." Niki scooped up Esmerelda and motioned for me to follow him.

Biscuits and tea sounded amazing. With the stress of opening the café and facing our first busy season—not to mention becoming entangled in yet another potential murder investigation—it was a joy to sit down with some nice folks and talk about a shared passion over something hot to drink and delicious to eat. For a few moments, at least, I would be able to forget about everything else.

As we were walking to the house, my phone buzzed with a text message.

MATT: The police have released the hotel room. Ethan and I are heading there as soon as his heat is over. Want to come meet us?

Sadly, it looked like my ability to put the real world out of my mind was going to be short-lived.

CHAPTER 10

After my meeting with the grower, I headed to the hotel to meet Matt and Ethan. The woman manning the reception desk barely looked at me as I hustled through the lobby and straight to the stairwell, which only reinforced my suspicion that anybody could have gotten up to the room without being noticed. Once upstairs, I knocked on the door and Ethan opened it a second later. The poor guy looked like he'd gone all night without sleep. There were dark rings under his eyes and his curly blond hair was sticking out in all directions, looking a little wild and frizzy.

"How are you holding up?" I asked.

"Poorly." Despite his sincere reply, he attempted a smile. Something told me that was Ethan in a nutshell—he was the kind of guy who always tried his hardest to stay upbeat, even in the crappiest of circumstances.

"But he still crushed his heat today. Finished on top with ease," Matt said from inside the room. "What a ripper. You should have seen him!"

I got the impression Matt was trying to cheer Ethan up, but it didn't appear to be working. Ethan motioned for me to come into the room and he closed the door behind me. "I have news."

"Tell me everything."

"The backpack turned up." He pointed to one of the twin beds, where a battered brown canvas and leather backpack sat. "Remember how I said it was weird that it was missing because Aaron never went anywhere without it? Well, here it is out of the blue."

I glanced at Matt, who was leaning against the wall, looking concerned. He, too, appeared to be running on little sleep. His leg bounced and he picked at a frayed hole in his jeans, as if a jittering energy coursed through his body and he was trying anything to get it out. I frowned. "Where did you find it?"

"Here. After the detective called to say they'd released the room, we came right over and when I opened the door it was . . . there. Sitting on the bed like it'd been there the whole time." Ethan tossed his hands in the air. "You guys were in the room. You *know* it wasn't here when we found Aaron, right?"

I closed my eyes for a moment and scanned my memory. Honestly, the time we were here was kind of a blur because it was shocking to find someone like that, even though it had happened to me once before. But I didn't recall there being anything at all sitting on the other bed.

"Maybe the police took it when we called 911 and they brought it back when they released the room?" I suggested, but Ethan shook his head vehemently.

"I asked the detective and she said they never took anything aside from Aaron's body, the pill jar and the handwritten note. I mean, there wasn't much else to take. Other than clothing and surfing gear, we travel light. I never bring my laptop with me and neither does Aaron, especially since we stay in these crappy hotels and the security isn't that good."

"Speaking of security," I said, snapping my fingers. "I wonder if the police looked at any security footage from the hotel to see who was coming and going?"

"I doubt it," Ethan replied bitterly. "They didn't take my concerns seriously at all. I bet they decided this was a suicide from the moment they walked in the room and saw the note, and didn't bother looking for anything that might contradict them. Why would they care? It's not like Aaron was a local. Heck, maybe they know about his past and think he was just some troublemaker who doesn't deserve their time."

"Ethan," Matt said, pushing off the wall and walking over to his brother so he could place a hand protectively on his shoulder. "That's unfair. I'm sure the police would investigate it the same regardless of *who* was in the situation. They believe it was a suicide based on the evidence they have and we disagree. So instead of wasting time putting words in their mouths, let's find something that shows them we're right."

Ethan let out a breath. I could feel his frustration thick and heavy in the air. "Yeah, you're right."

"We should see if the hotel will let us look at the security footage," I suggested. "But before we do that, have you looked in the backpack?"

Ethan shook his head. "I haven't, but I guess there's nothing to stop me touching it now. Not like they'll want to dust it for prints and they told me I could take Aaron's personal effects anyway, since I've promised to fly over to Florida and give everything to his family."

"You're a good friend, Ethan." My heart ached for the guy.

"I try." He shot me another half attempt at a smile. "Okay, let's open it up."

I held my breath in anticipation as Ethan undid the buckle holding the top closed and then flipped the backpack open. He reached inside and pulled out a stack of what looked like sketchbooks and set them on the bed. Next came a rather old-looking camera with a cap covering the lens, a tin of pencils, two different types of surfboard wax, a blue inhaler, a faded Orlando Magic baseball cap, some headphones, sunglasses, a beat-up cell phone with scratches and dings on it, a wallet and a Rip Curl water bottle.

"Let's see if there's anything weird on his phone." Ethan tried to power up the device, but the screen showed a blinking picture of a battery. "It's dead."

"We can charge it when we get back to my place." Matt reached down and tugged a charger out of the socket by the bed. "Don't forget this."

"Anything missing from his wallet?" I asked.

Ethan turned the wallet over in his hands and flipped it open. It was one of those simple folding types in a waterproof material that looked like the same thing wetsuits were made out of. Inside there was a piece of ID in the clear plastic pocket, a debit card, a few loyalty cards for different businesses, a transit card, a library card, a few crumpled low denomination bills and some coins.

There was also a medical information card which was bright red and had a cross on the front, inside which sat the caduceus—a winged rod with two snakes intertwining. It struck me as a responsible thing to have in one's wallet, especially considering that Aaron didn't seem to have a reputation for being that way.

"What's listed on the medical card?" I asked, remembering the empty orange pill bottle I'd seen on the floor beside Aaron's body. Ethan opened the folded information card.

"There are two medications listed: salbutamol and temazepam." Ethan wrinkled his nose. "I have no idea what either of those things are for."

I didn't either.

"I'll look them up." I pulled out my phone and typed "salbutamol" into Google after checking the spelling on the card. "Looks like the first one is an asthma medication, used for opening the airways and treating asthma attacks."

"Ahh, yes." Ethan nodded, reaching for the blue inhaler that was now sitting on the bed. The label confirmed it to be the one listed on his medical card. "He always carried this around with him. I've seen him use it a handful of times over the years. Whenever he traveled, I knew that if he were to have an attack I could find the inhaler in his backpack. He was serious about it. One time he ended up in the hospital because he accidentally left his inhaler at home when he went on a surf trip."

"The second medication is . . ." I tapped away at my phone. "Sleeping pills, by the look of it."

"Sleeping pills?" Ethan's brow furrowed. "I didn't know he was taking those."

I peered over his shoulder at the medical information card, which had documented Aaron's height, weight, date of birth, emergency contact information, blood type, medical conditions, allergies and medications. One thing I noticed right away was that all the information appeared in black pen ink, with the exception of the temazepam. That one was written in blue ink, though the handwriting appeared consistent throughout.

"Look," I said, pointing. "It seems like this was added after the rest of the card was already filled in. I wonder if that means he'd started taking it more recently. Also, we now have something with Aaron's handwriting on it in addition to the letter."

Matt looked at Ethan. "I told you she had an eye for this stuff."

"I'm hardly a detective." I flushed. "Let's just see what else we can find here. Then when we have something solid, we can take it to the chief."

We looked through the rest of Aaron's personal effects, after finding nothing else of interest in his wallet. The collection of black spiral-bound sketchbooks were visual journals, each with a date range written in metallic gold ink in the top right-hand corner. Most covered a six-month block, give or take. I flipped through one of the books and saw some beautiful sketches. Aaron had drawn a bunch of different beaches, capturing all the flora and fauna in great detail. It appeared that he also liked to catalogue cool shells that he'd found, collecting their images rather than the shells themselves.

The sketches occasionally depicted people. I recognized a few that I'd met so far, including Ethan, Mariah the Mermaid, Celina Sato the photographer, and the pretty girl from the beach who'd also been manning the door at the party. Kaila, I think was her name.

"He's super talented," I said, shaking my head in wonder. "These drawings are so evocative."

"What Aaron couldn't always put into words, he put into drawings," Ethan said, looking sad. "Used to be that way when he was young, too. Instead of apologizing if he did something wrong, he'd draw a picture and tuck it into my surf bag. That's how I knew he was sorry even when he couldn't say it."

I decided to put the sketchbooks in chronological order, so we could look through them in more detail later in case they showed anything that might be linked to the murder. That's when I realized that there was a chunk of time missing.

"Look," I said, pointing. "There's a gap in the dates. Nothing from February to April this year. Then the most recent journal starts up again in May."

"That's weird." Ethan wrinkled his nose.

"Maybe he didn't sketch during that time," Matt suggested.

"Aaron was *always* sketching." Ethan shook his head. "Seriously, if that guy wasn't on the water, he had a pencil in his hand."

This was supported by the fact that the pencils in the case had mostly been worn down to nubs.

"Could he have accidentally left one at home?" I asked.

"Nuh-uh. He was *way* superstitious about that. Carried the whole collection to every single competition. I even joked that in a few years we'd need to hire a U-Haul to transport them all around the country."

"Why was he superstitious?" I asked, staring at the identical black covers of the journals as though I might find answers there.

Ethan laughed. "Why is *anyone* superstitious? One time he had all the sketchbooks packed because he was in the middle of moving house and he brought them to a competition where he absolutely killed it. After that, he decided they were his lucky charms. One of many, just like rooming with me."

Interesting. I wasn't sure what to make of Aaron so far—he was young, had a gambling problem and picked fights, but he was also creative and superstitious and talented. An interesting dichotomy.

We packed everything up and gave the room a thorough look-over to make sure there wasn't anything hidden away. As we headed downstairs, Ethan said, "I'm not going to check out of the room in case we want to access it again."

"That's a good idea." I nodded. "You never know what you might need to look at."

"I just couldn't face sleeping in there." His eyes dropped to the floor and his brother placed a hand on his shoulder and squeezed.

When we made it to the ground floor, the hotel was as deserted as I remembered from the first time I came here. I had to wonder how a business could operate with such minimal capacity. Then again, I couldn't blame any potential guests for not being attracted to the hideous floral velvet chairs and peach shag carpet and so many shades of brown.

Behind the front desk, a young woman was standing, cracking her gum. She chewed like a dairy cow, blowing a bright pink bubble, popping it and then starting the whole process over again. Chew, blow, pop. Chew, blow, pop. She had dark hair streaked with purple that was shaved on one side, with the other side left long and combed over at an angle so that it hung slightly in front of heavily kohl-rimmed eyes. Eyes that, I noticed, kept flicking to Ethan with interest.

"She's looking at you," I said to Ethan. "Maybe if you go over there and talk to her, she might let us look at the security footage. Something tells me a place like this runs a lean ship and they probably don't have a whole security team."

Ethan looked over to the front desk, where he caught the young woman's eye and then she turned her head away, cheeks reddening. As a terrible flirt and rather awkward turtle myself, I knew these were telltale signs of attraction that would never be acted upon, unless the other party made the first move.

"Go," I said, nudging Ethan. "See what she says."

He looked between Matt and me, frowning. His brother shrugged. "You know I don't like leading people on, but this is for Aaron. It's for a good cause."

With a huff of reluctance, Ethan headed over to the front desk while Matt and I watched on.

"My stepdad raised him to always be honest," Matt said. "He's the moral compass in his group of friends."

"Sounds like your stepdad is a good guy."

"He's the closest thing I ever had to a dad, myself, since my own dad died when I was still a baby. I've got a great relationship with him." He bobbed his head. "I even kept his name after he and my mum divorced. Wilson is his surname and mum had my name changed when they got married. Far as I'm concerned, their split doesn't mean he's not my family anymore."

"Why did he and your mother divorce?" I asked, hoping I hadn't crossed a line in asking for that detail. But Matt was an open person, I'd found. He didn't hold much back.

"Just one of those things." He shrugged. "I think my mum never got over my father dying so young, and my stepdad always knew he'd be in second place. It's not easy to be 'the one after the one,' if you know what I mean. And he missed living in the States while Mum will never leave Australia."

"It takes a lot to pack up your life and move to the other side of the world." I knew it, because I'd done it myself.

When I left for Paris in my early twenties, I'd had a single suitcase to my name and that was it. It was an adventure, but also terrifying.

It wasn't a life choice that suited everyone.

We continued to watch Ethan chat with the young woman behind the hotel reception desk. Her interest in him was undisguised, even though she looked as far from a surfer girl as possible with her paper-white skin and dark, funky hair. But whatever Ethan was saying it seemed to be the right thing, and eventually he looked over his shoulder and motioned us over.

The woman, whose name tag read "Amanda," showed us to the back room and closed the door behind us before, presumably, returning to her post.

"We've got five minutes before her boss comes back from his break," Ethan said. "So we have to be quick."

There was a laptop hooked up to a screen which showed nine images on it. More than half were taken up by images of corridors, presumably one for each level of the hotel, but there was also a camera on the outside of the hotel where I'd parked in one of the short-term spots, another two on the longer-term parking structure out the back, and one for the foyer.

"How did you convince her?" I asked.

"I promised her an introduction to Makani," he said, laughing. "Turns out she was only interested in me because she's seen me coming and going with my surf gear and thought I might know him. Apparently, she's a huge fan. Follows him on social media and everything."

So much for my theory about unrequited attraction!

Matt sat in the chair and reached for the mouse. When he moved the cursor to the bottom of the page a menu popped up.

"She said the previous days' recordings are on the desktop, labeled by date," Ethan said.

Matt navigated to the files, stifling a groan at the chaotically cluttered desktop screen. "Some people don't realize you can store files in more places than just on the desktop."

"Resist your urge to organize it and find the one from two days ago," Ethan said, glancing back at the door. "We don't have much time."

Matt opened the file from the date Aaron died and we watched as the screen filled up with nine boxes, each bustling at extra speed. There didn't appear to be an easy way to zoom into any one screen, so we had to watch the one for Ethan's floor in small format. There *was* probably a way to do it, but the minutes were ticking down and we couldn't waste time fiddling with settings.

"Slow it down," I said, pointing as a figure entered the screen that covered Ethan's floor and Matt clicked the button for normal playback speed. It was Aaron and he looked pissed. His figure stomped up the hallway toward the room.

"This must have been right after the fight with Makani," Ethan said. The time on the clock showed it was about fifteen minutes after I'd arrived on the beach to witness the two men fighting.

He must have come straight back to the hotel from the beach.

Another figure appeared on-screen—a woman with a camera slung around her neck. Ethan pointed. "That's Celina, his girlfriend."

The picture quality wasn't the best and everything was in black and white, but it was enough that we could see Celina knock on the door and head inside. Before the door closed, Aaron leaned out of the room to look up and down the hallway, as if to check whether anyone else was there. We sped up the time again and approximately seven minutes later, Celina could be seen stomping out of the room and down the hallway. Aaron stepped out behind her, tossing his hands in the air, but he made no move to follow her. At the same time, another man entered the screen.

"Who's that?" I squinted as Matt slowed the video down again, trying to make the figure out.

"Bryce," Ethan replied.

Aaron's agent looked as though he was trying to calm both Aaron and Celina down, but Celina pushed past him and disappeared into the elevator. Bryce then followed Aaron into the room. About ten minutes later he left and Aaron could be seen watching from the doorway.

Then there was nothing. The time ticked over at rapid speed in the bottom corner of the screen, until a third figure appeared approximately thirty minutes after Bryce left. I recognized Makani instantly due to his long, dark hair and the rigid posture I'd seen him hold at the beach. He had a distinctive and commanding presence, like he was used to being noticed.

Makani walked down to Aaron's hotel room and knocked, but the door didn't immediately open. So he knocked again and it looked as though he was shouting something, but the quality was too bad for us to make out the words. I glanced at both Ethan and Matt, who were staring intently at the screen.

Aaron eventually opened the door, looked out into the hallway, and then Makani went inside. The minutes ticked by and about half an hour later the door opened again. It seemed like quite a long visit, given the tempestuous history between the two surfers. I'd assumed Aaron might kick Makani out more quickly than that. But when Makani left, I noticed something—Aaron didn't lean out into the hallway like he did with Celina and Bryce. In fact, when Makani left, we couldn't see Aaron at all.

We sped the video back up. Matt, Ethan and I were the next to appear on-screen, so we could confirm that nobody else had been to Aaron's hotel between Makani leaving and us arriving. Before we could discuss this new piece of information, the door to the security office opened suddenly. I gasped, but it was only the girl from behind the front desk.

"You need to leave, please. Now." Her voice was high-pitched with nerves. "My boss just pulled into his parking space out front."

Crap. There was so much else we didn't get to see—like if the cameras showed anyone lurking around the side of the building under Aaron's balcony. But I wasn't about to get arrested for trespassing, so I grabbed Matt's arm and pulled him away from the screen. "Come on, let's go."

The three of us scurried out of the office and into the hotel foyer just in time to see a tall barrel-shaped man wearing a poorly fitting suit enter through the front doors. He headed straight toward the room from where we'd just come. Letting out a sigh of relief, I looked to Matt and Ethan as we exited the hotel.

"I think we need to have a chat with Makani," I said. "Because if he's not the killer, he might have been the last person to see Aaron alive."

CHAPTER 11

We decided to head to the beach. But first, food.

I hadn't eaten a thing since breakfast and my stomach was growling louder than some of the monsters we had to fight in our Dungeons and Dragons campaign. Ethan wanted something healthy, since he was mid-competition and needed to keep his eye on the prize, even though it was fair to say we all had murder on the mind.

To support the healthy diet of our resident athlete, we decided to stop in at Sprout, Azalea Bay's LA-inspired health and wellness café. It was an Instagram haven with its dreamy white, peach sherbet, millennial pink and a powdery blue color scheme. There was even a designated "selfie spot" in front of a wall painted with all the brand colors in a soft watercolor design and the word "joy" spelled out in pink neon lights.

Their menu consisted of such items as antioxidant crystal-charged smoothie bowls, antitoxin charcoal bars (try eating *that* in public without your toothbrush), and anti–bad vibes power balls. I wondered what ingredients could claim to clear "bad vibes" and though I doubted any of it had scientific backing, if we had another murder in our small town I might just fork out to buy one for every resident in case it might help.

We pushed the door open to Sprout and headed inside. Usually at this time of day the place would be fairly quiet since the lunch rush was over, but most of the seats were full of tourists. We made a beeline for one of the banquette tables as a group vacated and I slid onto the peach velvet seat to claim the spot. There were two younger girls—late teens, I'd guess—waiting tables and the owner, Starr Bright (no, that's not her real name), was standing behind the counter.

"This place is . . . something else," Ethan said as he sat. "For a small town, you guys sure do have some fancy eateries."

"Tourism is big business here," I replied. "And people love a pretty picture for Instagram."

As if on cue, a group of women in their early twenties wearing colorful beach cover-ups positioned themselves in front of the selfie spot and one of them held up a phone so they could take a picture.

"If you want a healthy lunch, this is the place for it," Matt added. "And the food is really good. Not as good as yours, Chloe, of course."

I laughed. "I appreciate the loyalty but I can admit that Sprout is a great café, even if I have a different philosophy when it comes to food."

Starr thought my use of butter and cream was a crime against humanity and I thought peddling Goop-style wellness trends was a waste of people's money.

Before one of the two servers had the chance to get to our table with menus, Starr herself spotted me and headed over. In her late thirties, she had waist-length hair in a gleaming shade of platinum blond—today fashioned with two tiny braids, one on either side of her face, capped with shiny pearl beads. Her tan was glowing, her nails were far too perfect for someone who ran a hospitality business and she had a small tattoo of a dolphin gracing the inside of her arm.

"Had enough of your own café already?" she asked, laughing as though she'd meant it as a joke although the glint in her eyes said otherwise. She was always looking for a juicy tidbit.

"Of course not, but I don't hang out at work in my personal time. We business owners have to keep some separation between work and life, right?" I said, forcing a smile. "Self-care and all that."

She nodded. "Truth. Self-care is, like, *so* important to me."

Ethan looked at me and covertly raised an eyebrow. Starr was . . . a lot. In every sense of the word. And when my aunt had been accused of murder, she had been one of the people gossiping about it. To say that Starr and I weren't exactly the best of friends was kind of pointing out the obvious, and I'll admit I'd thought about mushing a freshly baked apple pie right into her suntanned face on several occasions.

However, at the risk of sounding completely hypocritical, the reason I'd brought Matt and Ethan here was the very thing that had put Starr and me at odds with one another: gossip. I didn't like it, but if there were rumblings around town about Aaron's death, then they would make their way to Sprout. That much I knew.

Starr handed us some menus, smiling at Matt as she did so. Everybody loved Matt.

"What's your tip for the surfing competition, huh?" I asked, leaning forward on my elbows. "I'm sure you have all the inside information, given all that time you spent in LA."

Starr loved to tell people she'd "grown up" in LA, but I knew for a fact that her family had moved away when she was five and she had actually spent most of her childhood and teen years in Idaho. But I was keeping that one up my sleeve for now.

Starr preened, shaking her long hair back and making the dangly earrings she wore tinkle like wind chimes. "I know a little."

"So spill."

"Well . . ." Starr crouched down next to me, her gaze darting quickly over one shoulder as if to ensure that nobody was listening in to whatever salacious tidbit she'd deigned to share with me. I could feel Matt's eyes on me, but Ethan had leaned over to show him something on the menu and he was momentarily distracted. "Makani Davis is the favorite. Anybody who knows surfing knows he's a big deal, and now that his main rival is out of the running . . ."

I shook my head. "It's such a tragedy. He was so young."

"*Too* young." Starr looked contrite but I wasn't sure if it was authentic. "Rumor has it that . . ."

Her eyes dropped and for a moment I sensed a flicker of true emotion. For some reason, it made me feel better about being here.

"That he took his own life," she finished sadly, shaking her head. "But not everybody thinks so. Certainly seems that Makani has a clearer path to winning now. Not to mention he doesn't need to worry about his sister anymore. Such history there. The two of them were canoodling right there in the back booth the night before everyone rolled into town."

"Makani's sister?" I glanced at Ethan, whose eyes widened.

"Uh-huh." Starr nodded. "It's almost a Romeo and Juliet story—star-crossed lovers, torn apart by feuding surf rivals. Gosh, Makani came in here and caught them. He was furious. Makes me wonder . . ."

"What?" I asked.

"Whether that poor young man actually killed himself, or if he was given a helping hand."

For once, Starr and I were on the same wavelength.

Without another word, Starr left the table. She liked a dramatic exit. A moment later, one of her staff members came over with a cheery smile to take our lunch orders. A farm-to-table chicken wrap with a side of roasted sweet potato for Matt, a hand-massaged kale salad with grilled wild-caught salmon and two slices of sour dough with hummus for Ethan, and a smoothie bowl for me.

Or rather, a mixed berry smoothie bowl with activated almonds, twenty-four-karat gold dust and moon powder (whatever the heck that was), that had been charged with jade for good luck.

Frankly, as much as I would love some extra luck right now, I knew it wouldn't come from the fact that a piece of semiprecious stone was waved near my food. But hey, on the microscopic chance that there *was* some luck up for grabs . . . I was hoping it came our way.

"You heard that, right?" I asked, leaning toward Matt and Ethan and lowering my voice, "Starr says Aaron and Makani's sister were in here 'canoodling' a few days ago, before the rest of the surfing folks came into town."

"Kaila?" Ethan shook his head. "I can't believe it."

The name rang a bell. That's right! She was the beautiful woman manning the door at the mansion party. Wow, good looks certainly ran strong in that family.

Matt looked at his brother with a raised eyebrow. "I thought they broke up ages ago."

Ethan nodded. "They did."

"Didn't Makani make a comment about Aaron dumping his sister?" I asked, remembering back to the night of the argument on the beach. "What happened there?"

"It's a load of stupid drama." Ethan huffed. "High-school stuff, really. Makani and Aaron always had beef, so Kaila was the forbidden fruit. Aaron wanted to date her because she was off-limits and he liked doing things to annoy Makani. And I think Kaila liked Aaron for the same reason. Given she's the only girl in that family, with four overprotective older brothers, I think dating Aaron was a way for her to assert her independence."

"But they broke up?"

"Yeah." Ethan paused as the food was delivered to the table, and then he reached for his fork and speared a piece of salmon. "They liked the notoriety of dating each other more than they *actually* wanted to be a couple, I think. They broke up and stayed friends. Aaron quickly moved on to Celina and posted a photo of them kissing before he'd told anyone about him and Kaila splitting, and Makani took that as Aaron publicly dumping his sister."

"You're right," Matt said through a mouthful of chicken wrap. "That *is* high-school stuff."

"And Aaron and Celina had been dating ever since?" I asked, looking dubiously down at my smoothie bowl which glittered like a makeup palette and seemed designed more for taking photos of than eating. I spooned a small bit into my mouth and was pleasantly surprised—sweet, zingy and flavorsome. Not bad at all.

"Well, if 'ever since' is a perpetual on-again, off-again thing . . . then yes." Ethan shook his head. "But Aaron and Kaila *weren't* dating again. He would have told me. Not that he boasted about getting girls or anything like that, but Aaron talked to me about everything. When he started dating Kaila, he came to me and I told him it was a bad idea. After they broke up, he said I was right and that he should never have gotten involved with her."

"Why?" I asked.

"Just because he knew it would cause drama and that he needed to get serious with his career." Ethan laughed. "And then he started dating Celina and it was one dramatic fight after another. Secretly, I think he loved the fireworks."

"Celina *did* hint at the fact that she'd been cheated on," I pointed out. "When I told her about my ex-fiancé cheating on me, she said, 'My ex had the same problem. Are some guys biologically wired to screw around?' Direct quote."

"And Aaron was her first boyfriend so . . ." Ethan shrugged. "She must have been talking about him."

"First boyfriend? Isn't she, like, twenty-three or something?" Matt asked, looking confused. "That's surprising."

"Her parents were strict. She told me once that they put a lot of pressure on her to go to law school and join her father's firm, which she didn't want to do. Instead she fell in love with the ocean and surf culture living in California, and has made a lucrative business for herself doing surf photography. Her parents decided to move back to Japan about a year ago because they felt America was a bad influence on her but she stayed here to be with Aaron. He told me it caused a *huge* fight with her parents. I don't think they've talked to Celina since."

"They weren't a fan of Aaron?" I asked.

"I don't think they knew much about him, to be honest. They didn't want to." Ethan reached for a piece of bread and took a bite. "Celina had been angling for a ring recently, but Aaron didn't want to get too serious too quickly."

"Now I can guess what some of the arguments were about," I said with a nod.

Ethan shot me a knowing look. "Spot on."

"So Celina stayed in America to be with Aaron after her parents left the country to go back to Japan, and it fractured her relationship with them. She wanted to get engaged but he wasn't keen. *Then* maybe she finds out that he's cheating on her with his ex-girlfriend . . ." I wrinkled my nose in thought. "Might explain why she was on the security footage looking madder than a wet hen."

"Mad enough to kill, though?" Matt looked at his brother.

"I saw her shatter a glass against a wall while they were fighting one time," Ethan admitted. "I like Celina, but she's fiery as all get-out."

"I mean, imagine sacrificing your relationship with your parents to be with someone, only for them to turn around and A, not want to get serious and B, start cheating on you . . ." It certainly added more weight to the idea that Celina could have been angry enough to kill. "I can't blame her for being furious."

Only *she* wasn't the last person to see Aaron alive. That, according to the security footage, was Makani. However, we couldn't ignore the fact that the door to the balcony had been open the night we found Aaron on his bed *and* that I'd seen someone exiting that way after the room had been closed up by the police.

The security footage showed us something . . . but I suspected, not everything.

After lunch, we made our way down to the beach. A crowd had gathered around a roped off space, separating what appeared to be a yoga class at the water's edge. I'd started taking yoga classes myself a little while ago with Sabrina, and I recognized some of the poses such as downward-facing dog (bend over and stick your butt in the air), warrior II (prepare for your inner thighs to ache), and tree pose (stand on one foot and try not to fall over).

Beach yoga was a fun way to mix up the standard exercises we did in the studio, and Sabrina had dragged me out a few times as the sun peeked over the horizon. That activity had, however, been put on hold ever since Baked by Chloe opened because if the sun was anywhere near close to peeking, then I was already at work.

I found myself itching to join in.

It dawned on me then that it was a bit odd for a beach yoga class to have a crowd watching. That was until I saw *who* was leading the class, however.

Makani stood at the front of the group, effortlessly working his way through the poses with a rock-solid balance that belied the malleable ground beneath his feet. Despite the sun beating down, there wasn't a drop of sweat on him. Several people in the audience held up their phones, filming the scene before them, including someone who bore a strong resemblance to Makani but looked several years older.

I leaned toward Ethan and, with my voice lowered, asked, "Is it normal for a surfing prodigy to be leading a beach yoga class right before a big competition?"

"It's normal for Makani," he replied without a hint of irony.

We watched as the class progressed through the final set of moves, finishing with everyone down on their mats in corpse pose—which I'd always thought was a morbid name for it. After a few moments, where everyone was so still and quiet that the only sound came from nature—the whoosh of the waves and the cry of gulls—the class came to an end.

The students got to their feet, dusting sand from their bodies, and one by one they went to Makani to express their gratitude. He dutifully stood around and took selfies and photos with the class participants, and I noticed what appeared to be a few official-looking folks off to the side, including one guy wearing a branded sweatshirt that had an image of a person doing the warrior II pose on a surfboard.

Clearly this was some kind of promotional event.

"Makani is big into yoga as part of his prep for surfing competitions," Ethan explained as we waited around. "He posts a lot on his social media about his daily yoga and meditation practice, and he's been signed by a few brands that focus on the holistic side of sports. Some cynical people think he's trying to make himself the next Kelly Slater in every sense of the word, but he seems to genuinely love it. I tried it once but eh, it's not for me."

I laughed at Ethan's wrinkled nose. "What's so bad about yoga?"

"It's just so slow," he groaned. "I love surfing for the rush of chasing a wave and the tension when you have to wait. With yoga there's no tension."

"I think that's the point," Matt replied, looking as amused as I felt.

"Then yoga and I will never be friends," Ethan replied resolutely.

It took a while for the crowd to clear and while we waited, I kept an eye on the happenings at the beach. One of the men who resembled Makani was off to the side, chatting with a group of three people. I decided to take a walk past them to the water's edge to see if I could catch anything of interest. As I got closer, I realized Kaila was one of the three people—I hadn't recognized her because all her hair was pulled back into a bun and she had a baseball cap partially covering her face.

She seemed to be in a heated discussion with the man I'm guessing was one of her older brothers.

"I guess you don't have to worry about it now, do you?" she said, her tone sharp. "The problem is gone. Yay for you."

"Don't be like that. I know you're sad, but it's for the best. You'll see." He went to reach for her, but Kaila pulled back.

"Don't act like you understand what's best for me, Hilo. You have *no* idea."

I pulled my phone out of my pocket and paused to snap a photo of the ocean, which I hoped would give me a few more seconds to eavesdrop. But Kaila turned on her heel and walked away from the group, leaving strong indents in the sand with her bare feet. Hilo, who I would have put in his mid-to-late thirties, was built like an ox and was the tallest of the group, and had traditional Polynesian tribal tattoos covering one arm. Like Makani, he also had jet-black hair, although Hilo's was cut shorter. The other two men standing with him were smaller in size, by comparison, but would still have each been close to six feet tall.

I snapped my photo, but didn't hear anything else as the men had started to drift away, putting enough distance between us that I couldn't hear their conversation anymore. When I made it back to Ethan, I asked, "Do you know the men who were standing around there? I think Hilo was one of their names."

Ethan nodded. "They're Makani's crew. Hilo is the oldest brother—he competed for a short time, but never made it to the pros. He's helping Makani set up a surfing school and charity on the island to help more Hawaiian kids make it onto the tour. The other two guys are their cousins, I think. Or maybe they're family friends. I know one of them manages Makani's social media accounts, because I've seen him at almost every competition."

"There seems to be trouble between them and Kaila." I relayed what I'd heard. "I'm starting to think she was the person I overheard in the bathroom at the party."

The voice had sounded similar, although at the party the person talking had sounded on the verge of tears so I couldn't be one hundred percent certain.

Could she have been talking to Makani or Hilo? Or someone else?

As the crowd dispersed, Makani spotted Ethan and lifted his hand in a wave. As he came over, a grave expression marred his handsome features. "I'm sorry for your loss, man."

To my surprise, he drew Ethan in for a strong hug. Whatever grudge he might have held with Aaron, it didn't seem to have spread to any of his friends. I watched his face to see if it looked like he was putting on the gracious act, but he appeared genuine.

It was easy to see why he was doing well on social media—he was the entire package. Model good looks, a sense of authenticity, name pedigree and boundless talent. Plus the whole yoga thing would draw a crowd outside surfing. On some level, Makani was everything that Aaron was not. He was a smart businessman and a brand as well as an athlete.

Perhaps it pissed Makani off that Aaron was keeping pace with him while being so undisciplined.

"Thanks." Ethan nodded as he stepped back.

"We were wondering if you'd heard anything about Aaron's

death," I said, almost blurting the words out before Makani had a chance to walk away. Given I hadn't seen him at the party the other night and I got the sense he didn't do anything but work and train while the competition was on, I doubted we'd have many opportunities to ask him questions.

He looked at me closely, as though trying to read what was going on in my head. There was an intensity and focus in his dark eyes. "I heard that he overdosed."

Interesting. We hadn't yet heard from the police whether the autopsy had been conducted, although I assumed the empty pill bottle next to Aaron's body was the cause of his death. The quick reading I'd done about the sleeping medication he was on had told me that it was definitely possible to overdose, especially if combined with alcohol. Or randomly, grapefruit juice. Apparently, it increased absorption into the bloodstream.

"Where did you hear that?" I asked.

"Celina." He raked a hand through his long, dark hair and I swear it looked like he was in the middle of a shampoo commercial. "She said Aaron started taking sleeping pills and she was worried about him getting addicted."

It was likely that the police would have spoken to Celina about what they found—or that she'd proactively gone to them. Makani didn't seem like the kind of guy who was easily rattled, so I decided to shake his cage a little and see what happened.

"What did Kaila say about it?" I asked, pressing on despite the flare of anger on his face. "You know, since they were dating again."

"I'm sorry, *who* are you?" he asked, his eyes fixed on me in a way that was slightly unnerving. He might be all chill yoga dude for the cameras but I got the sense that Makani's temper explosion on the beach the other night was not an isolated incident.

"Chloe." I smiled and barreled on. "I heard you practically dragged Kaila off him when they were at Sprout. Small town, you know. People talk. And then I heard her talking to you on the phone from the party the other night. Said you and Aaron had a huge spat at the hotel right before he died."

I was totally bluffing of course—I had no idea *if* the woman speaking was Kaila, nor whether the person on the other end of the line was Makani. But given how the man in question had suddenly gone white as a sheet, I had to assume I wasn't far off the mark.

He shook his head. "You think he didn't overdose on purpose."

"No, I don't."

"*We* don't," Ethan added, stepping closer to me as a show of support.

"And you think *I* was responsible?" He gaped at us. "Are you nuts? Why on earth would I kill him?"

"Maybe you were protecting your little sister since Aaron was no good for her," I said. "It's totally understandable. I get the impression family is really important to you. If Aaron was going to hurt your sister again—"

"I didn't do it." Makani's eyes swung to Ethan, and the warmth and compassion from earlier evaporated like smoke. "You should know me better than that."

"We're not accusing anyone." Ethan held up his hands to show he wasn't looking for a fight. "I just want to know what happened to Aaron."

"She's accusing me." Makani pointed to me.

I copied Ethan's pose and held up my hands, too. "Look, we're just gathering evidence to take to the police so that they'll look into things further. We're not trying to start a witch hunt or anything, we just wanted to make sure Aaron gets justice."

For a moment, he didn't reply. I could practically hear the

cogs in his brain turning as he figured out what to do next. But my hopes of him telling us anything fizzled when his mouth set into a grim line.

"Stay out of my family's business," he said, glaring at me. "And let the police do their job."

Before I could ask anything else, Makani stalked back toward where his crew were waiting along with an older man who I assumed was either a sponsor or his agent. Hilo threw a nasty look in our direction before the group headed up toward the stairs leading away from the beach.

"What do you think about that?" Matt asked, looking between me and his brother.

"If he wasn't involved, it was certainly a strong reaction to have," I replied. "We need to find out what they were arguing about."

CHAPTER 12

That night it was my turn to host our Dungeons and Dragons group. We played every other week on a Thursday night, and rotated between a few people's homes. Not everyone had the space to host, but Grandma Rose had been kind enough to let me have everyone over to her place—well, *our* place until I eventually decided to go out on my own—even though she still didn't quite understand what Dungeons and Dragons was.

"Wait, *how* do you fight again?" she asked.

We stood in the kitchen as I prepared food for our guests. After the encounter with Makani at the beach, I'd taken my car past Baked by Chloe to see how they'd gone for the day and to help out with the closing procedure. Another sellout day! Packing some of the unused white macaron shells into a box, I'd come home and whipped up a simple chocolate buttercream and sandwiched it, along with a dollop of Grandma Rose's homemade blackberry jam between the shells.

The plan was to order pizza from La Bella Cucina for dinner. Hey, even professionals use Uber Eats sometimes.

"Well, everybody rolls a d20—that's a die with twenty sides—and the person with the highest total score goes first. Then on every turn we have an action, a bonus action and some movement," I explained as I opened a bag of tortilla chips and poured them into a bowl. Along with the macarons, I'd made fresh guacamole and roasted garlic hummus. Quick things that would keep everybody satiated until it was time for a break and some "circle food" as Sabrina liked to jokingly call it. "People can use their weapons or cast spells according to their characters' abilities."

"But you can't see anything." Grandma Rose looked utterly perplexed. "How do you know where to move?"

"Sabrina usually brings grid paper and has rough maps drawn out for the encounters we might have. Then we use markers or tokens to represent the characters, so we know where everything is."

"Sounds like a whole lot of make-believe to me," she muttered.

"That's *exactly* what it is. Think of it like a video game of the mind." I grinned.

We carried the food items out into the dining room, where we placed them in the center of the table along with a jug of iced tea and some sparkling water. Down by my feet, there was a blur of black, white and tan as Antonio raced past me with something in his mouth. It was a stuffed plush toy in the shape of a slice of pizza.

"It's not time for pizza yet," I said crouching down and laughing as he jumped back and forth in front of me, waving his pizza around like the proudest pup in existence. I grabbed the end and we had a little tug of war.

"You should have seen him today running around with that thing." My grandmother laughed. "You would have thought he'd found the Guinness Emerald."

I scooped Antonio up and cradled him against my chest, extracting the stuffed pizza slice from his mouth and tossing it into his basket of toys. He had a few around the house, since my grandmother was intent on spoiling him and although we'd tried to teach him to put the toys away, he was much better at pulling them out and leaving them in trails around the house than he was at putting them away.

The little dog snuggled into the crook of my neck and I stroked his velvety head. That's when I noticed that Grandma Rose was looking rather dressed up for a Thursday night. After I'd come home and started preparing snacks for the D&D group, she'd changed into a pretty pink dress with a sheer white cardigan over the top and a pair of flat white shoes. She was wearing sheer stockings, which I never understood given the heat of where we lived. But it seemed to be a leftover of the style from her day.

"You look lovely. Where are you headed tonight?" I asked. Antonio nudged my hand when I stopped stroking him momentarily, and I started up again to keep him happy.

"Just to Betty's. We're having our cards night."

Just like I had my Dungeons and Dragons night, my grandmother and her group of girlfriends had a biweekly cards night. For as long as I could remember, I'd grown up listening to the sounds of their cackling laughter and the gentle thrum of music. After, the sink had always been full of glasses, with empty wine bottles stuffed into the recycling bin and plates scattered with cake crumbs piled onto the countertop. I loved that my grandmother had always been surrounded by such fierce and loyal friends, and I felt like I was starting to build that for myself now, too.

Recently, the cards night had been "rebranded" to "Screw Cancer Night" in support of Grandma Rose. But usually it wasn't a dressy affair. In fact, her friend Luisa had on more than one occasion turned up at our house with her hair in rollers and her feet jammed into a pair of fuzzy slippers.

Then it clicked—if Betty was hosting, that would mean that her brother, Lawrence, might be there.

"Don't you say anything," she said, as if reading my mind.

"As I believe you said to me, I dress for myself, thank you very much."

I stifled a smirk and looked at Antonio. "I think the lady doth protest too much."

He yipped in response.

"Oh, hush," Grandma Rose grumbled. "Why do you tease me so?"

"Because I love you." I pulled her in with one arm and made a squishy little family hug with Antonio nestled right in the middle. "And I think it's great that you've found someone after Grandpa."

She looked at me warily. "Really?"

"Of course." Then it dawned on me why she might have been acting so coy about her crush on Lawrence all this time. I released her. "Were you worried I'd be upset?"

"Oh, I don't know." She shook her head. Twin pearls dotted her ears and they dangled from a tiny gold stud that winked in the light. "You loved your grandfather very much, as did I. He was the love of my life. My soulmate."

The little crack in her voice almost brought tears to my eyes. "Oh, Grandma. I know he was. Just because you might fall in love with someone else now that Grandpa's gone, that doesn't negate your feelings for him. You know that, right?"

"I've felt guilty," she admitted.

My grandfather had been dead for two decades and I still missed him. *That's* the kind of person he was—a big personality, someone who made a lasting impact. Of course my grandmother had loved him with all her heart. And he'd loved her back just as fiercely.

"I think getting cancer has put some things into perspective for me," she said. "I knew Lawrence had taken a liking to me a long time ago, but I never encouraged it because . . . well, I thought true love meant one person forever. But when it becomes apparent you might not have all the time left in the world, you can start to wonder about things."

"None of us know how much time we have," I said softly. That had been hammered home even more of late—Aaron had barely been an adult, yet his life had ended so suddenly. "We have to appreciate and value what we've got. We have to *live*."

"That could be some sage advice for yourself, Chloe," she said with a wise nod. "Being afraid of getting hurt isn't a recipe for living."

"Touché." I squeezed her shoulder. "And point taken. But just in case you need to hear it spelled out in absolutes: I will not be mad if you want to have a relationship with someone else after Grandpa. I think Lawrence is a wonderful man."

"You approve?" She looked up at me—and yes, even though I was quite vertically challenged myself, Grandma Rose was even shorter—her eyes shining. "You know I value your opinion, dear."

"Of course I approve." I reached in to hug her once more and this time we lingered.

Coming home to Azalea Bay might have been the best decision I'd ever made, even if the universe had needed to give me an almighty shove to make it happen. Nothing was more important than this. In that moment, my mind drifted to Aaron's family. I didn't know them. But they would never have this moment with him again—this connection, this love, this comfort.

They were owed the truth.

"There, from the depths of the shadows deep within the cave, you hear a low rumble. The noise builds and builds and builds and suddenly it feels as though the whole cave is shaking. Small rocks and debris begin to loosen from above and it showers down as the dragon steps back into the light. It's still alive." Sabrina's voice had everyone at the table totally enraptured. As she described the dragon we thought we killed a few moments ago, her eyes almost glowed with energy. Her descriptions were so vivid I could practically see the beast before me. "What do you do, Yasmine?"

Immediately I panicked and looked at my character sheet. I only had one spell slot left and my character, a human cleric named Yasmine Fridenot, was right in front of the dragon. I stuck my hand out and squeezed my eyes shut. "I cast Guiding Bolt."

"Yeah, Chloe. Get some!" Erica yelled and I heard Ben and Archie whoop in response.

"Describe it to me," Sabrina said.

"I hold out both hands and you see my hair fly up around me. A flash of pale blue light shoots in the direction of the dragon." I reached for my d20 die, knowing what she was going to ask of me.

"Make an attack roll."

I rubbed the die back and forth between my palms and blew on it for good luck, anxious energy coiling in my stomach. If I missed, then I was totally out of spells and being a lower-level Cleric meant I was *not* great in close combat. I was, as everyone kept reminding me, squishy. Low hit points, which had already been reduced from the previous part of the battle, and no more spells to cast healing on myself or others.

But that was always the question I had to ask—attack or defend? And right now it felt like I needed to attack.

"Come on, you can do it." Archie reached over and grabbed my shoulder, giving me a little shake. His gold wire-rimmed glasses had slid down to the tip of his nose but he barely seemed to notice. "You just have to roll over seventeen."

I took the twenty-sided die, which was maybe the strangest looking shape I'd ever seen in my life—called an icosahedron and, yes, I'd looked it up—and I willed it to roll my way. It was made of clear plastic chock-full of pink and purple glitter, part of a matching set that was a gift from Sabrina when I agreed to join her D&D group. I released the die into my velvet-lined dice tray and clamped my eyes shut.

Everyone at the table burst into a roar.

I opened my eyes and gasped. "Natural twenty."

The best possible roll.

"That's a critical hit. Roll two d6 and double the total," Sabrina said, barely concealing her grin. Even though, as Dungeon Master, she played the role of the baddies we fought and all the NPCs—those were the random characters we encountered as an adventuring party—I knew she loved it when her friends did well.

I reached for my set of two d6 dice and rolled them, quickly adding the numbers and doubling the score. "Twenty-two points of radiant damage."

"That's more than you needed. How do you want to do this?" she asked and the table erupted.

This was my first time killing a monster in the game and I took a moment to describe it to everyone, while they all cheered and clapped. Afterward, Sabrina called break time and Archie headed off to grab his phone so we could order our dinner.

"Your first monster kill, well done!" she said. Her dark, curly hair was pulled back into a poufy bun at the back of her head and she was wearing a black T-shirt with a picture of a set of dice on the front, with the words *That's how I roll* written in scrolling font. "I'm so proud of you."

"You're a natural," her boyfriend, Cal, chimed in. "I almost can't believe you've never played before."

Cal and Sabrina were both proud, self-confessed nerds who met at Comic-Con a few years ago, while cosplaying characters with a romantic history. Talk about an adorable meet-cute! He worked remotely as a computer programmer by day and, after moving to Azalea Bay to be with Sabrina, now helped to manage the online portion of her family's business, the local bed-and-breakfast.

In real life, Cal was a friendly giant. His big booming voice belied his gentle, caring personality and big mushy heart. He was head over heels for my best friend in every sense of the word. But when it came to D&D . . . Cal played a raging half-orc Barbarian who loved to Hulk out and smash things. It was fun to see him transform in role-play. It was fun to see them *all* transform.

"Thanks." I ducked my head, feeling a little self-conscious from the praise. "Sometimes the dice just go your way."

"Ah yes, but Dungeons and Dragons is all about strategy." He slung an arm around my shoulders and squeezed. "Knowing what spells to cast and when."

"Or which rocks to smash with your hammer."

"Technically it's a Maul. But yes, I do like to smash things." He grinned.

Archie went around and got everyone's opinions about what pizza flavors we should order—a process I knew would take a good fifteen minutes because Archie was the kind of person who wanted to make sure that everyone was fully accounted for and had their say. It was a great personality trait to have . . . but also a time-consuming one. I was almost at the point of hunger that literally cardboard-flavored pizza would have sufficed.

I made my way into the kitchen to sneak some chips. There I found Ethan sitting on my grandmother's counter, looking at a phone that was plugged directly into the wall. He'd accompanied Matt over but wasn't taking part in the D&D session, even though everyone had tried to include him. He'd wanted to sit with Aaron's phone while it charged so he could start going through the texts and emails.

"Hey," I said and he looked up, his mouth downturned. "Find anything of interest?"

I gestured to the battered older-model cell phone in his hands. There was a crack running along the back of the case, which probably started out life as a light blue but had transitioned into a dull grubby gray over time.

"Nothing major." He sighed. "It looks like Aaron cleared out a bunch of his text messages recently. He doesn't have cloud access or anything, so he was always getting warnings about his phone storage. Especially since this thing is basically an ancient artifact."

"Right." I stuffed my hand into the chip packet and pulled out a few crispy rounds, popping one into my mouth.

"I *did* find something, though. I don't know if it means anything, but there were several entries in his notes section that looked like payments to a debt he owed." Ethan showed me the phone. In the notes section, there were several listings with names that didn't make much sense, but each one featured a series of dates with a dollar amount next to it and a total at the bottom.

"I wonder why he didn't keep this in a spreadsheet," I mused as I looked through the notes.

"Aaron wasn't the most technical guy. I tried to show him how to use Excel one time but he said he found it too confusing. I guess this seemed easier."

"Adding up numbers manually?" I laughed. "Not for me."

"Aaron was actually really good with numbers, even though he flunked out of school." Ethan smiled. "He was one of those people who was naturally smart but hated authority. School never suited him."

"The names of these notes are funny. Little Thruster?"

"That'll be Stuart Simons. He's another surfer in the Challenger Series." Ethan laughed at my confused expression. "We always called him Stuart Little, like the mouse, and a thruster is a three-finned surfboard. It's Stuart's favorite board."

"Oh, so these are nicknames?" I looked over the list. "What about Aggro Benny?"

"Ah, that'll be Benji Parker. He's a . . . piece of work. He's got a rep for being a bully on the waves. But a 'benny' is also a term for someone who's not local, and Benji isn't from a surfing place even though he likes to act like he grew up in Cali."

"Well, if Aaron borrowed money from someone who's super aggressive . . . ?" I looked up from the phone.

"It's a solid idea, but Benji is in Hawaii at the moment. It's all over his socials." Ethan sighed. "Maybe all these loans have nothing to do with anything."

"Well, I have to give it to him, the naming system is very amusing. I would say it makes the names hard to figure out, but you don't seem to have any trouble."

"I know Aaron well." He shrugged. "But to anyone else looking at the phone? It's meaningless."

I looked through a few more. "This one's interesting. Lady Gray Suit. Looks like he owed her a fair bit—over five thousand and not a single payment."

"Lady Gray Suit." Ethan wrinkled his nose, thinking.

"Like the tea, maybe?" Lady Grey was a variation of the more well-known Earl Grey.

"I don't think so. Aaron wasn't exactly the tea-drinking type." He cocked his head. "The 'men in gray suits' is an old-school nickname for sharks. So a lady who is a shark?"

"Or one who wants to *work* with sharks," I said, thinking of the conversation I had in the café earlier that day. "Like Mariah the Mermaid."

"Five grand?" Ethan shook his head. "She doesn't have that kind of money lying around. I've seen the beater she drives."

"Not to mention she's paying her way through school," I added. Then I remembered something. "Did anything ever happen between you and Mariah?"

Ethan blinked at me like a deer in headlights. "Why do you ask that?"

"Well, she came into my café today and I was chatting with her. I mentioned that you'd told me about her recovery after the shark attack and how she wanted to study marine biology. She said she never knew you kept such close tabs on what she was doing," I relayed. "And then she said, 'Especially not since the thing with Aaron,' or something like that."

"Oh yeah, that." Ethan flushed and raked a hand through his curly blond hair, looking rather sheepish.

I raised an eyebrow, letting him know I wasn't going to be content with a vague "oh yeah, that" kind of response.

"I'd had a crush on Mariah ever since I was in high school. She was gorgeous and talented and funny." He got a dreamy look in his eyes, which was the most adorable thing ever. "We dated on and off for a while, but it wasn't anything serious because of all the pressure and travel of competing. Then after the shark attack she had this kind of . . . epiphany. Said that when she saw her life flash before her eyes that it brought everything into focus."

"Okay." I stretched the word out, not quite sure where the story was going.

"She told me that she'd been in love with Aaron since they met at surf camp when they were kids." Ethan hung his head. "She'd always been too afraid to ask him out, because he never seemed interested and they lived on opposite sides of the country."

"Whereas you were interested and on the right coast." I cringed. "Oh Ethan."

"I was the safe bet and Aaron was the . . . dream guy." He blew out a breath. "I told her to go for it and said that I didn't want to hold her back."

"So she asked him out?"

"Yup. Aaron shot her down immediately, because he said it would make him a terrible friend if he dated her knowing how I felt. She and I haven't spoken much since. It's kinda awkward."

"Clearly she and Aaron were in touch, if she loaned him

money." I looked down at the phone. Why would he want to borrow money from the woman who broke his best friend's heart?

Desperation, perhaps.

"Mariah wouldn't hurt Aaron. She was in love with him."

"Love makes people do very ill-advised things," I replied. "And if she needed that money back for school . . ."

"No way." Ethan shook his head vehemently, but I wasn't sure I shared his confidence.

Not a single payment had been made back to Mariah, if Aaron's note could be believed. I wondered if this was who Makani was referring to when he'd said, "Him borrowing money and not paying people back is not petty crap, either." I made a note to find out how I could "bump into" Mariah and ask her about it. Maybe her social media would let me find out where she was working next.

"Besides, if she *did* kill him and steal his backpack to go through his things . . . wouldn't she have deleted the note?" Ethan said, nodding toward the phone. "Why steal the backpack if you're not looking to destroy evidence."

That was a good point. "Unless she didn't know it was on the phone? Who the heck keeps anything important in their notes? I think you're onto something about someone else wiping the phone, though. If the backpack had been taken for twenty-four hours before the police released the hotel room, it's certainly possible it wasn't Aaron who deleted a bunch of texts."

"True." Ethan nodded.

"I'm starting to wonder if the person I saw sneaking out of the hotel didn't go there to *steal* something, so much as return it." I munched on another chip. "What if the murderer took the backpack and I saw them after they had put it back in the room?"

"Maybe you're right. Maybe someone took the backpack,

stole the journal, wiped the phone and then returned it all the next day, hoping no one would notice it was gone." He bobbed his head and held his hand out for the chip bag.

"Did the missing journal turn up?" I asked.

"I went back to the room before we came here tonight to have another look. It's definitely gone." Ethan sighed. "But *who* took the bag? We saw the security footage of the hotel hallway. The last person out of the room before we found Aaron was Makani and he didn't have it."

"The door to the balcony was ajar when we found Aaron," I replied. "I thought it was strange at the time. But perhaps whoever took the backpack got in the same way they left—via the balcony. You're only on the first floor and there was some furniture underneath from the room below. It might be possible to climb up that way to avoid the security cameras. I doubt they have any trained on that little side alley that leads down to where the dumpsters are."

Ethan's eyes were back to sparkling again, like he'd gotten a second wind of energy. "There's only one way to find out."

CHAPTER 13

As soon as the Dungeons and Dragons session was over, Ethan, Matt, Ben and I headed to the hotel to conduct an experiment.

"Isn't this breaking and entering?" Ben asked nervously as we got out of the car. It was dark out and the inky sky gave us plenty of shadows to work with.

"We're not going to break anything and entering isn't a problem when you're paying for the hotel room." I patted Ben on the shoulder. "It'll be fine."

"I'm surprised you're not playing a Rogue for your D&D character," he muttered in response.

"Why don't you go up to the room and wait for us," Matt suggested gently. "We don't need everyone standing around the bottom while I climb up."

"Who says *you're* climbing up?" Ethan asked. "I was going to do it."

"No way. You're competing in two days and if you injure yourself, your dad will kill me." Matt shot his younger brother a stern look. "Don't worry about me, I'm fit as a fiddle."

He wasn't kidding. Matt was currently wearing a fitted black T-shirt that showed off arms corded with muscle. He wasn't bulky like a gym bro, but rather had the physique of a runner. Strong, economical, lean. If someone could haul themselves up to a first-floor balcony, my money was on him.

"So long as I don't need to do it," I joked. "I've got the upper body strength of a marshmallow."

"Come with me," Ben pleaded, grabbing my arm. "This place gives me the creeps."

"You two go upstairs." Ethan thrust the room key into my hand. "And come out to the balcony."

Ben and I went through the hotel's front entrance and, for the first time in all the times I'd been here, we saw someone beside the check-in associate in the foyer. Only this person wasn't someone I'd expected to see.

"Detective Alvarez," I said, my voice pitched up to a squeak.

"Chloe, what a surprise." The detective was dressed in her usual attire of a pair of smart slacks with a crease down the front, a white shirt and sensible black shoes. Her seemingly endless collection of glasses today included a pair of funky green and purple tortoiseshell frames in a bold square shape. "Hello to you as well, Ben. I suspect we're all here to see the same person."

She must have assumed that Ethan was still staying at the hotel.

Oh crap. Ethan . . . who was currently with his brother trying to see if they could scale their way up to the first-floor balcony. That wouldn't look suspicious at all, would it?

I gulped. Then a nervous giggle bubbled out of me, immediately making the detective narrow her gaze. "Well, who else would we be seeing in this place? I suspect they only have one room booked at a time."

The detective's lips twitched but she managed to stifle the smile before it fully bloomed. "The choice of decor is . . . interesting."

"That's one way of putting it," Ben muttered beside me.

The detective turned like she was going to head toward the elevators and I felt my heartbeat kick up a notch. I couldn't let her catch Matt or Ethan climbing up into the room from the balcony. What if the police had now found something suspicious and they turned their attention toward Ethan? I wasn't sure what was worse—them not believing him when he claimed Aaron was murdered, or them suspecting he did it.

Probably the latter.

"So, uh . . . has the autopsy been done yet?" I asked. "For Aaron."

Detective Alvarez's eyes flicked over me, but her face revealed nothing. She was a tough nut to crack, I'd found. Professional, always with a firm eye on boundaries and hardened from working homicide in LA for the last few years of her career, she never gave much away.

"Not yet," she said. "We've requested one but it likely won't happen until at least next week or the week after."

"But everyone will be gone by then!" I blurted the words out without thinking about the consequences.

"What do you mean *everyone will be gone*? Aaron's family is in Florida and we'll notify them as soon as we have the reports back from the coroner's office." She reached up and adjusted her glasses, an action I'm sure was meant to make her seem like she was slightly distracted, but I knew better.

I glanced toward the elevators. Matt and Ethan would have probably only made it around the side of the building by now. I had to stall the detective. Given she was usually a woman on a mission, I needed to do something that would make her stand her ground.

"Well, because he was murdered, of course," I said, throwing my hands in the air.

Ben looked at me like I'd sprouted a second head and started speaking Elvish. "Uh, Chloe?"

The detective let out a long breath and pinched the bridge of her nose. "I understand that what happened last time might have caused you to distrust the abilities of the chief and I—"

"I don't distrust you," I said.

The police *had* missed critical clues last time. In my opinion, this was because they were too focused on the wrong people, like my aunt. But I also knew from firsthand experience that catching a killer wasn't exactly child's play. It was easy to miss things. To not be in the right place at the right time. To overlook the needle in a haystack.

But I didn't believe that the police were incompetent or incapable of doing their jobs. I simply thought that sometimes they were too swayed by policy and procedure, and that sometimes they were too stubborn to listen to the average Joes. I guess that was to the advantage of a murderer, who didn't have to follow any rules.

"We're confident that Aaron ended his own life," she finished. "I understand this is extremely devastating news to hear. I mentioned to Ethan that we have grief counseling resources available, not just for him but for anyone who is hurting. It might help to talk to someone—"

"He was murdered," I said resolutely. "Did you know the balcony door was ajar when we found the body? And that his backpack was missing and now his phone has a bunch of messages deleted. And one of the journals he always carries with him is gone!"

"His backpack *was* missing?" She raised an eyebrow.

"It was missing when we found him. But then when you released the room the next day it was there again." As I spoke the words out loud, I was aware of how it would come across.

"Perhaps the backpack was simply tucked away somewhere and it got moved after the room was cleared," she said.

"It wasn't. It was gone and things are missing from it." I stepped around her, standing between the detective and the path to the hotel rooms. "Can't you look into things? Aaron was making plans to get out of debt, he was excited about the upcoming surfing competitions. Does that sound like someone who doesn't want to live?"

"We never know what's going on in someone's mind," she said. Her dark eyes blinked behind the lenses of her glasses and I swear for a moment I saw a flash of regret there. "Sometimes people have good days and bad days, and they hide those ups and downs from their loved ones. Perhaps this bad day outweighed the good."

There was a slight shake in her voice—a tremble that told me she knew all too well what it was like to witness someone riding that emotional roller coaster.

"Detective, please," I pleaded with her. "Ethan knew Aaron better than anyone. They were like brothers. He's convinced that there was foul play."

"When we get the autopsy and toxicology reports, if there's anything strange at all then I promise we will take appropriate action—"

"I saw someone leaving his hotel room." This was the very last thing I could use to get her to believe me. An ace up my sleeve? Not exactly. But it was all I had.

"What do you mean you saw someone leaving his hotel room?" she asked.

"The day after we found Aaron, you'd closed the room off," I explained. "I came by the hotel and I saw someone jump off the balcony from their room. They were dressed all in black."

"What were you doing here?" she asked sharply.

"Shouldn't you be more interested in why someone was jumping off a dead man's balcony than why Chloe was here?" Ben asked. I'd almost forgotten he was there for a moment, he'd been so quiet.

"Because Chloe has a habit of putting herself in dangerous positions," the detective replied, adjusting her glasses again.

This time it seemed more of a nervous tic than something to disarm us. "And . . ."

"Sticking my nose into other people's business," I said, anticipating her words.

"You said that, not me," she replied, but I could tell she *would* say something along those lines, although maybe not to my face. "I was going to say that last time you got lucky and it was nothing more than a bump on the head."

"But why would I have anything to worry about if Aaron's death really *was* suicide, like you say?" Hmm, maybe I'd got her there.

"How do you know the person didn't jump down from a higher balcony onto Aaron's, and then down onto the ground?" she asked.

I hadn't thought of that.

"It's also possible if someone knew the room was empty, then they assumed there might be something to steal," she said. "It could be any number of things."

I folded my arms across my chest. "Or it could be murder."

"At this time, however, the directive is that we're treating this as a suicide. People never want to believe that someone we care about would willingly leave. Trust me, I know this." She sighed. "But sometimes they do."

I looked down. If the autopsy wasn't going to happen for another week or two, then the chance of them ever catching Aaron's killer was slim. After the weekend, all the tourists would scatter to the wind. All the people staying in town who could be involved would get on planes and trains and in cars and go in a million different directions.

"I'll call the coroner's office and ask if there's any chance we could have Aaron moved up," she said gently. "I don't like my chances, but I'll ask, okay?"

"Thank you."

Whether she would actually call the coroner's office, I had

no idea. There was even less chance that they would bump Aaron up the list, even if she did. The detective looked like she wanted to say more, but instead she pursed her lips as if trapping her reply in.

That's when I noticed that she wasn't the only law enforcement here. Chief Theodore Gladwell exited the office where Ethan, Matt and I had previously looked at the security camera footage, and I saw him shaking hands with the hotel manager. The chief was in his fifties and, unlike the detective, was dressed in full uniform. His shirt was tucked neatly into his pants and a black belt dug into his slightly protruding belly. Age had softened him some, but he was still a strong man with an intimidating physical presence when he needed it.

He headed toward us, a crease deepening between his brows. "Ms. Barnes, why am I not surprised to see you here."

"Chief." I nodded. "You know I'm all about frequenting local businesses."

His jaw twitched. Chief Gladwell was not the biggest fan of mine as of late. He'd seen me as meddling with his investigation while my aunt was a murder suspect, and I hadn't heeded his advice to mind my own business.

"Shall we go upstairs?" the detective said, likely before I had a chance to say anything else that might tick off her boss.

We faced off in the hotel lobby and out of the corner of my eye, I saw the girl at the reception desk watching us with interest. Eventually, the chief broke his gaze away and began heading toward the stairwell. The rest of us followed.

I had stalled as long as I could. Hopefully, Ethan and Matt had finished conducting their experiment by the time we made it up to the first floor. Ben shot me a worried look and we followed the chief and the detective toward the stairwell—clearly, she didn't trust the elevator, either. No one said a word as we clomped up the stairs.

As we made it to the landing, the door to Ethan and Aaron's

room suddenly swung open and Ethan burst out, cheeks pink and curly blond hair in disarray. "Guys, we totally did—"

His voice died off when he saw the detective.

"Oh, hello, Chief Gladwell. Detective Alvarez." He glanced around the hallway as if wanting to see whether they'd brought anyone with them. "What can I do for you?"

Matt poked his head out of the door and raised an eyebrow at Ben, who was standing with me behind the detective. Ben shrugged.

"Could we talk in private a moment?" she asked.

"Anything you have to say to me, you can say in front of my friends." Ethan stood straighter and I saw Matt place a protective hand on his shoulder.

The chief made a noise under his breath, but the detective nodded and motioned for us all to head back into the hotel room. It had been refreshed—I could tell because the beds had been made in that way the twenty-something boys would never do on their own. And a glimpse in the bathroom as we walked past showed all the towels hanging neatly on the rack, instead of crumpled in piles on the floor or slung over the shower railing.

It also smelled less like boy.

"What did you want to talk about?" Ethan asked once we'd all settled on the various surfaces around the room—Matt and Ben on one bed, myself on a rickety desk chair with Ethan purchased on the desk itself next to me, and the detective leaning against the wall that separated the bedroom and bathroom. The chief stood rigid as a board by the door.

Nobody went near Aaron's bed, however.

I could tell Ethan was equal parts wary and curious about what they had to say, and he nervously tugged at a strand of hair at the nape of his neck.

"I wanted to share some information that we came across," she said. "With Aaron's family's permission, of course. The chief had a thorough conversation with his aunt, and confirmed that Aaron had attempted to harm himself in the past."

"When? How?" Ethan shook his head.

"There was an incident about six months ago, where Aaron was on the roof of their double-story house threatening to jump off," she said. "His aunt managed to coax him down at the time."

This was pretty damning news. No wonder they seemed adamant there was no foul play.

"I don't know what to say," Ethan replied, shaking his head. He looked shell-shocked.

"I understand there are still some concerns around your friend's death . . ." The detective glanced in my direction.

"This is a safe town," the chief interjected, his voice brittle. "We don't have murders committed left and right. Just because there was one murder, doesn't mean others will follow. Azalea Bay is not that kind of place."

This is the view that concerned me—the chief's undying love for his hometown clouded the reality that bad things could happen in good places. Bad things could happen anywhere. And I suspected there had been an increase in concern from residents of the town about safety, something that probably rubbed Chief Gladwell the wrong way. It sounded like it wasn't the first time he was speaking these words.

"Our job is to follow the evidence," the detective said, as if trying to soften her boss's message. "And I can assure you that we've reviewed all the evidence very thoroughly. I understand how shocking a sudden loss can be, so if there's any support you need . . ."

"Thank you." Ethan's reply was barely a whisper and his eyes were fixed into the distance. "I need a moment to think."

The detective nodded. "We'll be in touch."

The chief strode out of the room and she followed, pausing to throw a glance over her shoulders, her dark brows creased in concern. Then she was gone. Their leaving was punctuated by the soft snick of the door closing, leaving us sitting in silence, all eyes trained on Ethan, who continued to stare blankly into space.

"Maybe I never knew him that well after all," he said, his voice rough. "Maybe if I'd checked in more . . ."

"Let's go home," Matt said gently. "Nothing is going to be solved tonight."

"And here I was thinking we'd figured something out when we found out how easy it was to climb up onto the balcony from the ground below." He shook his head and looked out to where the balcony sat, empty except for a single potted plant. "Maybe it was all for nothing."

I wasn't sure what to think. The police had plenty of evidence to suggest there was no foul play and today's news had only further supported their theory. But there were also several people who had a grudge against Aaron and now we knew for sure that they could have entered the hotel room away from the prying eyes of the hallway security cameras.

Not to mention the missing text messages and journal.

It was a mystery, that much I knew. At this point, it might be *all* I knew.

When I made it home there was a strange car in the driveway and the light was on in the living room. One of Grandma Rose's friends must have driven her home from their card night, since we only owned one car—the Jellybean—and I was driving it. Besides, Grandma Rose hated driving at night. Her eyesight wasn't what it used to be.

I parked on the street and walked up the driveway, turning over the day's events in my mind. Something wasn't adding up. If there was no foul play, then why would *anyone* have taken the backpack and altered its contents? Why delete the messages from the phone? Why climb into his room when it was sealed by the police and risk getting caught?

Someone was trying to hide something.

Yet so many signs pointed to the police being right about their theory—Aaron's attempt to harm himself, the bottle of pills matching the information listed on his medical card, the note with his handwriting.

I unlocked the door and stepped inside. While toeing off my shoes, I heard voices floating through the house from the kitchen. Grandma Rose's voice . . . and a man's voice. It was Lawrence St. James, I was sure of it. My grandmother's laugh carried in the air—the sound of pure girlish delight. It could have been the giggle of someone half her age, a little flirty, a little sweet.

I couldn't help but smile. I meant every word of what I'd said to my grandmother earlier: I hoped she felt free to find joy with another man after my grandfather. Life was short. I was reminded of that every day when I saw the scarf around her head and the tiredness that her treatments imposed on her. She deserved to be happy.

Antonio was sleeping in his little doggy bed, curled up into a bean shape and snoring lightly. His stuffed hamburger was tucked into his side, like he was a small dragon guarding his treasure. Grandma Rose and Lawrence were sitting at the table in the kitchen, with mugs of steaming tea in front of them and a small plate of brownie slices in the middle.

"Oh Chloe!" My grandmother was so shocked to see me standing in the doorway that she almost leaped out of her seat. "I uh . . . I wasn't expecting you home so soon. I guess, well it is kind of late. I must have lost track of time."

Her cheeks were bright pink, as if I'd caught her making out with Lawrence instead of innocently sharing a cup of tea and some brownies I'd made—the non-weed kind.

"It's nice to see you, Chloe." Lawrence got up and gave a little bow, ever the gentleman. He wore gray slacks with a pleat in the front and a tweedy sports coat over a white shirt. He smelled like a nice cologne, clearly having dressed up for my grandmother.

It made my heart happy.

"Good to see you, too, Lawrence."

"Would you like some tea, dear?" My grandmother went to stand, but I waved her away.

"I hope I'm not interrupting anything," I said as I grabbed a mug from the cupboard. I'd recently bought a fresh tin of peppermint tea leaves and I spooned some into my infuser. I needed the calming aroma of peppermint right now.

"We were actually having a very interesting discussion about the mating rituals of bowerbirds," Lawrence said and I stifled a snort. My grandmother's cheeks graduated from pink to fuchsia. "Did you know they build extravagant structures out of twigs and they cover the floor with all manner of natural treasures, like bones and shells and pretty stones? They even get flower petals to decorate. Anything they think the female will like. These structures are actually called bowers. Some males even resort to sabotage by destroying the bowers of other males, so they can attract the best female."

Lawrence seemed so excited by this information and eager to share, that his whole face was lit up. Grandma Rose, however, looked like she wanted to sink into the floor.

"That's so interesting," I said, pouring the hot water over my infuser of peppermint tea leaves. "Is this a general discussion of mating rituals, or just specifically about the bowerbird?"

Grandma Rose shot me a silencing look.

"Oh, we actually started talking about some birdwatching that I've done." Lawrence seemed completely oblivious to my grandmother's mortification. "Since I retired, I've been trying to keep myself active and busy. After years of deadlines and late nights and worrying about what critics will say about my books, it feels good to simply explore the world and see what beauty it has to offer for no other reason than personal enjoyment."

"So you don't think you'll write another book again?" I asked as I took a seat at the table with my tea.

"I'm writing my own story now," he said with a charming smile. My grandmother looked on at him dotingly. She was totally smitten! "With actions rather than words."

"That's a wonderful sentiment." I watched the steam curl up from my mug, carrying with it the fresh, green aroma of the peppermint. I sucked it in, eager for it to loosen the circular thoughts in my mind. "I bet you must be good at solving mysteries, though. Given you wrote them for so many years. Can you even watch an episode of *Law & Order* without figuring out who the killer is before anyone else?"

He chuckled. "Well, my sister does say I'm rather annoying to take to the movies. I usually know what's going on before she does and she hates that."

"Sounds like Betty." I giggled and my grandmother nodded in agreement. "She loves being in the know."

"What did you get up to tonight after your Dungeons and Demons thing?" Grandma Rose asked, clearly happy we'd moved along from the conversation about mating rituals.

"Dungeons and *Dragons*," I replied. "And actually, we're trying to solve a mystery of our own."

I filled Lawrence and Grandma Rose in on what was happening with Aaron.

"That is very peculiar." Lawrence nodded his head. "I wrote a book once with a murder that was made to look like a suicide. It takes an intimate understanding of a person to make such a bait and switch feel authentic, you know. Someone who knows their fears and weaknesses. It's not simply a matter of scribbling a note and leaving it at the scene. If it's going to fool anyone, then the killer has to know them extremely well."

"That could cover several of the people who have a motive,"

I replied. "We've got the lifelong rival, the betrayed girlfriend, and the rejected crush."

There was also Kaila, Aaron's previous girlfriend and possibly the person with whom he was cheating on Celina. Not to mention Kaila and Makani's older brother and cousins. Killing Aaron could have had a twofold benefit—get revenge for and/or protect Kaila from Aaron, *and* remove Makani's main threat in the surfing competition.

"Oh, and there was a competition judge that he had some issues with, apparently," I added. "That seems to be the only suspect who doesn't fit into the 'intimate knowledge' category."

"If you don't mind me asking, how did the poor young man die?" Lawrence asked.

"The police are still waiting on the autopsy results, but he was found with an empty bottle of pills beside him. Since they suspect it was suicide then I'm guessing nothing on the body indicated there was a struggle, and Aaron was taking sleeping pills regularly enough to write them on his medical card. I did a little Googling and death is one of the symptoms listed for overdose."

Lawrence nodded. "If anyone knew he was taking those pills, then it would have been easy to slip him a drink laced with a sedative and then have him ingest a lethal dose. Or maybe they gave him something to amplify the quantity he'd taken, say a glass of alcohol."

"Or grapefruit juice!" I gasped, remembering the article I'd read. Many medications required a specific enzyme in the small intestine to aid metabolization. Grapefruit juice, however, was able to block this enzyme, resulting in a higher quantity of the drug both entering the blood *and* staying in the body for a longer period of time . . . which could lead to overdose. "Oh my gosh, I have no idea how I missed that. There was a bottle of grapefruit juice sitting on the bedside table when we found Aaron *and* the person I saw leaving his hotel room was carrying an empty bottle of juice."

I immediately texted Ethan.

CHLOE: Do you know if Aaron drank grapefruit juice? Or do you drink it?

ETHAN: Random question. No, neither of us drank it. That stuff is nasty.

CHLOE: Are you sure Aaron didn't drink it?

ETHAN: Definitely not. He told me once his doctor said it was bad for his medication. Weird, right?

Only it was not weird at all. It was murder.

CHAPTER 14

The following day at the café, we were absolutely packed!

People had flown in from all over the country—and beyond—to watch the later stages of the surfing competition. But before heading to the beach, they were packing out Azalea Bay's eateries. I saw a few familiar faces come in over the course of the day, including Ethan's agent, Bryce; Mariah the Mermaid (Again! Gotta love a repeat customer); Makani's older brother and one of the cousins, and Fisk Clemmens, the judge that Aaron didn't like.

Fisk was sitting in the back corner by himself, talking loudly on one of those Bluetooth earpiece things about the movie he was involved with. I bet he thought all the people looking over were impressed and excited that a Hollywood type was sitting close to them. In reality, however, I noticed several people roll their eyes and complain about how loud and obnoxious he was.

Currently, Aunt Dawn was working the register, and Erica was busing orders out to the tables and making drinks. Our food items were flying off the shelves so fast that I'd been out the back most of the day trying to keep our front counter stocked.

Erica poked her head into the kitchen at one such moment. Her cheeks were pink and she looked slightly out of breath. "We're out of the canna-gria."

"Again?" I gaped.

"It's really popular!" She grinned. "Looks like we should take it off the specials board and add it to the permanent menu."

I loved how she used "we" in that scenario—Erica had really invested herself in making sure Baked by Chloe was a successful business, and I love that about her.

"Looks like we might," I replied. "Okay, I'll start another batch."

The "canna-gria" was Aunt Dawn's idea—a sangria-inspired drink that was cannabis-infused, but alcohol free. She'd spent several summer vacations in Spain over the years and had fallen hard and fast for the fruity yet quenching wine-based drink often served there. She loved to make up a big batch for our summer barbecues.

Together, we'd brainstormed how we could possibly bring the fruitiness and color of sangria into our cannabis café, minus the alcohol since we'd made the decision not to be licensed for serving it. That had started the hunt for a substitute base. Thankfully, low-alcohol and nonalcoholic beverages were trending so I'd managed to find some great alcohol-free wines, including a sparkling rosé that made for the prettiest peachy-pink base color.

I started making the canna-gria by chopping up apples into cubes (leaving the skin on), slicing the oranges and lemons into rounds (leaving the peel on) and de-stemming and halving the strawberries. I had plans to also try adding some peaches when I could get more from a local supplier, but today I had to make it with whatever fruit we had left. I put all the fruit into a large receptacle, and added cranberry, orange and lemon juice. I let all of that rest while I prepared another tray of brownies—

peanut butter–flavored, which had been much requested—and another batch of savory scones.

When the fruit was done macerating (well, the minimum amount of time I could afford to leave it anyway), I opened a couple of bottles of the nonalcoholic sparkling rosé. The bottles were *so* pretty! They were made of pink cut glass, with glittery text on the label. The foil at the top was rose gold and everything about it matched the vibes of my café to a T. I'd even decided to keep a few bottles on display behind the counter, because they looked so good. Plus, the woman who ran the company was super nice and she'd been very supportive of my business, so I was more than happy to give her some extra advertising.

I poured the wine into the sangria mix and gave it a gentle stir to make sure everything was well combined. I then ladled the canna-gria into a more easy-to-manage jug that we could keep in the fridge behind the counter and we'd top it up from the big container whenever it got low. We'd decided to dose each drink individually, rather than dosing the whole jug. Yes, it was a little extra work, but this way we could ensure that each drink contained the correct dose and customers would have the choice of either THC *or* CBD, since we were adding the tincture right before serving.

I carried the fresh jug out to the serving counter. The line had slowed some, though all the tables were still full and I saw two eagle-eyed people hovering to one side, waiting to snatch a spot as soon as one became available. Aunt Dawn was chatting with a gray-haired woman in a long, floral dress, who wore a pretty shell necklace and matching earrings.

"Oh, there you are! This is my niece," Aunt Dawn said, gesturing to me. "She's the Chloe behind Baked by Chloe."

"It's so nice to meet you," the woman said. "I asked your aunt if you were in because I wanted to tell you how wonderful your macarons are. My daughter lives in Paris, so I'm there every other year for a visit, and none of the macarons I've had in this country even come close to the amazing ones there. But yours are as good as the ones I buy at Pierre Hermé."

"I am sure I'll never be as good as the master." I ducked my head in modesty. "But that is a huge compliment, thank you."

"And thinking to infuse them with cannabis?" She made a "chef's kiss" gesture. "My husband has Parkinson's and his tremors are terrible some days. Very debilitating. We tried getting him to use cannabis and it really helped, but he always felt a bit uncomfortable with the idea, you know? Being able to eat some sweet treats—he's such a sweet tooth!—has really helped him to feel like it's a more normal thing, and I'm taking a whole box of these home for him after the surf competition tomorrow."

I pressed a hand to my chest. "I'm so glad you found something that works for him."

Hearing these stories was one of the things I loved most about my business—whether a customer enjoyed the use of cannabis for relaxation, creativity or medical relief, knowing that I could help people with my baking skills was the biggest buzz of all.

"Your husband isn't alone. I know a lot of people who don't like the idea of smoking and find dispensaries and all the different products to be a bit intimidating." I nodded. Grandma Rose had been like that in the early days, too. She'd stuck to gummies, but always complained that they tasted a little funky. "But food is accessible, right? We all eat. I really wanted to create a warm, welcoming environment with the café so that nobody ever felt too afraid to step in and speak with us."

The woman beamed. "You have done exactly that."

She gave a wave with one hand as her other hand clutched the medium-sized box of macarons, which housed a dozen neatly. I glanced over at the top shelf of our display cabinet, where I had special holders to keep the macarons upright—

there were only four left. Two chocolate and passionfruit, one raspberry, and one of the experimental flavors.

"I made twenty percent extra today," I said, shaking my head. "I'm going to have to advertise for a junior pastry chef quicker than we thought. I can't keep up with the demand."

Aunt Dawn patted me on the shoulder while wearing a very smug smile. "I told you so."

"I thought you were just being nice." I continued to stare at the near-empty macaron shelf. I had one last batch of pink shells cooling on racks in the kitchen and half a stand mixer bowl's worth of chocolate buttercream. Strawberry and chocolate it would be!

"Do I look like someone who says things for the sake of being nice?" She looked almost affronted.

"I never thought saying someone was nice would be considered an insult." I chuckled.

"Call me authentic. Call me dramatic. Call me that weird hippie lady who wears too much patchouli perfume. But don't call me nice." She winked. "And no, I wasn't being *nice*. I was serious. You're going to work yourself into the ground at this pace and a sustainable business is more likely to be a successful one."

"You're right." I nodded. "I'll write up a job ad on my break. I figure if we can get someone in to cover the basics— like making the cookies and mixing buttercream and prepping ingredients—that will leave me to the trickier things like the macaron shells and the pastry doughs."

"Exactly. *And* you can train them over time." Aunt Dawn nodded. "It would be a great opportunity for a young baker to be mentored by someone with your experience."

"You're going to give me a big head," I warned.

"Modesty is overrated." She gave me a gentle shove back toward the kitchen. "Now, please make some more macarons, because we're still open for another four hours and this empty shelf is making me sad."

* * *

It was well past lunchtime and I was desperate for a break. A quick check of my phone revealed a text from Matt saying they were done with the heats for the day (at least, for Ethan's section of the competition) and that it looked like Ethan would be going through to the quarterfinals! Great news. I admired his perseverance in the face of his friend's death.

Tenacity like that would take a person places in life.

But before I could head out for a break I had to pipe and sandwich the last batch of macarons, whip up another batch of cookie dough, and put in my order for the next month's worth of basics—including butter, milk, flour etc. Oh, and I had to tweak the roster for the next week after asking Erica if she would be willing to take on some more shifts.

So I put my head down and got to work until everything was done.

I *really* needed to write the job description for the junior baker. But first, I needed something to eat. Desperately. I grabbed two slices of bread and cut off a hunk of the cheese I'd been using for the scones and made myself a quick grilled cheese sandwich. Then I picked up the cup containing what was left of the coffee I'd bought and mostly ignored earlier that morning. It was stone cold but caffeinated, and I wasn't in a position to be picky.

Outside the air was warm and thick, our hottest day for the year so far and a great indication that the surf competition would have optimal weather. I wandered toward my usual lunch spot, the green space across the road from the café. I nabbed one of the benches under a cypress tree and sucked in a scent of tangy ocean air mixed with the rich scent of butter and cheese coming from the sandwich I'd hastily wrapped in parchment paper.

Just as I opened it all up and took a big, cheesy bite, I saw something that made my heart stop. A tall man wearing a white shirt with a heavy gold chain around his neck came out of the fresh-pressed juice shop three doors down from Baked by Chloe. It was Fisk Clemmens and he was carrying a large, plastic container with a thick straw poking out the top. Inside, the juice was a bright pinkish-orange color.

Maybe it was grapefruit juice!

He walked along the street, heading in the direction of the beach, his steps slow and leisurely. I looked down at my sandwich and then back up at Fisk, before quickly deciding that I was a modern woman who *could* have it all. In this case, lunch and clues. I darted across the street, draining the rest of my cold coffee and tossing the empty container into a street trash can. Then I ducked into the juice shop.

The shop, named Main Squeeze, was a little more than a year old and was run by some businessman who had stores peppered along the coast. I'd never seen him around. But I happened to know the woman who managed this particular one—because she was the daughter of Aunt Dawn's friend Michelle, and was also part of the family from whom we adopted Antonio.

"Hi Chloe." Tanisha held up her hand in a friendly wave. She was in her early twenties, with warm brown skin, closely cropped black curls and a smile that could melt even the frostiest stranger. Her makeup was always bold and fun, and today she wore a bright aqua-blue eyeliner that made her wide-set eyes stand out. "How's Antonio doing? Mom said he's really settled in well with you and your grandma."

"He's a delight. Truly." I glanced behind me to make sure there was no one within earshot. "This is very random, but there was a guy in here a minute ago . . ."

"Older dude with all the chains and chest hair?" Tanisha waved her hand in front of her, fingers spread. I noticed her nails had a French tip design, but instead of the traditional white they were the same aqua blue as her eyeliner. "He was spouting something about being a Hollywood director and then suggested I could be an extra in a movie because I'd look good in a bikini. Creep."

"That's him." I cringed. "What did he order?"

Tanisha raised an eyebrow. "He got the Sunset Supreme. Why?"

I glanced up at the electronic menu above Tanisha's head, which flicked between options for smoothies, juices and even some frozen yogurt variations, all with brightly colored pictures. Sunset Supreme. Grapefruit juice with a dash of ginger. Ordering grapefruit juice didn't make him a killer, of course, but my gut was telling me the juice was an important clue. If neither Aaron nor Ethan drank it, then it *had* to have gotten into the room somehow. Maybe Fisk was there and he returned later to remove any evidence that he'd been in the hotel.

"No time to explain. I hope you told him to get lost!"

I was almost the entire way out the door when I heard Tanisha's laughing response, "You know I did, girl."

I took a hearty bite out of my sandwich as I hurried up the street in the direction Fisk had gone. Thankfully, he hadn't turned a corner yet, so I could see him almost a full block ahead. My stomach groaned from the unusual mix of scoffing my food and exercise—not a great combination, by anyone's standards. But I was a busy business owner *and* an amateur sleuth.

There were not enough hours in the day to do things separately.

I closed the gap to Fisk, who was walking far more slowly than I was. At the next intersection, he turned onto the main strip and headed immediately across the road in the direction of our local surf store, Offshore, which had rainbow racks of surfboards and boogie boards out front, rails of colorful T-shirts cluttering the street, and swimsuits strung like a garland over the large front entrance.

Slowing my pace, I hovered at one of the T-shirt rails as if I was a browsing customer, making sure to keep the butter-covered fingers away from the fabrics, of course. Taking another bite, I peered into the shop.

The store was huge—there were entire sections for surfing equipment, wetsuits, waterproof technology as well as all different kinds of apparel: sneakers, hats, sunglasses and other accessories. I came in every couple of years to pay for the indignity of buying a new bathing suit, which was about as fun as buying jeans or bras or anything else that seemed made to prey on the insecurities of women and their bodies. Especially those, like me, who did *not* have the washboard stomachs and toned limbs of actual surfers.

I saw Fisk heading toward the escalator that went up to the second floor, where the women's section was. I headed into the store and followed him, keeping several paces behind and my eyes drifting around like I was just another shopper. As we were on the escalator, I realized he was on the phone and talking into his earpiece. Outside it had been too loud to hear him say anything, and thankfully the store didn't have the music pumping today.

"Yeah, I'm here," he said, keeping his voice low. "She's . . . going to . . . no, I won't."

I quietly went up another two steps to get a little closer.

"I don't know how she found out. He must have told her." Fisk swore under his breath. "I thought I was going to get away without forking out any more money. But he's screwing with me from beyond the grave."

I bit down on my sandwich and was thankful the fluffy bread and gooey cheese stifled my squeak of surprise. Was he talking about Aaron? He had to be!

I thought back to all the loan tracking on Aaron's phone. How was he paying those loans, especially with everything he needed to fork out to be on the competition circuit? Was it possible he had some dirt on Fisk and was blackmailing him?

The escalator seemed to move slower than an escargatoire of snails traveling through peanut butter—and yes, I knew the collective term for snails because it came up at a trivia night one time. Fisk lowered his voice again, glancing back over his shoulder to see me standing close behind. I averted my eyes, glancing around the shop while I finished my sandwich. On the other side of the escalator, I saw someone hustling down the stairs with their head bowed as though they were in a hurry to get outside. Weird.

I glanced back as they got to the bottom and sprinted toward the door. That's when it clicked that they were dressed all in black—black hoodie with the hood up, baggy black jeans, black sneakers. A strange sensation settled in the pit of my stomach.

Could that have been the same person I saw jumping off the balcony at the hotel?

I shook my head. It was more likely to be some kid shoplifting than anything else. Yeah, Azalea Bay was a safe town with a low crime rate—generally—but theft still occurred. I saw a few people go to the edge of the store and peer outside, roused by the strange sight of someone running, but nobody seemed to quite know what was happening. I finished the last bite of my sandwich and stuffed the parchment paper into my pocket.

Fisk stepped off the escalator and took a few steps, his head swinging back and forth as though he wasn't quite sure where to go. But then he moved sharply to the left. When I got to the top a second later, I walked in a curve to head in the same direction without it being obvious that I was following him. Up here there were racks and racks of bathing suits, bikinis, board shorts, T-shirts, dresses and all the other feminine beachy bits and pieces.

But Fisk was heading straight to the changing rooms. Weird again—he didn't have anything to try on . . . and all the men's gear was downstairs.

I grabbed two bathing suits off one of the racks without

checking the size and followed behind Fisk. There didn't seem to be an attendant anywhere—which was unusual. Then I heard a big burst of laughter and cheering from downstairs, followed by the squeal of a microphone. Sounded like they were setting up for an event.

Fisk stalked straight into the changing rooms and then counted the doors along the righthand side. When he got to the fourth one down, he paused and knocked. I ducked into a free stall on the opposite side and pulled the door closed, still listening. Another knock.

Then the creak of hinges.

An ear-splitting cry shattered the quiet air of the changing room, almost too high-pitched to have come from a man. Was he hurting someone? I burst out of the changing room, fists up as if ready to defend whoever Fisk was thinking about attacking when I saw him standing in the doorway of the changing stall across from me, face white, eyes like giant round cookies, and his mouth hanging open.

Inside the stall the crumpled body of a woman lay on the floor. Long black hair was spilled around her face, and on her ankle were two distinguishing features—a tattoo of a dolphin and a dainty silver ankle bracelet.

It was Kaila.

"Call 911," he said to me, his voice shaking. "I think she's dead."

CHAPTER 15

Thankfully, Kaila *wasn't* dead.

But she had sustained a forceful blow to the head and had been unconscious for an indeterminate amount of time, which was not a good thing. Paramedics had arrived at the surf shop quickly and whisked her off to the hospital, but since I hadn't done anything more than call 911 I wasn't required to hang around and provide a witness statement. It wasn't until I got back to the café that I remembered the person in black whom I'd seen running out of the store.

If that was the same person who'd entered the hotel room *and* killed Aaron (which was nothing more than a gut feeling, at this stage) then I was starting to feel less confident about Makani or anyone in his camp being involved. Not to mention that Fisk had slipped down the list, too, since he'd been in front of me almost the entire time at the store. I'd only been in the other changing room for a few seconds, not long enough for him to attack Kaila and knock her out cold. And he certainly wasn't the person dressed in black who'd run out of the store, because he couldn't be in two places at once.

But *was* the person in black the same one from the hotel?

I searched my memory, trying to think about what I'd seen

in both situations. The person, whoever they were, had been very good at obscuring their face and the baggy black clothing had disguised their frame. Plus, they'd moved too fast to me to catch anything else.

Slumping further down into one of the chairs at the café, I sighed. We'd closed up shop half an hour ago and I'd tried to shoo Aunt Dawn away, but she'd resisted. Now I was seated at one of the tables after we'd finished cleaning up, and she was making CBD chai lattes for us.

"Did you get any updates about that poor girl?" she asked as she brought two mugs to the table.

I eagerly reached for mine, desperate for the comforting warmth of the mug against my palms and the scent of cinnamon and cloves and cardamom. Not to mention I could really use the calming effects of the CBD right now. It was too hot to drink, so I blew on the steam, watching the delicate curls dissipate and re-form.

"Ethan texted me. She's been stabilized at the hospital but they've had to put her into a medically induced coma for the time being. Apparently it's to prevent brain swelling after a serious head injury." I shook my head. "So scary."

Aunt Dawn made a sympathetic clucking sound. Her hair was dyed a deep purple and when the light hit the halo of frizz, it made the edges look almost magenta. Without her uniform apron, I could see the full breadth of color in her outfit, a paisley maxi dress—purple, green and yellow—over which she had a belt made of braided suede in a bright mustard. Normally her colorful appearance put a smile on my face, but today I was finding it hard to be upbeat.

"I think it's connected to the man who died in the hotel," I said. I'd been keeping her updated when we worked together before the store opened each morning. "I saw someone fleeing the scene wearing all black, just like the person I saw leaving the hotel room via the balcony."

My aunt pursed her lips. "Chloe, I don't know that it's a good idea that you're getting involved in all this. People are getting hurt."

"Do you trust the police to get the job done before everyone leaves town?" I asked.

She shot me a look. "I know the answer you want me to give."

"I'm genuinely interested in your answer. Your *real* answer." I brought the mug to my lips and took the tiniest sip, wincing a little at the heat. "Because they don't even believe that Aaron was murdered."

She let out a long breath and I could tell she was being very considered about her response. For my aunt, this wasn't her usual way of communicating. She was more one of those speak-from-the-heart, no filter, too-blunt-for-her-own-good types of people.

"No, I don't trust them to get the job done that quickly," she admitted. "I think the chief has an idea of what this town is—that nothing bad ever happens here—and he overlooks things out of his own stubbornness."

This exactly echoed my own concerns.

"And the detective?" I asked.

"She needs his support if she wants to climb the ranks here. She might be looking to take over his job and rocking the boat would be counter to that."

It was an interesting point. "I get the impression she would speak up if she thought something was going on. But she really seems to believe this was a suicide. And if they're so set on that theory, they might not even see Kaila's attack as being linked."

"But you think it was?" My aunt's blue eyes searched my face. I could tell she was interested despite her protests about my safety.

My aunt loved a puzzle as much as I did.

"I do." I nodded. "The guy who found her was there to

meet up with her about something. I overheard him talking on the phone and he said, 'I don't know how she found out. He must have told her.' Then he made a comment about having to fork out more money and someone screwing him from beyond the grave."

"Okay, so I can see why it's got you all in a twist." My aunt gave a sheepish smile. "So you think the guy who died knew something and he told the woman who was attacked?"

"Yeah, I do. Only, the guy who found her wasn't the one who attacked her. I had my eyes on him practically the whole time and he was the one who asked me to call the ambulance."

"You saw him find her?" she asked.

"Well, I was in a changing room for a few seconds. But he was outside her stall before I closed the door and there were no sounds of a struggle. I didn't hear her speak or anything. I'm confident he found her like that." I nodded, playing it all over in my head again. My gut told me Fisk wasn't the one who attacked her. The way he screamed, so high-pitched and terrified . . . he did not strike me as someone who was comfortable with violence. "He waited around with the paramedics and he was going to hurl the whole time."

"Doesn't sound like a killer."

"Nope." I shook my head. "Makes me wonder if Aaron's girlfriend, Celina, is the one who did it. He was supposedly cheating on her with Kaila, and now Kaila is in the hospital. Maybe it was a crime of passion?"

"Seems extreme." My aunt wrinkled her nose.

"She basically cut ties with her whole family for Aaron. They went back to Japan and she refused to go with them, which caused a huge rift between her and her parents." I shrugged. "It's more complicated than just a jilted love interest. She gave up so much for him."

We sipped our chai lattes in silence for a moment. My brain was whirring harder than an old fan on a hundred-degree day.

Something wasn't adding up but I couldn't quite put my finger on what felt off about all this. I wanted to know what was going on with Fisk Clemmens.

"Hey," I said, turning to my aunt. "What's the fanciest place to stay in town, do you think?"

"I suspect there's possibly a few nice Airbnbs in the rich section of town," she replied, wrinkling her nose. "But if you're talking about regular accommodation, probably Sabrina's bed-and-breakfast. They built a couple of free-standing luxury suites there about a year and a half ago for guests who wanted to stay on the grounds but didn't want to mingle with other people so much."

"Oh, yeah! I had totally forgotten about the expansion." I grabbed my phone and fired off a text to my best friend.

CHLOE: Hey girl! Any chance you have someone named Fisk Clemmens staying with you?

SABRINA: You know I can't give out confidential guest information. But I did hear chatter that some pompous Hollywood type was trying to recruit bikini extras in my dining room which is so *not* okay.

I glanced at my aunt and grinned. "Feel like coming on a fact-finding mission with me?"

"I'll come," she said, grinning right back. "But only to make sure you're safe."

"Sure." I rolled my eyes. "And I bet you'll hate every minute of it."

"Absolutely," my aunt replied in a way that told me quite the opposite would be true.

The Azalea Bay Bed-and-Breakfast was located at the edge of town, up on a hill, with a wonderful view of the ocean and part of a large swath of walking trails and natural green land. From the front, it looked rather modest—a quaint white building, with a pretty stone path bracketed by colorful flowers and foliage, and a welcoming air.

But once you got inside, it was easy to see that an immense amount of care and thought had been put into the place. This was mostly Sabrina's doing, in fact. Instead of going off to college, she'd stayed in our hometown to take her parents' bed-and-breakfast business from being on the brink of bankruptcy to becoming one of the most Instagram-worthy accommodation spots in all of Azalea Bay and the surrounding areas. These days, they were constantly booked out. And they had a huge social following, all thanks to when Sabrina had decided to document the renovation process on Instagram—sharing all her clever decorating hacks and tips along the way.

Instead of the floral duvets and couches and dark, claustrophobic shades I remembered from my childhood playing here while Sabrina's parents worked, now everything was light and airy and stylish. It was all white walls and furniture made from reclaimed pine and accents in warm gold, silvery eucalyptus green and hazy turquoise. A feature wall behind the front desk was wallpapered with a muted, elegant design of palm leaves in a bluish gray. While overhead, an incredible light fixture dangled from the ceiling, large, pearlescent baubles strung from gold wires, so it looked like bubbles floating in the air.

On the reception desk was a floral arrangement of native flowers including bright yellow pops of golden yarrow, the delicate white petals of Californian aster and the pretty sunset pink of lewisia.

"Hello you two." Sabrina came out from behind the front desk. Today she looked extra-professional with her curly dark hair pulled back into a braid, and a navy blazer over a white silk top and pair of straight-leg cream pants.

It was a far cry from her all-black Dungeon Master look.

"Hey, is uh . . . our Hollywood friend around?" I asked, keeping my voice low.

"I think he's hanging around by the pool," she replied, pulling a face. It was clear she was not a fan of Fisk.

"Crap. Maybe I should have picked up a bathing suit while I was at the surf shop," I muttered. "It's going to look weird if we hang out by the pool fully clothed."

"Not me." Aunt Dawn pulled a pair of large sunglasses out of her bag and slipped them on. "Hand me that hat, dear."

She pointed to a large floppy straw hat that was hanging on the wall behind reception as part of the decor. Sabrina sighed and reached for the hat, handing it over. There was no point arguing with Aunt Dawn. The hat coupled with the maxi dress and sunglasses, she could have been mistaken for an aging starlet hiding her identity on a luxury cruise.

"What about me?" I looked down at the outfit I'd changed into before we came to the B&B. I had on a pair of loose jeans with rips in the knees, a pink-and-white–striped T-shirt and white sneakers—not exactly the attire of someone with poolside aspirations.

"There are fluffy toweling robes and slides in that cupboard," she said, handing me a key. "You can change in the staff toilets."

"You're the best." I threw my arms around her neck and squeezed.

"I don't even want to know *what* you're up to," she said, hugging me back. "But please don't give my business a bad name, okay? And don't do anything illegal."

"I promise." I made a cross shape over my heart and then darted off to change into my robe and slides.

I stashed my clothes in one of the staff lockers, leaving it ajar since I didn't have a lock with me. But I figured nobody would be inclined to steal my sweaty sneakers, anyway. I threw my robe over my underwear, got my sunglasses from my bag and slipped my feet into the fuzzy white slides that had the bed-and-breakfast logo embroidered on the side. Very luxurious.

When I walked back through the foyer to drop Sabrina's key off, I noticed Aunt Dawn was gone. Already soaking up the sun by the pool, no doubt. I traipsed through the sliding glass doors and out to the pool area. It might not be common for a lot of bed-and-breakfasts to have a pool, but we *were* in California and we had great weather for swimming for most of the year. In fact, the pool had been built when Sabrina and I were kids but she'd updated the area during the renovation phase.

Now it has a cool 1960s pool party vibe, with large umbrellas in pale blue and white stripes with white fringing around the edges, and banana lounges with cushions to match. There were blue and white polka dot floating donuts in the pool, a covered space with rattan chairs and tables flanked by a longer trestle table with jugs of fruit-infused water, and an outdoor rainforest showerhead for people to wash the chlorine off before they went back to their rooms.

I spotted Fisk immediately.

He was sunning himself on a banana lounge, wearing a pair of white board shorts that were entirely *too* short and leaving his chest bare, save for the thick gold chain tangled in the ample amount of curly hair growing there.

It was certainly a look.

Thankfully, the lounge next to him was free and I made a beeline for it before anyone else could nab a spot. Most of the other lounges were full and I saw Aunt Dawn sprawled out on the other side of the pool, chatting with someone I didn't recognize. Typical. She could make friends anywhere.

The lounge chair squeaked as I lowered myself down and Fisk's gaze flicked in my direction before he returned back to looking ahead, dismissing me. I'd already figured my curvy pastry-loving figure would not solicit an offer to be a bikini babe extra in his movie.

His loss.

"Hey, are you . . ." I turned to look at him, gasping like I'd just figured out who he was. "Oh my gosh, it *is* you!"

Fisk took his time turning to look back at me, his sunglasses perched on his head despite the fact that it was very bright out and he was definitely squinting. Something told me he wanted to be recognized and wouldn't let sun protection stand in his way.

"I'm sorry, I can't talk about the movie—"

"No, from the store today! You found that girl." I pressed a hand to my chest. "I called 911 for you."

Now I had his attention. His eyes narrowed at me, as though trying to figure out if I was telling the truth. Earlier, when he'd screamed and I'd come flying out of the changing stall, he'd barely been able to tear his eyes away from Kaila's crumpled body. But when I pulled my sunglasses off, recognition flashed across his face.

"That was so terrifying. I can't even imagine what a shock you must have had finding her like that." I reached out to touch his arm, hoping that none of the giant ick factor I felt inside was visible to him or anyone watching. "Especially since you know her."

"Excuse me?" His arm went rigid under my fingertips and I pulled away.

"From the surfing world. Kaila, I mean." I watched him like a hawk for any sense of guilt or shame. But instead his eyes welled up with tears. "Makani's sister."

"Yes. I've known her since she was a little kid," he said, sniffling. "She came to all the competitions with Makani, following him around like a puppy. She was always a sweet girl, kind to everyone she met."

Admittedly, I was a bit surprised by his reaction. I hadn't expected an emotional response.

"She had a big heart," I bluffed. "I hope she's going to be okay."

At least that much I could be truthful about. I hoped that

Kaila would be well enough to leave the hospital and be with her family as soon as possible.

He brushed a tear away with the back of his hand, but his eyes immediately welled again. "Her dad and I used to surf together when we were kids. God, poor Greg. He's going to be devastated knowing someone hurt his little girl."

Fisk let out a sob and I blinked.

"Why were you meeting her in the changing room?" I asked and now it was his turn to blink. I kept my voice low enough that nobody around us would hear. "That's a bit of a strange place to meet up with the daughter of your close friend, isn't it?"

"I . . . I . . ." he stammered. "I didn't . . ."

"You were meeting her there because she wanted money from you, right? She was collecting a debt for Aaron."

His eyes widened comically and he shrank back against the banana lounge as if I'd announced that I was a witch about to put a curse on him. "How do you know about that?"

"I know a lot more than you think, Fisk. And I can go to the police if I think it's necessary." I gave him a look that said I wasn't messing around.

I was glad we were in an open space with lots of people close by, so he wasn't tempted to try anything funny. But Fisk surprised me again. His face crumpled and he buried his head in his hands.

"It was one time," he moaned. "One freaking time and I was desperate!"

"*What* was one time? You'd better not lie to me."

"I fixed a competition." He shook his head. "I blackmailed a surfer to throw a huge competition that he was sure to win, so I could bet against him and make good money. I used a bookie and . . . I needed the cash, you see. I had a problem. Dogs, ponies, blackjack."

Something clicked—Fisk wasn't the only one with a gambling problem.

"Aaron saw you at a gambling addiction meeting and put two and two together," I said. "He figured out what you'd done."

Fisk nodded, lips quivering like he was a naughty child who'd been told off for stealing from the cookie jar. "He wanted money for his silence. I thought the first payment would be enough, but periodically he'd pop up and threaten my career whenever things were tight for him. This went on for the last three years. I should have told him I was done with his games and if he wanted to ruin my career, so be it. My judging days are over, anyway. Hollywood is where I belong."

Part of me was surprised that he was willing to tell me his story . . . but then again, he struck me as a person who enjoyed the sound of his own voice. Perhaps he was the type of person who lived to have an audience. Whatever the reason, I wasn't going to question it.

"But you think he told Kaila about the match fixing?" I asked.

"He must have. They were close, even after they split up. Then right after he died, she told me to come meet her." He shook his head. "I knew she was going to ask me for money like he'd been doing."

"You knew or you guessed?" I probed.

Across the pool, I caught sight of Aunt Dawn keeping an eye on me. It felt good to know she was there, but in my heart I knew Fisk wasn't a killer. He was a guy with an addiction who'd made some poor judgment calls. That was all. And if he was ready and willing to leave his judging days behind him for a new career . . . then why would he murder Aaron to keep his secret safe and risk going to jail for something much bigger than match fixing? It didn't seem plausible.

"She never said that was what she wanted exactly. But she said she needed my 'help' and I thought that was code for 'money.'"

"But she never mentioned the blackmail and the match fixing specifically?"

He shook his head. "No, she didn't. But my gut told me she knew from the way she was speaking to me."

But what if she didn't know? What if Kaila really *was* looking for help from Fisk? He was friends with her dad, after all. He'd known her since she was a kid, by his own admission. Maybe he was someone she trusted.

Or maybe Fisk had picked up a Hollywood trick or two from his actor friends.

"You know that's a pretty big motive for murder, right? The guy who was blackmailing you suddenly turns up dead . . ." I cocked my head. "Where *were* you the night of the murder?"

"I was . . . at a beach party . . ."

Fisk suddenly turned green. His eyes bulged and he clamped a hand over his mouth, shaking his head furiously before he tumbled off the banana lounge and went to throw up in the bushes behind the pool. I cringed.

Not exactly the reaction of a killer, was it?

I got up off my lounge and motioned for Aunt Dawn to follow me out of the pool area. She came up beside me and hooked her arm through mine.

"Find anything out?" she asked, her head bowed to mine.

"Yeah . . ." We walked toward the glass doors leading inside and I glanced back over my shoulder to where Fisk was still on hands and knees by the bushes. "And I owe Sabrina money for cleanup."

CHAPTER 16

"Fisk didn't kill Aaron."

A group of us sat around the outdoor table at my aunt's house. It was a little early for dinner, but we'd decided to have a group discussion about what was going on, so everyone was on the same page. In my mind, it was always best to have important conversations with food.

Matt and Lawrence stood at the barbecue, grilling shrimp skewers and flank steaks. Lawrence seemed entirely too dressed up in his button-down shirt, gray slacks and brown leather loafers, but now that I thought about it . . . I didn't think I'd ever seen him dress any other way. Aunt Dawn was currently pouring glasses of water and freshly squeezed orange juice for everyone, while Grandma Rose, Ben, Ethan and I sat back in our chairs.

Ben had come straight from work and was still in his work clothing—neat chinos and a checked shirt, though his hair was a little mussed. I was sure there was tension at home for him and Matt, and I wished we were closer to an answer for everyone's sake.

In the backyard, Moxie played with Antonio. They'd become fast and unlikely friends, given the black-and-white border collie was about ten times the Chihuahua's size. In truth, Moxie was also *way* smarter than Antonio, and she ran rings around him, doing tricks and playing hide-and-seek. It was a good thing Antonio was the cutest dog on the face of the earth, because he was easily and happily fooled.

"How do you know?" Ethan asked. He was sitting cross-legged on one of the outdoor chairs, wearing a pair of lime-green flip-flops and board shorts, his hair textured with salt from being in the water all afternoon.

"Admittedly, it's just a feeling. But it's a strong one," I said. "And he definitely didn't hurt Kaila. I've gone over it in my head a dozen times and he just wouldn't have had time to do it. Given I also saw someone dressed all in black fleeing the store right before he found her—possibly the same person I saw sneaking out of the hotel room— I'm positive Aaron's killer is also the person who hurt her. It's got to be related."

"Do they have any idea when she can come out of the medically induced coma?" Ben asked Ethan, his face creased in concern.

Ethan shook his head. "Not yet. They're still doing tests and waiting for results from scans and stuff. Makani is devastated. He hasn't left the hospital since it happened. It was a good thing his heat was first thing today, so he'd already competed when he got the call."

Grandma Rose made a sympathetic tutting sound. "There's nothing more stressful than having a loved one be attacked."

Both she and Aunt Dawn exchanged a look and I knew they were thinking about me. Thankfully, I wasn't left with any lasting injuries. But things could be dire for Kaila. And, with her being unconscious, it wasn't like she could tell anyone what happened.

"Do you know if the police have a suspect?" I asked. "I assume they checked the security footage from the surf shop."

"I heard from someone who's good friends with Makani

that the police have nothing," Ethan said. "Apparently all they saw on the security footage was someone dressed in black enter the store, follow Kaila upstairs and into the changing rooms. But there's no cameras in that section, obviously. That would be a major violation of privacy. They saw the person leave and then Fisk went in. Shortly after that, 911 was called."

Great. So the police had nothing more than I had, simply from being there when it happened. I wished I'd been able to get a better look at the person in black! I was so busy trying to eavesdrop on Fisk's phone conversation that I hadn't been paying enough attention to my surroundings.

"And they have no idea who it might have been or why they attacked her?" Aunt Dawn asked, her arms wrapped around herself despite the warm temperature. None of us liked the idea that someone was lurking around town attacking people. It had unnerved us all.

Ethan shook his head. "They suspect that her head was slammed against the wall. Apparently, there was a dent."

I shivered. "That's brutal. Poor Kaila."

"I hope she wakes up and there's no lasting effects," Grandma Rose said. Her hair was wrapped up in a pale lavender and pink floral scarf, and she'd fastened a jeweled brooch to the front to give it a little extra pizzazz. I noticed she'd been wearing more jewelry of late, and even with the somber mood after Kaila's attack, I was happy to see my grandmother sparkling like the gem she was. "I will keep her in my prayers."

"Who else is on your suspect list?" Lawrence asked as he carried a plate of shrimp skewers to the table and set it down, while Matt sliced up the flank steak.

As soon as the food hit the table, everyone began to dish themselves up.

"There's Aaron's main rival, another surfer named Makani. There's a lot of bad blood between them and he was the last person who went to Aaron's hotel room, according to the hotel security footage," I said. "But he's also the big brother of the girl who was attacked *and* we figured out that it's possible to get into the hotel room by climbing up onto the balcony, circumventing the security footage. So this whole thing makes me question whether he was involved."

Ethan nodded. "I agree. There's no way he would hurt his own sister."

"I think the only way that Makani is involved would be if two different people hurt Aaron and Kaila . . ." I said, reaching for a glass of water and taking a big sip. "But my gut is telling me it's the same person. And, to your point from the other day, Lawrence, I don't know that he'd have the knowledge of Aaron's medical history to fool a coroner. We're still waiting on the results, but if it comes out that he *did* die from an overdose of his sleeping tablets . . . how would Makani even know that was an option?"

"Exactly! He does not have the intimate knowledge of the victim." Lawrence took the seat next to my grandmother and I saw him reach over to clasp her hand. It gave my heavy heart a moment of sweet reprieve. "Now, if it were a spontaneous murder, perhaps. But a faked suicide is more than likely planned, because there cannot be any injuries or evidence that might detract from the story the killer wishes to tell."

I noticed Matt, Ethan and Ben all nodding along, enraptured by Lawrence's voice. I really *did* need to borrow some of his books from my grandmother, because I could tell he would be a great writer. He clearly had a keen understanding of people and behavior.

"I fear your friend's rival is not the killer." Lawrence bobbed his head. "There are too many signs pointing away from him, rather than to him."

I nodded in agreement. We could potentially strike Makani and anyone from his family off the list, as well.

"Kaila's attack makes me more suspicious of Celina," Matt

said. Everyone was seated with full plates and glasses now, and the scratch of silverware over porcelain filled the gaps of our conversation. "Maybe the jealous girlfriend killed her boyfriend and attacked the woman he was cheating with—doesn't seem a huge stretch, I reckon. Who else has ties to *both* people and motive for both attacks?"

That was a good point.

"And don't forget, an intimate partner would have medical knowledge," Lawrence added with a nod.

"I still find it hard to believe that Aaron would cheat on Celina, though," Ethan said, blond curls bouncing as he shook his head. He forked a piece of steak into his mouth and chewed. "I know Celina wanted to get engaged and he was resistant . . . but that's only because he hated the idea of marriage. Not because he didn't care about her."

"I think you put Aaron on a pedestal," Matt said gently. His green eyes drifted over to his brother, brows knitted in sincerity.

"I don't," Ethan protested. "I know he was flawed. But we all are. He used to talk about Celina a lot—he admired her. How hard she worked, what a talented photographer she was, how independent she'd become even with her family trying to stifle and mold her. Aaron might have been a lot of things, but he wasn't a cheater."

"And then there's Mariah," I said. "The friend he rejected romantically, who'd also loaned him money. Now we know she's struggling financially, trying to pay for college herself, and she probably needed that money back."

"But if she kills him then she *definitely* doesn't get that money back," Aunt Dawn pointed out, jabbing the air with her fork as if to emphasize her point.

"Maybe she'd come to the conclusion she was *never* getting the money back," Ben suggested. "And she killed him out of revenge?"

It was certainly possible, but something about the theory didn't feel right.

Silence settled over the table. There was a big, black hole in our knowledge of what happened these past few days, and I was sure Aaron's deleted text messages and missing journal had something to do with it.

Then my memory jolted. "Did you end up finding anything *else* of interest on Aaron's phone? Other than the notes with the loan payments?"

"The only other thing I found was a text from someone asking him to meet up the night before I arrived, which was odd. For starters the number wasn't saved as a contact in his phone and secondly, I didn't realize that he'd come up the day earlier. We checked into the hotel together so I have no idea where he would have stayed."

"Weird." Matt cocked his head. "Did you try calling the number?"

"Yeah, it rang out. No voicemail or anything."

"What about the camera in Aaron's backpack?" I asked.

Ethan shook his head. "There was no SD card."

"Huh." I cocked my head. "So, whoever stole the backpack took one of the journals, wiped a bunch of messages off his phone *and* took the SD card out of his camera."

"That sounds mighty suspicious to me," Grandma Rose chimed in with a nod of her head while she speared some cherry tomatoes and lettuce onto her fork. "Aaron knew something and someone has erased it."

"But what?" Ethan tossed his hands in the air. "Whatever it was, he didn't tell me a thing."

"Maybe he told Celina?" Matt suggested.

"A lover's confession." Lawrence bobbed his silvery head, eyes narrowed in concentration. I could practically hear the gears turning in his head. "Even if she didn't know exactly what was going on, she probably knew more than most."

"Either that or she killed him," I mumbled.

"We need to talk to her," Ethan said. "She's doing some sunset photos down at the beach tonight. Why don't we head there after dinner and see what we can dig up?"

I chewed on my shrimp, too distracted to enjoy the naturally sweet flavor. "That is an excellent idea."

After dinner, Lawrence agreed to take Grandma Rose home— no doubt to share a cup of tea and possibly some conversation about another strange mating ritual in the animal kingdom. Aunt Dawn and Maisey were off to some new bar in a town close by named Twin Parks, while Matt, Ben, Ethan, Antonio and I headed to the beach to find Celina.

We squished into Ben's car, a sporty little thing that felt only marginally bigger than the Jellybean, and made our way to the water. It took us a few minutes to find a free parking spot, and we ended up having to walk an extra block to the boardwalk. Not that I minded, it was beautiful out. The sun would probably be setting in another half an hour, and the sky was filled with rich, golden light.

Out on the waves, the surfers glided and twisted and flew. Holding Antonio in my arms because his little legs struggled with the big wooden steps, we made our way down onto the beach. The sand was scattered with people, music floating up into the air from portable stereos and some groups with picnic baskets and games. There were a few folks in the shallower section of the water tossing a brightly colored beach ball around, and three children burying an adult in the sand. They'd given the poor forty-something man one hell of a sand bra, and were in the process of sculpting his lower half into a tail.

Something told me that guy would be finding sand in his nether regions for weeks to come.

"There's Celina." Ethan pointed out to the water.

It took me a moment to find the figure bobbing in the waves, a large bulky camera in front of her face. How on earth did she take photos in the water without ruining her camera? It must have been enclosed in a special casing or something.

She disappeared suddenly, and then bobbed back up at the end of a large, curling wave, facing a surfer who was barreling right toward her. I clamped a hand over my mouth, watching as she held her ground—or rather, her water—to get the shot. Then she ducked beneath the waves again, letting the surfer glide by.

A few minutes later, I spotted her standing closer to the shoreline in knee-high water while she checked her camera. It had been hard to see at a distance, but she was actually wearing a black helmet that blended in with her dark hair. Maybe that's how she felt confident staying so close to the surfers to take their photos. After her checks were complete, she waded out of the waves, a pair of bright blue fins slapping at the shallows, and a large camera on a stick dangling from one hand. She had one of those rash guard tops, with long sleeves and a high neckline that kept her chest, shoulders and most of her stomach completely covered. On the bottom was the lower half of a bright red bikini.

She immediately headed to a patch of sand where a bucket of water was waiting and she dropped the camera into it. I noticed there was a small cord attaching the camera to her wrist, and she removed it, tossing it to one side before giving the camera a shake in the bucket and then pulling it back out to set it on top of a small case to dry. She pulled her helmet and fins off, yanked down the half zipper on her rash guard to open the neckline and then peeled the wet fabric from her skin. Underneath was the red bikini top to match the bottoms.

I glanced at Ethan and he nodded, then we headed over to her.

"That's one beast of a camera," I said as we approached.

Celina looked up as she squeezed the water from her hair.

When she caught sight of Ethan, a small smile flickered across her face, though it was fleeting. "The camera is just a camera, but I suppose the AquaTech housing makes it look pretty big."

"That's to keep the water out, huh?" I peered down to look at it. The housing was a bright orange with a handle on either side and then a stick protruding from the bottom. There was a big clear circle at the front, and getting a closer look I could see there was a regular camera nestled inside.

"Yep. You pop your camera inside and snap these clamps shut to keep it secure. I have a Nikon D6 inside."

Matt let out a low whistle. "That's some serious gear!"

She glanced at him, eyebrows raised with interest. "You shoot?"

"I've dabbled," he replied. "But nothing like what you do and never in the water."

"He's being modest," Ben chimed in, slipping an arm around his boyfriend's waist. "We had a few of his photos blown up and framed for our house. He's got a natural eye for it."

Matt blushed.

"Hey, you're the creative one in this relationship. Own it." Ben bumped his hip against Matt's.

"Does it ever get dangerous?" I asked Celina, genuinely curious. "I saw you were wearing a helmet. I didn't know people wore helmets in the water."

She nodded. "The ocean is an uncontrollable environment and there's a lot that can happen. The helmet keeps me protected from any sharp fins if I collide with a surfer, but it would also work for rocks and reef structures if I got pulled under by a riptide or something like that. If I'm shooting around really rocky areas, I also have an impact vest to protect my torso."

"Safety first." I nodded. "That's smart."

"And using the pistol grip means I can keep my other hand free." She pointed to the stick coming out of the bottom of the camera's housing. "It has a button so I can take the photos easily while holding the camera with one hand. That way I can use my other arm to swim or protect my face or whatever else I need to do. I have a bodyboard leash to keep the camera attached to me in case I drop it, and the fins help me move with speed, so if I need to get out of the way quickly, I can."

"You've thought of everything." I shook my head in wonder. "So, this is your career, huh? That's really cool."

"It is." I could sense the pride radiating from her. "I started out taking shots for friends and then some surf influencers started to hire me, and eventually I got more and more work with the big brands and the WSL."

"What's the WSL?"

"It stands for World Surf League," Ethan explained. "They run the show as far as the competition circuits and other major pro events are concerned."

We stood around chatting about her work for a few minutes, and Celina's face glowed as she showed us some of her shots. It was clear she was thrilled to have found success and respect in her chosen field. Based on what I knew, she'd probably never had any interest in her work from her family, since they'd always wanted her to work in her father's firm. It must have been validating to have other people be so keen to hear about her chosen path.

I leaned over to Ethan and whispered, "Can you take Ben and your brother for a walk or something? I want to have a girl chat with Celina."

I couldn't get Lawrence's suggestion out of my head—if she wasn't the killer, then there was a chance she knew *something* useful, even if she didn't think it was valuable information.

Ethan nodded and herded the two other men toward where a young guy with a large yellow surfboard tucked under his arm stood by the water.

"Did you hear about Kaila?" I asked. Celina took a seat on the towel and I followed her down without waiting for an invitation. Thankfully, she didn't shoo me away. I wasn't sure if she remembered me from the party or not, but I guess since it was clear I knew Ethan and Matt, I must be automatically vouched for.

"I did." She turned to me, her dark, upturned eyes boring into mine. There was an iron strength to this woman. I could almost feel the determination crackling in the air around her—she was someone who was always prepared to fight for what she wanted.

But would she kill for it?

"I take it by the way you're looking at me that you know she was the person Aaron was cheating with," she said, her voice unemotional and unwavering. I respected her control. I hadn't been quite so strong when I found out about my ex knocking up his mistress.

"I understand how painful it is. I understand the betrayal and the need to get the rage out," I said, meaning it.

"I get my rage out in the water," she replied. "I didn't put Kaila in the hospital. And I didn't kill Aaron either, if that's what you're thinking."

"I never said that." I held up both hands.

"I'm not naive, I know people are thinking it." She sighed and turned to look out over the water. The sun was so low it was barely a blip on the horizon now. The rest of the sky was a hazy purple and dotted with brilliant stars, and portable lanterns started to flick on along the beach. It looked like people were preparing to stay awhile. And why not? The weather was perfection.

"It doesn't matter what people think," I said with a shrug. "Only the truth matters."

"And why do you care? You don't know me." She drew her knees to her chest and wrapped her arms around her shins, propping her chin down. The position shrank her and she suddenly looked very young and very vulnerable. "I'm nobody to you."

There was a sadness in her voice that tugged at my heart-strings. "I know what it's like to be in another country far away from your family when everything turns to crap. I know what it's like to feel utterly alone in the world."

Those days felt like a strange and distant memory, even though in reality they weren't that far behind me. But I remembered the aching loneliness, the regret, the feeling of being isolated and homesick.

She glanced at me. "But you're not like that now, are you?"

I shook my head. "No. I came out the other side and you will, too."

She chewed on the inside of her cheek and I felt some of her guardedness ease. "Makani sent me a nasty text saying that if I hurt his little sister then I'd be hearing from him."

"I'm sure he's just freaking out because his sister is in a coma," I said gently. "I doubt he means it."

"If I *had* done anything wrong then I would have reason to be scared. Family is everything to him." She let out a breath. "How nice it must be to have blood relations feel so passionately about protecting you."

There was no anger in her voice. Not even bitterness. Just a deep, pulsing sadness. I wanted to reach out and hug the poor woman. Nobody should ever have to feel like that.

"But I didn't do it," she said. "Any of it."

"You confronted Aaron about it the night he died," I prodded. The hotel security footage had shown them arguing in the hall as she left.

Celina seemed so lost in her own thoughts that she didn't even ask me how I knew that piece of information. Instead, she nodded. "I went to his room and told him . . . I told him I had proof."

"Proof?"

"He'd been denying it." Tears welled in her eyes and she sniffed. "I asked him weeks ago and he said nothing was going on between him and Kaila. The night we arrived it was late and

I went out for a walk because he wasn't answering his phone. I saw them. I had my camera with me . . ."

Her voice broke off and she used the back of her hand to whisk away a tear.

Then she reached over to her bag and pulled out a more compact camera than the one she'd taken into the water. "I never bring my good one to the beach outside the housing because I don't want to risk getting sand in it. But I have this little one in my bag all the time for happy snaps and if something grabs my eye."

She turned it on and started to click through the photos. Then she turned the display screen toward me. The photo was beautiful. It showed the high part of town, with a stripe of orange along the horizon feathered by the tall grass that surrounded our walking trails. There were two people in the photo, shadows mostly. I squinted.

"Keep clicking right," she said.

The next one was zoomed in, showing an area glowing from an overhead streetlamp. Two people were entwined in an embrace. The light reflected off Aaron's ginger hair, making it gleam like the setting sun. The girl in his arms was slender, with long, dark hair. At first one could have mistaken her for Celina, but the next photo showed their faces and it was unmistakably Aaron and Kaila. The photos showed them hugging and in one photo Kaila even looked like she might be crying.

I was waiting to see a picture of them kissing or touching in a more sexual way, but there wasn't anything.

"Are you *sure* he was cheating on you?" I asked, a seed of doubt taking root inside me. There was nothing sexual or romantic about the embrace in the photos. At least, not to my eye.

"You saw the pictures," she said, gesturing with a sharp, flicking hand toward the camera. "They're in love. He was going to leave me."

I wasn't sure I agreed. They were hugging, yes, but the vibe seemed almost . . . like he was comforting her. In one picture in particular, Kaila looked almost distressed. Perhaps Celina thought it was simply the other woman's ploy to steal her man, but something about the photos sat funny with me.

"Now you know I'm a stalker," she said, taking the camera back and turning it off. She toyed with it for a moment, flicking one of the dials back and forth. "But I'm not a killer. I *loved* Aaron. I loved him enough to destroy my relationship with my family to be with him. It's pathetic, but I would a thousand percent rather him be alive and be with someone else, than have him not around at all."

I believed her. The raw grief in her voice was unmistakable.

"And I hate Kaila for what she did, but I would *never* risk doing anything to piss off her family. They're royalty in this world. One word from her father and I'd never work again. So, I would have lost the only other thing I love, besides Aaron. What would be the point of my life then?"

That was a damn good question and I was now officially stumped.

Fisk, Makani and Celina were all effectively struck off the suspect list. Who else would be motivated to kill Aaron and harm Kaila?

"Hey, so Ethan noticed that one of Aaron's journals was missing from the backpack in his room." I didn't bother to relay the whole story about the missing and then *not* missing backpack. "It was the one that covered the period from February this year through to May. Did anything major happen during that time?"

"Things were really tense with my parents then and I was . . ." She huffed a piece of damp hair out of her eyes. "I was difficult, I'll admit it."

"What about with Aaron? Was there anything going on with his family or his money troubles or anything else?"

Celina thought for a moment. In the silence, the sounds of the beach flooded in—waves, laughter, music. "He started disappearing a lot around then."

"Disappearing?"

"Yeah." She nodded. "It was like he got obsessed with something. He was always on his computer reading articles and calling people, but never while I was in the room. Then he would take off at night and come home at all hours. It was strange."

"But you have no idea what had got him so worked up?"

She shook her head. "All he would tell me was that he'd figured out something terrible was going on in the surf community."

For a moment I wondered if she was talking about the match fixing with Fisk . . . but Aaron had been blackmailing him for a few years. So it must have been something else.

"I wish I knew where that missing journal was." I let out a sigh of annoyance. "It's got to be the key to figuring out what happened to him."

Celina looked at me, baffled. "You didn't even know Aaron. Why do you care what happened to him? You're here, asking all these questions and . . . I can't figure out why."

It probably seemed strange to her. To most people. *Why* would I get involved in something that, arguably, wasn't my business?

"And I, like an idiot, just keep answering your questions," she muttered, shaking her head. I got the impression that Celina didn't have anyone to unload on. Anyone to lean on. Maybe my talking to her gave her a chance to get some things off her chest.

"I guess I hope that if something terrible ever happened to me that someone would try to find out what went down." I shrugged. "I would hope that someone cared enough to try, you know."

Celina looked down at the small camera in her hands. "Aaron

would have liked you. For all his faults, he always wanted the best for everyone around him. He would totally get himself embroiled in an investigation because it spoke to his moral center."

We sat there for a moment, not speaking. Frustration built behind my chest—it was like a bubble that continued to swell and swell without release. I *needed* that missing journal.

"I think I would have liked him, too," I replied.

Beside me, Celina stashed her camera away in her bag. She rifled around inside it for a minute and then pulled out a piece of paper.

"I . . . I tore this page out of his journal about six weeks ago," she said, hanging her head in shame. "We'd had an argument because I found out he'd been speaking to Kaila on the phone. I was feeling petty, so I took it."

She handed me the piece of paper, the edges jagged as if they'd been torn from a spiral-bound notebook. The sketch was incredible—completely lifelike right down to the light in Celina's eyes. It showed her holding a camera, dressed similarly to how we'd found her tonight, with a rash guard top, bikini bottom, flippers and helmet. Behind her, the waves crested. I could feel how much he admired her in the careful strokes and smudges of the pencil.

Down the bottom, a date was scrawled in messy handwriting. April tenth.

But when I flipped the paper over, there was a drawing on the reverse side with another date—April eleventh. It was a sketch of a pill bottle sitting open, pills spilling out and scattered along a surface. Next to it was a martini glass sitting on a napkin with a logo in the center. The writing on the pill bottle said "temazepam," which was the same type of sleeping pills that Aaron had listed on his medical information card.

My heart stalled for a minute. "Huh?"

"I don't know what it means. Aaron never mixed his pills

with booze." She shook her head. "He was super careful about that, because the doctor had been very clear when he pre-scribed the pills that he shouldn't drink alcohol while taking them."

"Or grapefruit juice," I muttered.

"Yeah." She cocked her head, looking surprised that I knew that detail. "Weird, right?"

"Then why would he have a picture of the pills next to a cocktail?" I mused.

"I have no idea. It's funny that it's a martini, too, because Aaron *hated* those kinds of drinks." She smiled sadly, as if lost in a memory. "He was unpretentious like that. It was beer or nothing. Maybe a vodka and Coke if he was feeling extra. Never a cocktail. He thought they were girls' drinks, which is funny because a martini is way too strong for me. I think they taste like rocket fuel."

Something tickled in the back of my mind, information I'd read while searching for information about temazepam. I grabbed my phone out and brought up the article I'd kept in my browser.

Benzodiazepines are commonly prescribed to treat patients suffering from anxiety, panic attacks and insomnia. These drugs have a high potential for misuse and have been known to be used in drug-facilitated sexual assaults.

CHAPTER 17

The following morning was the busiest we had seen in Baked by Chloe since we opened. While the surfing competition had been going on since Wednesday, today and tomorrow were the big drawcards. Today had both the quarter- and semifinals, while tomorrow was the grand finale. Azalea Bay was at peak capacity and it felt like our cozy little town was bursting at the seams, our normally quiet streets lined with cars and every eatery with a line out the door, ours included. It was like opening day but on steroids.

Frankly, I was grateful for the distraction.

"How are you doing?" Erica asked as she breezed into the kitchen to collect a batch of scones that had been cooling on a rack on my preparation bench. She looked perky and upbeat as ever, despite the intense speed at which we were all working.

I, on the other hand, did not look quite so fresh. Sweat dripped down my spine and pooled uncomfortably at my lower back, causing my uniform top to cling to me. My chef's cap felt like it was cooking my brain, and I'd given myself a burn on my wrist while rushing to get a sheet of macaron shells out of the oven. I caught a glimpse of myself in the reflection of the oven door and shuddered.

"Like I'm regretting all my life choices and wondering how expensive it would be to move to a remote island and collect crabs or something," I quipped.

Erica laughed. "But then how would you play Dungeons and Dragons, huh? I bet crabs aren't too good at tabletop roleplaying. Hard to grip a d20 when you only have claws."

"True." I tried to squeeze out every last bit of energy I had to keep kneading the dough I was working on. My hands were aching and I was very grateful that we'd be shut Monday and Tuesday next week. "I'm just tired."

Erica patted me on the shoulder. "Even the best jobs have days where a desert island and an army of roleplaying crabs seems preferable."

"I appreciate the pep talk." I flipped the dough around and it slapped against the workbench. "I'll be back out there as soon as I've got the last few trays in the oven. We've got another round of the galettes, a batch of cookies, the cheesy herb mini loaves, and a mixed batch of macarons."

"Great! There was a customer who missed out on the last galette and she was super disappointed. I'll let her know that there are more coming." Erica bounded out of the kitchen and I swear she left a trail of pixie dust behind her.

The positive energy was very welcome and I, once again, was thrilled she'd joined our team. Through the din of a very full café, I heard my aunt's cackling laughter and couldn't help but smile. How lucky was I to be surrounded by such wonderful people?

As if on cue, there was a click behind me and my grandmother came into the kitchen via the back entrance. She was all dressed up for the surfing competition, in an adorable pink Hawaiian-print shirt, white breezy slacks and sandals. From her ears dangled two small pink surfboards, and she wore a cute straw sunhat with a pink-and-white–striped ribbon around it.

"Don't you look fabulous," I said as I shuffled the dough around between my hands, forming a small ball. It would need to sit for a while to rise.

"I normally wouldn't invite myself in through the back but I couldn't even get close to the front door!" She shook her head, blue eyes wide. "You must be run off your feet."

"That's accurate, yeah." I laughed. "But we have to make hay while the sun is shining, right?"

"Very true. Come winter it will be a different story." She nodded. "At the same time, your pace needs to be sustainable. It's a good thing I raised a hard-working daughter and grand-daughter."

I noticed that she said daughter, singular, instead of daughters, plural. I wondered if that was because my mother had been a slacker when she was young or if my grandmother had essentially written her out of her head. It had been years since I'd heard from the woman, with the last contact being a twenty-first birthday card that turned up six months after my birthday.

I was glad that Grandma Rose didn't put my mother and me in the same category.

"Are you off to watch the festivities?" I asked.

The surf competition was going on for most of the day. From what Ethan had told me, the quarterfinals were taking place in the earlier part of the day, where he would be in a heat with three other surfers. The top two would go through to the semifinals. The semis usually drew a big crowd, so we'd decided to open early and close early both days this weekend, since by the afternoon, the beaches would be jam-packed and the streets would have cleared out.

I was really hoping that Ethan would make it through to the next stage, so I could see him in action.

"I certainly am," Grandma Rose replied. "Luisa and I are meeting Betty and Ida down on the boardwalk."

"Did someone say my name?" My grandmother's Italian friend, Luisa, poked her head through the back door. Clearly, nobody was able to make it through the front.

"She has hearing like a bat, that one." My grandmother smirked. "Never utter anything around her."

"You don't mind if old Luisa comes into the kitchen. You know I was born to be in the kitchen." Luisa Fusco's mother had opened an Italian restaurant back in the 60s and Luisa had done her time managing it before her daughter and two granddaughters took over. La Bella Cucina was a fantastic restaurant and a favorite among both Azalea Bay residents and the tourists who flocked to our shores. Luisa herself was, indeed, a fabulous cook.

"Of course, come in, come in," I said, even though Luisa had not waited for an invitation.

That was her in a nutshell, charmingly pushy. I loved her for it . . . but I also made a mental note to get better at locking the door after I came in from my break. Today I'd been so busy and distracted that I felt like my brain couldn't keep up.

"These are wonderful." Luisa's face sparkled with delight as she looked at a tray of macarons ready for the display cabinet out front. She wore her hair in a fluffy dark brown perm which was barely specked with gray, and had a penchant for red lipstick, leopard print—which today was a big, sweeping blouse over cropped tan pants—and heavy, gold earrings. "Look at how each shell is exactly the same size as the next and no cracks. Perfetto! Such a clever girl you are."

"I hope you ladies have fun at the beach," I said, hoping they would get the hint to leave me to my work. As much as I loved my grandmother and her friends, I really needed to buckle down and get this last lot of items into the oven so I could go back to serving out front.

"You're coming later, right?" Grandma Rose asked, raising an eyebrow. "With Jake?"

Luisa gasped. "The handsome young man next door!"

I narrowed my eyes at my grandmother. I didn't exactly want to broadcast the thing between Jake and me before I even knew what it was.

"Yes, after work I'll be heading down to the beach," I said, purposely leaving out any comment about *who* I would be going with.

"I hope you're going home to get changed before your date," Luisa said, sniffing the air and looking disapprovingly at me. To be fair, I would probably look disapprovingly at me if I went out into public like this, too.

"I thought men liked a sweaty woman," I said, keeping my face totally still. "Something about pheromones."

Luisa looked horrified before realizing I was joking. "Darling, the only pheromone you should put into the air is one that comes from a Chanel perfume bottle."

I snorted. "Is that rule number one in Luisa Fusco's Guide to Catching a Man?"

"No, darling. Rule number one is always remembering that you are a goddess and they would be lucky to have you. Rule number eight is to wear Chanel."

I wasn't sure I wanted to know the details of rules two through seven, *or* how long the list went. But Luisa was onto her third husband, and frequently joked about finding number four whenever poor Giorgio was annoying her. Frankly, I knew several of the older generation of men around town would be lining up to apply for that spot. But I also knew that underneath all her man-eating persona, she loved her third husband very much and would do anything for him.

The femme fatale schtick was more for show than anything else.

Grandma Rose and Luisa bid me good luck for my "date" and left me to my devices, thankfully. As fun as it was chatting with them, I had work to do.

* * *

We closed up shop by two p.m. I sent Erica off as soon as the doors were shut, and Aunt Dawn and I tackled the closing procedure together.

"My goodness, I am *starving.*" Aunt Dawn broke off the side of a cheese and herb cannabutter scone, one of only three items left in the otherwise barren front counter. She stuffed it in her mouth and chewed, sighing in relief.

"I told you to take a break earlier," I admonished. I was currently stacking all the chairs upside down on the tables, so I could sweep and mop the floor.

"And leave you and Erica to manage the crowd?" She shot me a look. "There's no way you would have gotten that extra round of scones and galettes done if you had to be out front."

She had a point.

"You *really* need to get on to hiring someone to help you in the kitchen," she said, tearing off another piece of the scone and popping it into her mouth.

"Don't you eat too much of that," I said, pointing. "It takes a while for the cannabis to kick in and you don't want to flake out during your catch-up with Maisey tonight."

"Girlie, I was smoking joints and going to raves before you were even a twinkle in your mother's eye," she replied loftily. "I can handle a scone."

I laughed. Hard as it might seem to imagine my fifty-three-year-old all-hippie-vibes aunt in kaleidoscopic rave outfits waving glow sticks around in the early nineties, I had seen the pictures.

"But here, we can split it." She tore the remainder in half and placed my portion on a napkin.

I glanced at the broom, but my stomach growled angrily. I, too, had forgone a break today. I eagerly took a bite and chewed. "Thanks."

"How's it all going with Ethan?" Aunt Dawn asked as she

wiped her hands off with a napkin. "Did you manage to speak with the girlfriend? Serena?"

"Celina," I corrected before stuffing the last of the scone into my mouth and reaching for the broom. I finished chewing before speaking again. "And yeah, we spoke to her. She seemed very in love with Aaron, even if she did suspect he was cheating on her. I honestly can't see her as a killer."

Then again, the person who'd turned out to be a killer last time was someone I hadn't suspected . . . so maybe my murderer radar was broken.

I dragged the broom under the tables, collecting little piles of crumbs and other debris. There was an abandoned receipt, a bobby pin and the lid of a pen. "She showed me a drawing that Aaron had done, however. It was of a martini glass and a bottle of pills . . . the same pills that Aaron was taking. *And* there was an empty bottle of pills on the ground when we found him."

"Pills and drink aren't a good combination." Aunt Dawn frowned. For all her quips about smoking joints and raving, my aunt was also very serious about responsible consumption— for both herself and others. "Do you think that was foreshadowing that he wanted to take his own life?"

"I don't think so." I shook my head as I corralled the little piles of dust into one corner so I could sweep it up with a dustpan. "Celina specifically said he hated drinking cocktails of any kind. So why would he draw a martini for himself if he would never actually drink it? In fact, she said he specifically said he thought cocktails were for girls."

"That's silly, but okay." Aunt Dawn's bangles clinked and chimed as she vigorously wiped down the countertops of our serving area, making sure the surface gleamed. "What do you think it means?"

"Sleeping pills and a strong drink . . ." A cold, uncomfortable feeling seized my gut. "Made me think of drink spiking, to be honest."

My friends and I had been terrified of it back in our college days, and we'd always watched one another's drinks. There didn't seem to be *any* good reason why someone might combine sleeping pills and alcohol. But did Aaron's drawing imply that he was doing it himself—maybe as a coping mechanism— or was the drawing in reference to someone else? My mind drifted back to the conversation I'd had with Celina yesterday.

"Celina *did* mention that Aaron thought there was something bad going on in the surfing world," I said, leaning on the broom and scrunching up my nose. "But he never told her what it was. She said he got obsessed and that he was always on his computer reading articles and calling people. He was definitely speaking with Kaila, that girl who was attacked in the surf shop."

"Maybe she knew what Aaron was up to," Aunt Dawn suggested. "Maybe Aaron found out something terrible and whoever killed him realized that he'd told her."

"I'm starting to wonder that, too." I nodded. I thought back to the photos that Celina had shown me, the ones of Aaron and Kaila embracing. What Celina saw as a romantic interlude, I had seen as something else—friendship, comfort.

What if Kaila's drink had been spiked and she had gone to Aaron for help or support, which caused him to do some digging? Didn't Celina intimate something to that effect?

He would totally get himself embroiled in an investigation because it spoke to his moral center.

Had someone spiked Kaila's drink? Surely it wasn't Aaron. But it could be someone taking the same medication as him. Or was that image meant to be some kind of metaphor? Without the rest of the journal it was hard to tell. There were too many pieces of the puzzle still missing.

All I knew was that my gut told me that Aaron's murder and Kaila's attack were very much linked.

* * *

After Aunt Dawn and I finished closing up the café, I headed straight home to wash the long workday from my skin. I let the warm water soothe my aching muscles and I massaged my scalp as I washed my hair, as though it might help to percolate all the bits of information in there. But I could knead my head until the cows came home—nothing was making the clues fit together.

I realized I'd been in the shower longer than planned when the hot water started to run out.

"Ah crap." I wrenched the taps off with a squeak and then I hopped out of the shower, glancing at where my phone was sitting on the countertop. "Double crap!"

I was supposed to meet Jake in five minutes and I was currently doing my best impression of a drowned rat. Hastily, I towel-dried my hair and decided the walk to the beach would have to do the rest, and then I darted into my bedroom to put some clothes on.

But the eternal question arose . . . what to wear?

Jean shorts and a T-shirt or a skirt and top combo? What about a cute little flowing dress . . . or did that look like I was trying too hard?

Ugh!

Knowing how to act around guys was *not* my strong suit. Never had been. Add to that the unusual beginning to my friendship with Jake and it was even harder to make these kinds of decisions. Through my bedroom window I could see into his lounge room, and I caught movement down near where his front door was.

Sadly, there was no time for a 2000s romantic comedy dress-up montage.

I grabbed a cute chambray wrap dress from my closet which I knew would be comfortable but also enhance all the bits I liked about my curvy figure, and threw it on. Then I stuffed my feet into a pair of white sneakers and grabbed my purse.

As I was about to leave my bedroom, I glanced back at my

vanity where a weighty fluted glass bottle sat, a gauzy pink ribbon tied around the neck and a fancy, scalloped gold cap decorating the top. I'd bought it on a whim as a birthday gift to
myself when I was feeling homesick my first year in Paris because it was called Rosy Dawn and it smelled like a garden
after a rain shower.

Rolling my eyes at myself, I went over to my vanity and gave
myself a spritz. It wasn't Chanel, but it would have to do.
Clearly, Luisa was getting into my head.

I went downstairs to pop Antonio into his harness and meet
Jake out front. Before I locked up, I sent him a cheeky text.

**CHLOE: I hope it's okay, but I'm bringing another man
on our date.**

I cringed the second I hit send. Was it too cheesy? Gah!
How could I be a smart and successful businesswoman at work
and then the second it came to my love life, I reverted back to
my awkward fourteen-year-old-never-been-kissed self?

**JAKE: Is this where I make a joke about being
uncomfortable with the idea of a ménage à trois?**

I snorted and Antonio looked up at me, head tilted and ears
pricked.

"He's a funny guy," I said to my little friend. "And I am a
sucker for a man with a sense of humor."

I was also a sucker for a man with dimples, a great smile and
working hands that could put together any piece of IKEA furniture with ease. And Jake had all that in spades.

"Promise you'll tell me if I'm embarrassing myself?" I asked
the dog and he yipped in response, although something told
me Antonio would love me no matter how much of an awkward turtle I was.

Outside, I locked up the house and saw Jake heading over

to the bottom of our driveway with a small bag in his hand. As I got closer to him, I saw the side of the bag said "pawsitively delicious."

"I figured I should butter up the competition," he said, handing it over. I peeked inside, grinning like a fool, and saw a bunch of handmade dog treats. "Keep your enemies close and all that."

I laughed. "That is so sweet. Thank you!"

He crouched down to give Antonio a scratch behind the ears and the little dog's tail wagged so fast I was worried he'd give himself a stitch. Humans could learn a thing or two from dogs. They loved freely and without reserve, they always seemed to be happy with what they had, *and* they focused on the important things in life—cuddles, sleep and enjoying a good walk in the fresh air.

"You'll have to give me the lowdown on the whole surfing thing," Jake said as we started our walk to the beach. The sun was high in the sky and it beat down on us with force. Thank goodness I kept a bottle of sunscreen in my purse as I'd need to slather some on my arms and legs when we got to the beach. "Growing up on the East Coast, the closest I ever got to surfing was the one time the subway flooded and I had to climb a flight of stairs in ankle-deep water."

I snorted. "You're really selling the East Coast city life there."

"Cockroaches, rats and rude people—what more could you ask for?" He grinned, a dimple forming in his right cheek and his hazel eyes twinkling with mischief. My heart fluttered. Oh boy, the dimples got me every time! "But it's not all bad. New York really is a fun city and the people aren't nearly as rude as you think once you understand the rules."

"The rules?"

"To living in New York City. Walk with purpose, don't waste people's time, mind your own business and for the love of god don't eat pizza from a chain restaurant."

"I mean, those rules should be enforced everywhere." I nodded. "Especially the pizza one."

Antonio veered across the path to sniff something interesting and I had to encourage him to keep on track. By the time we made it to the beach—by way of the ice cream parlor on the main strip, the aptly named Dripping Cones—we'd covered all manner of topics, including what I knew about surfing (not much), my sporting knowledge in general (microscopic) and my experience with making ice cream (don't skimp on the fat).

I licked at the round scoop of delicious dessert—one of their signature flavors: the spicy and sweet ginger pineapple. Jake had gone for a more traditional mint choc chip.

"Wow, this is . . ." Jake's voice trailed off as we reached the boardwalk, which ran parallel to the beach but on higher ground. "Something else."

Normally Azalea Bay locals would come to the beach for the expansive views of golden sand, pristine blue ocean, silver waves and the rugged cliff-faces of the coastline. Today, however, it was impossible to see anything but the crowds packed onto the beach and the brightly colored tents and stands where judging officials, commentators, brands and fans were all camped out. People had brought deck chairs, all manner of shade-making structures and some industrious folks had even set up some little tables and chairs to watch the action.

Temporary food and shopping stalls cluttered the boardwalk, selling everything from hats to sunscreen to bikinis to flip-flops. The scent of ice cream, French fries and nachos filled the air, and the sound of general merriment put a smile on my face. Everything had felt so serious of late, so it was a relief to be out in the sunshine for no other reason than enjoyment.

"Welcome to Azalea Bay's silly season," I said, laughing. "Now you know why a bunch of people on our street all decided to get out of town this weekend."

"No kidding." His eyes were wide. "I mean, living in a huge city for so long I'm very used to crowds. But this . . ."

"It's different when you're in a place like this, because you're not expecting it." I chased a melting dribble of ice cream with my tongue. "Come on, let's find a spot to camp out."

I scanned the beach for familiar faces and caught sight of someone waving their arm madly in our direction. It was Ben and he had a huge grin on his face.

"Looks like there might be good news," I said, motioning for Jake to follow me.

"I love good news."

As we walked down the stairs to the beach, Jake held my ice cream cone so I could carry Antonio as his little legs couldn't handle the big steps. When we got to the bottom, Jake handed the ice cream cone back to me and our fingertips brushed, sending an unexpected tingle of awareness scurrying up my arm. His eyes darted to mine as though he'd felt it too.

In the midst of the chaos of opening a new business and trying to solve the mystery of what happened to Aaron and Kaila, it was good to feel something like that. Something normal. Something sweet.

Something that I wanted to feel again.

CHAPTER 18

"Our boy made it to the semis!" Ben shouted as Jake and I approached the group on the sand. Matt was grinning from ear to ear, radiating his usual amount of happiness and vibrancy. I knew the last week had been rough while he tried to support Ethan in the aftermath of his friend's death, so it was good to see him smiling so wide.

I also loved how Ben had basically adopted Ethan as his younger brother, too.

"That's amazing!" I clapped my hands together.

Ben eyed Jake with interest as we came to a stop where my friends were gathered around. A few feet away I could see Ethan chatting with Bryce, both their faces serious, likely making game plans for the next part of the competition. Ethan was wearing a bright red long-sleeved top with the WSL—World Surf League—logo on the front.

"Everyone, you all remember Jake," I said awkwardly. "Jake, this is Ben, Matt, Sabrina, Cal, Archie and Erica."

He'd been at the surprise celebration after my first day of opening Baked by Chloe, but I took a moment to say everyone's names in case he hadn't been formally introduced. Jake smiled as he shook everyone's hands one by one and I noticed him repeating the names under his breath. That was a sign of a good person, wasn't it? Someone who took those things seriously, like remembering people's names when they met. I appreciated a level of conscientiousness, because I sometimes found it sorely lacking in the world.

We settled down to watch the show. Matt and Ben had brought a big blanket for the sand and I unclipped Antonio's leash so he could trot around, hopping from lap to lap as he liked to do. He was indiscriminate like that—any welcoming lap was a good lap! I saw him make a beeline straight for Erica, his ears quivering in excitement, and her whole face lit up as she scooped him up and popped him between her thighs. Archie, ever the dad, immediately cooed.

"So this is a big deal, huh?" Jake looked around, eyes wide.

"That's West Coast life." I grinned. "Sun, sand and surf. They've been holding this competition here for as long as I can remember. Since I was a kid, at least. Maybe longer."

I was down to the part of my ice cream where it was mostly cone and I took a bite out of the hand-poured waffle cone that Dripping Cones was famous for. They sometimes did fancier designs that had the top dipped in chocolate and sprinkles or crushed nuts. But I liked the good old-fashioned plain waffle cone. The smell of the batter always made me remember being a kid, barely tall enough to look into the glass cabinet and buzzing with excitement over which flavors to pick.

"You never took up surfing yourself?" he asked.

"Balance and coordination are not my strong suits." I cringed. "Just ask my yoga teacher. I fell over in tree pose the other day and almost sent some poor old lady flying."

Talk about the ultimate mortification.

Matt came over to Jake and they began chatting. Jake looked relieved that he'd received a warm welcome and it made my heart swell with happiness. That's the kind of people my friends were—the "more the merrier" type, rather than the cliquey type.

Ben shuffled over to me on the other side and leaned in conspiratorially. "He's cute."

"I know." I flushed.

"This isn't a first date, is it?" he asked.

I glanced over to where Matt was talking about a time where he got chased by a kangaroo back home in Perth, and Jake was wiping tears of laughter from his eyes.

"I don't know," I said, honestly.

"How can you not know?" Ben looked aghast. He was wearing a T-shirt with the original *Point Break* movie image on the front. It felt like Keanu Reeves and Patrick Swayze were listening in to our conversation.

"Well, it's kind of . . . complicated."

"Girl, you are *all* complicated. Why do you think I prefer men?" he quipped and then he gave my shoulder a squeeze to let me know he was joking. Well, kind of.

"I find first dates to have a whole lot of pressure and build-up that inevitably leads to disappointment," I admitted.

I'd had more than my fair share of dating disappointment. Enough to write a book about it. Awkward blind dates, Tinder creeps, a guy that got so drunk when he tried to kiss me on my doorstep he ended up vomiting into my favorite potted plant. Then there was the one guy who asked me to pay for his taxi fare because he was broke . . . and that was after I'd paid for dinner because he'd conveniently left his wallet at home.

"So you bring him to hang out at a surfing competition with all your friends?" Ben raised an eyebrow. His dark eyes narrowed at me. "Mama Wong would be so disappointed in you."

I chuckled. "Is your mom a romantic?"

"Absolutely. She rejected my dad's proposal the first time because she said he didn't put enough effort in." He grinned. "Which explains the two of them in a nutshell. Mom wants everything to be movie-level perfect and my dad is practical to the core. They balance each other out."

"Maybe that's why I suck at relationships. I've never had a

good example at home." As much as I'd loved my grandfather, he passed when I was still so young. Boys weren't even on my radar yet! And with both Grandma Rose and Aunt Dawn staying single my whole life until very recently, I'd never gotten an idea of what love looked like from anywhere but Disney movies and funny-but-unrealistic rom-coms.

But I wanted it . . . that special sparkle that Matt and Ben had. That easygoing affection that Sabrina and Cal had. That giddiness that Grandma Rose felt around Lawrence St. James. The click and connection that Aunt Dawn and Maisey had. I wanted it all.

"After the competition is done, go for a romantic walk up to the lookout," Ben suggested, keeping his voice low. "Put some moves on."

My face suddenly felt like the molten core of the sun.

"I believe in you, Chloe." He patted my arm. "Don't be a wimp."

Ben dragged Matt away from his conversation with Jake under the guise of them going to check on Ethan, and the others were engaged in a card game on the blanket. Jake turned to me and popped the very last bite of his waffle cone into his mouth.

"Your friends are cool." He bobbed his head. "It's great that you've been able to find a solid group after moving back here."

"I owe it all to Sabrina," I replied, finishing off my own cone and digging a cleansing wipe out of my bag to clean my hands off. There was nothing worse than having sticky *anything* at the beach. "They're her friends and she brought me into the fold. Sometimes it just takes that one person, you know?"

"I know exactly what you mean." The way he was looking at me made me wonder if he thought *I* was that one person for him. Ben's words danced in my brain.

Don't be a wimp. Don't be a wimp. Don't be a wimp.

"We should go for a walk after the competition is over," I

said, my voice a little high-pitched and squeaky. "There's a nice lookout up on the big hill."

"You're inviting me up to a secluded lookout, huh?" he teased, the smile deepening his dimple. "Should I take that as a good sign?"

"I think you should," I replied without meeting his eye. Maybe if I was better at flirting, I would come up with something wittier to say then, but, like tree pose, wit was not my forte. Instead I dug the dog treats out of my bag and tossed one toward Erica so she could feed it to Antonio.

"Good." Jake leaned back on his elbows, getting comfy for the competition. His fingers brushed mine and I didn't pull my hand away.

It felt nice.

I soon sensed a buzz and movement around the beach that told me the semifinals were about to begin. I glanced around the crowded beach and spotted a familiar face—Mariah. She wasn't in her full mermaid outfit today, but she *was* mermaid-themed. Her long hair was curled and had some strands of something shimmery woven through it, and she was wearing a T-shirt that said *Mermaids Have More Fun* in glittery writing. But despite her cute, whimsical look, there was a tension in her face. The line between her brows was deep.

That's when I noticed she was talking with someone, but it almost seemed like she was speaking under her breath. I sat forward, trying to get a better look at who she was talking to. What I saw almost made my heart stop in my chest. The person was wearing all black! Black jeans, black sneakers and a black T-shirt and baseball cap. Sunglasses covered the person's eyes, though I guessed they were male based on the sharp shape of their jaw. He was on the shorter side, but had long lanky arms. Porcelain pale skin, a leather bracelet around one wrist.

It was hard to tell much more about who it was beyond that.

But it could *definitely* be the person I saw leaping off the balcony of the hotel room and running out of the surf store after Kaila's attack.

The squeal of a microphone snapped my attention away from Mariah and the mystery person. Bryce was standing down by the water with a portable speaker and microphone.

"I want to thank you all for being here today to witness these awesome athletes doing what they do best," he said. Even with the somber tone he still sounded a bit like Keanu Reeves in *Bill & Ted's Excellent Adventure*—another '80s movie Aunt Dawn had made me watch on repeat when I was a kid. "But I humbly ask for a moment of your time."

Oh, he must be giving a speech about Aaron before they got started with the competition. I glanced over at Ethan, who stood at the front of the crowd next to Bryce, board tucked under his arm.

"Before we start the semifinals competition, I'd like to recognize someone we lost in our community recently." Bryce dropped his head for a moment. "Aaron Gill was someone many of you either knew or, at least, knew of. He had a big personality, was aggressive and sometimes chaotic on the waves, but he had that magic that all surfers desire. He could communicate with the ocean. He had an incredible ability to read the water, to feel what would happen next and to change his approach on the fly. If you've ever seen him hit a perfect ten, you know it's truly awesome."

Ethan was looking down, letting his curly blond hair create a curtain around his face. He sniffled, eyes misty, and someone near him placed a hand on his shoulder and squeezed. It was Makani. He was wearing a WSL top almost identical to Ethan's, only in green. I was almost surprised to see him here, given Kaila was still in the hospital.

But I guess surfing was like theater—the show must go on.

"With the blessing of the WSL, I'd like to propose a minute

of silence for a fellow lover of the ocean who's now watching down over all of us. I know he would want everyone here to enjoy the waves and for his competitors to give it their all."

It was eerie to hear the rush of the waves so clearly with such a full beach. But everyone bowed their heads and, bar a few sniffles here and there, it was silent. I took a moment to send some good vibes out into the universe for Aaron's family, for his little brother, especially. It sounded like his childhood bore similarities to my own and my heart ached for the boy left behind.

"Thank you everyone," Bryce said as the minute was up. "May the best surfer win."

As Bryce handed the mic off to someone in an official event T-shirt, the booming voice of the announcer came over the speakers. The first heat was up, but we would need to wait for heat number two to see Ethan.

The surfers in the first heat headed out into the water and I felt the tension rise in the air. Everyone was waiting with bated breath.

"Give us the lowdown, Matt," Sabrina said. She was wearing a yellow bikini top and a pair of white denim shorts under a cream crochet beach cover-up that contrasted with her long curly black hair. "How does this all work? I honestly have never paid much attention to the surfing comps before."

"You can see up there," Matt said, pointing up to a platform structure that had been purpose-built for the competition. People in matching T-shirts sat at a table running the length of the platform, while several others stood behind them. "The guy on the end is the announcer. He lets the surfers know how much time is left in the heat, plus other critical information. The five men and women next to him are the judges, who will individually score the surfers. There's also a head judge—he's the guy with the long hair who's standing up. He makes sure no waves are missed and that all the judging is aboveboard."

"Right." I nodded. I spotted Fisk Clemmens sitting there, dressed in the same aquamarine T-shirt as everyone else, though he had a fat gold chain sitting around his neck.

"Every wave a surfer takes is judged out of a possible ten points," Matt continued. "The judges look for things like speed, power, flow, commitment, the variety and difficulty of maneuvers that the surfer is able to perform. They then knock off the highest and lowest judging scores, and average the other three for the total score."

"Do they have a set number of waves to surf?" Jake asked.

"The surfers can take as many waves as they like so long as there's still time left," Matt replied. "But only the best two waves will count toward their final score. Then the top two performers make it through to the finals and the other two will be knocked out. In the semis, there are two heats of four surfers. So the finals will have the top four from the whole week."

"And Ethan is up in heat two of the semis, right?" I asked.

"Yeah. He's in a really tough heat, though. Makani is the favorite so that's a rough draw for Ethan. And the other two are accomplished surfers as well. The older guy has been on a great run this year and is tipped to make it to the Challenger Series. The other one is a bit of a wild card—he's young, but he's been smashing it the last few comps. I reckon he could cause a bit of an upset."

We watched as the four surfers in the first heat took turns attacking the waves. Matt described what was going on using words like "cutback," "bottom turn," "curl," "kick out" and "pumping." I tried to follow along, but most of it went over my head. Jake would occasionally glance over at me, a questioning look in his eyes, and I would simply shrug, making both of us laugh. We just cheered when everyone else cheered, like we had a clue what was going on when we absolutely did not.

Every so often I glanced through the crowd, looking for the

person dressed all in black. He was with Mariah for a period of time, but eventually disappeared into the crowd. I noticed that she looked more relaxed after that, whooping and cheering along with everyone else. I wondered what their conversation was all about.

The surfing was fun to watch, though. Especially when the second heat started and Ethan made it out onto the water. Matt could barely sit still.

"Jumping around like a cat in a bag isn't going to do anything," Ben admonished. But I could see there was an anxiousness in his posture, too. We all wanted Ethan to do well.

"Some of these waves are uncontestable," Matt huffed, his knee bouncing. "We had bigger swells for the heats yesterday."

I learned quickly that the reason the surfers were wearing the bright, single-color tops was to help track the surfers and for allowing the announcer to call out who had preference for the next wave, because the surfers couldn't just catch any wave they wanted to after the first one was taken. Matt pointed out that, near where the judges sat, was a board with colored squares matching the Lycra tops worn by the surfers, each with a number next to it that was changed out as the competition progressed, so the surfers always knew where they were in the priority lineup.

Ethan was up next. He paddled on his board toward a wave and then hopped up onto his feet with grace and agility. The wind blew his curly hair back from his face and he stuck his arms out to the sides, squatting down as he rode just ahead of the foamy portion of the wave. Then he flicked the board, scooping up to the top of the wave and then sharply back down, followed by another smaller version of that movement, with a quick change of direction.

"Okay, okay. Not bad, not bad." Matt bobbed his head, bringing his hand up so he could chew on his fingernails. Ben reached out and smacked his hand away. "That should be good for a seven-something. Maybe closer to an eight if they're feeling generous."

Ethan rode as far as he could, bailing out into the water and then climbing back to a paddle position on his board, so he could head out in time for his next shot. Makani was up next. Now, I might not know much about surfing. Not the rules or the names of the techniques or the jargon or anything. But I knew, watching him, that this man was born to be out on the ocean.

The water seemed to move as if he'd commanded it, the swell rising and lifting him up. He was inside the front of a curling wave, staying just ahead and almost disappearing out of sight at one point. But he maintained control, effortlessly and easily. It looked as natural as breathing to him.

"Dammit." Matt thumped a fist on the ground. "That's got to be a nine-something."

I glanced back to the judges' table and the score flashed up on a screen: 9.2

Ethan currently had a 7.0. The other two surfers were sitting at 7.5 and 7.9 respectively.

"Seven on the nose?" Ben spat. "Harsh."

"He got unlucky there." Matt shook his head. "There's only so much you can do with a flat wave."

We spent the entire heat on the edge of our seats, nail-biting and glancing eagerly back at the judges' table to watch the changing scores. Even Antonio must have picked up on the tension, because he sat in my lap, giant ears pricked skyward, as he swung his head around, checking on everyone in the group. His big, buggy eyes looked up at me, pleading for some reassurance.

"It's okay, bud. You can relax."

But only a few waves in and Makani was in a league of his own.

"He wouldn't be cruising to victory uncontested like this if Aaron was here," Matt said with a sigh as the time trickled down. There was only a minute and a half remaining for the heat. "Even if they ended up in different heats in the semis, Aaron would have given him a run for his money in the finals. Now he's probably going to take it all without breaking a sweat."

It was also becoming clear that without some kind of divine intervention, Ethan wouldn't be progressing to the finals. With Makani streets ahead and Ethan on the bottom, the other two surfers were trading watery jabs for the second finals slot. I could sense Matt's deflation as his shoulders dropped, the seconds ticking down and the ocean remaining frightfully calm. There didn't seem to be any quality waves for a Hail Mary shot, unfortunately.

"And that ends heat two of the semifinals," the announcer declared. "Makani Davis and Felix Hough will progress through to the final round. Be back here tomorrow to watch the action."

Ben leaned in to give Matt a hug. "Ethan did his best."

"I know." Matt nodded. "I'm disappointed because I know how hard he works. It's not his time. But next year, things will be different."

As the crowd slowly started to disperse, our group hung around to congratulate Ethan on making it to the semis. He seemed disappointed but grateful that he had such a supportive group around him.

"I'm going to take Ethan back to our place for a quiet night just the three of us," Matt said as I leaned in to give him a hug. He raked a hand through his long blond hair. "This week has been a lot."

"That's a good idea." I looked up at him. "Is there anything I can do to help?"

"You've done so much already, Chloe. The competition will

be over tomorrow and then everyone will get back on their planes and into their cars and . . . it will all be over. We might not ever find out what happened to Aaron." He sighed.

"Any news on Kaila?" I asked, biting down on my lip. I didn't know her at all, but she kept popping into my head and I truly hoped she would come out of this okay.

"Not that I know of. Makani left immediately after time was called to head straight back to the hospital. The family has been with her day and night. Her folks got in yesterday, which they'd planned to all along but their mom missed Makani's heats today because she didn't want to leave Kaila alone."

"They sound like a good family," I said.

"I've met their parents, Greg and Pualani. Nice folks. Very family-oriented." Matt hung his head. "This isn't supposed to happen. Azalea Bay is a safe town and now we've got one young person dead and another in a coma. Sorry to sound so bloody negative, I'm just feeling overwhelmed at the moment. Maybe *I'm* the one who needs a night in."

"Take it easy, okay? But don't give up hope."

I was sure that the page I saw from Aaron's missing diary had *something* important to tell us. I just had to figure out how to connect the dots, and there was one person I wanted to ask about it: Mariah the Mermaid. Tonight she had an appearance at a bar a few towns over and I was going to ask Jake to come with me.

The question was, did I admit that, once again, I was asking him to get embroiled in a murder investigation with me?

After everyone in our group had said their goodbyes, Jake and I stood alone. I'd clipped Antonio back into his harness—much to Erica's disappointment, as she'd been making jokes about stealing him all afternoon. So I had promised that she could have him around for a sleepover one night, provided Grandma Rose was okay with it. Antonio *loved* Erica, especially because she'd popped around more than once with doggy treats she'd baked herself.

"I know I mentioned going for a walk after this was all over. But how do you feel about going for a drink and something to eat, instead?" I asked, fidgeting with the gold necklace and charm hanging around my neck. "There's a cool bar called Salty's Flamingo Shack that's about half an hour out of town. I thought maybe we—"

"Yes." Jake smiled and the edges of his hazel eyes crinkled.

"You really should wait until I finish making my suggestion," I said, laughing. "What if I was going to suggest we grab dinner while also checking out a murder suspect?"

"Chloe, when it comes to you, I know to be ready for anything," he said, holding out his hand. "And whatever wild situation that is, I'm in."

"That is a bold and possibly stupid amount of trust you're putting in me," I replied. But I took his hand anyway.

He shrugged. "When your gut says something is right, you just have to go for it."

"I know exactly what you mean."

Because right now, my gut was telling me to put all my baggage to one side and have a great night with this man.

CHAPTER 19

When we got home, I raced inside to get changed. After helping Antonio out of his harness and making sure his water bowl was full—and palming him a treat from the bag Jake had given me—I headed upstairs to have a shower and wash all the salt and sand from my body.

I don't know how sand always got *everywhere*, but it did. That stuff was like the glitter of the natural world. One interaction with it, and you'd be finding it in all your nooks and crannies for days.

"Chloe! Is that you?" Grandma Rose's voice floated down the hallway as I stepped out of the bathroom, wrapped in a fluffy robe with my hair bundled up in a towel.

"Yes, Grandma." I scurried into the bedroom and pulled on my underwear and slipped on a bra. "I'm not home for long, though. Heading back out."

"With Jake?" she asked hopefully.

I chuckled to myself. I swear, she acted like I was at risk of dying alone sometimes because I was in my late twenties and still single.

"Yes, with Jake," I called back as I rifled through my wardrobe looking for something to wear. "We're going out for a drink."

I didn't know much about the bar. All I'd seen was that Mariah had tagged their Instagram account in a post saying she was performing tonight, and how cool it was to work at a place with a permanent built-in mermaid tank. Seemed it was some kind of shipwreck-inspired tiki lounge place. Apparently, she would be there working from six to nine p.m.

Hopefully, we could catch her after her shift.

I held up two dresses in front of the mirror—one a rich royal-blue linen and the other a pale gray with a short hemline, ruffled sleeves and shimmery threads running through it. The gray one still had the tag swinging from it. I'd bought it for my bridal shower . . . the bridal shower that never went ahead. I'm not even sure why I still had the dress, to be honest. I'd thought about burning it a few times. Before I moved back home, I'd cleaned out my apartment in Paris and had almost added it to the pile of things to send to the charity shop. But it was such a pretty dress, with its feminine details and pretty, delicate color.

Would it be bad luck to wear a dress meant to celebrate an engagement on a date with another man?

"That is some superstitious bullshit right there," I said to my reflection. Why was I letting the past hold me back so much? Why did I get bogged down in worrying that bad things would repeat themselves?

I yanked the tag off and tossed it into the wire trash bin under my vanity unit. I was going to wear the dress and attach new memories to it. It deserved more than to languish in the back of my closet forever, and *I* deserved more than to hold myself back from new relationships because one bad egg tried to break my heart.

Today was as good a time as any to move on.

I unzipped the dress and slipped it over my head just as Grandma Rose knocked on the door. When I opened it, I was surprised to see her in a fancy dress, also.

"I was just about to say that was good timing, because I

need a hand with this zipper," I said. Laughing, she turned to show me the back of her dress was also undone. "And then I remembered that you said Lawrence was taking you to Foam tonight."

"That's right."

I reached for the zip on her dress and pulled it up. There was a fiddly hook-and-eye closure at the top, and it took a few attempts but I got it closed properly. Then I straightened the little sash around her waist where it was twisted. The dress wasn't new—she'd worn it to my college graduation ceremony years ago—but it was *so* Grandma Rose. Dark pink and light pink stripes, some thick and others thin, with a collar and mother-of-pearl buttons. She had pearl studs in her ears and had even put on some of her rings, which most of the time she didn't bother wearing because they were tough to get on and off with her knuckles these days.

I noticed that she had also put on a pretty gray wig.

"Do I look okay?" she asked me, self-consciously touching the fake hair. Pre-cancer, Grandma Rose's hair had been fine and always permed into a fluffy cloud. The wig, however, was thicker, smoother and sat in a shapely bob. "The lady at the cancer treatment center told me about this place to buy wigs and it came in the mail yesterday. Aunt Dawn helped me with ordering it online."

"You look *wonderful*." I gave her a hug to hide the fact that my eyes were sparkling with tears. "If Lawrence doesn't fall over when he sees you, then he needs to get his eyes checked."

"Does it look real?" she asked, frowning.

I took a moment to look at the wig closely, so she didn't think I was brushing away her concerns—even though I didn't think it mattered if anyone knew she was wearing a wig.

"It does. I wouldn't know it wasn't your real hair unless you told me," I concluded. "The hairline is very convincing."

"That's good." She let out a breath. "I mean, people who

know me will be able to tell it's a wig because they know I don't have much hair right now."

"True. But nobody will care. You're not sitting at home feeling sorry for yourself. You're getting out there and enjoying your life." I pressed a kiss to her cheek. "That's what matters! Wig or no wig."

"I have always enjoyed my life, Chloe. Getting to raise you was a great privilege and something I am very proud of." She motioned for me to turn around so she could do my zipper up. "You have turned into an admirable young woman."

"I love you, too, Grandma."

In that moment, we felt like two sisters helping each other get ready for an exciting new step in our lives. The years between us melted away like ice cream on summer pavement. It felt strange to be going through the same thing—reentering the dating pool—together. But I could practically see my grandmother as she had been when she was young—vibrant, feminine, a capacity for love and affection that rivaled anyone I knew. No wonder my grandfather and Lawrence had both fallen for her.

"You have fun tonight," she said, nodding. "Make sure Jake gets you home safe and sound."

"Of course," I replied.

I had no idea of knowing it, but my ready answer was one of ignorance. The end of the night would be anything but fun *or* safe.

When Jake and I arrived at Salty's Flamingo Shack my mouth hung open in awe. As soon as we walked inside, I could see across the bar to the mammoth water tank that took up an entire wall. Three mermaids were swimming inside and the tank was decorated to look like a shipwreck, with a portion of a ship poking into view, a treasure chest open on the bottom with gold coins spilling out, and brightly colored coral and sea vegetation filling the space.

It was spectacular.

"How have I never been here before?" I asked as we inched forward in the short line to get inside. The place already looked pretty busy, but they were still letting people in. "This is amazing."

We found an empty high table to sit at. The stools were upholstered in a rich teal velvet and the frame was made from a bronze shade with a deep patina. There was a flamingo made of pink neon lights above the bar that flashed two images so it looked like the flamingo was dancing. When I looked closer, the flamingo's body was actually a martini glass, and the bird had an olive in its mouth.

The menus were covered in a brown canvas and had the same logo embossed on the front in gold. Something about it struck me as familiar, but I couldn't quite place my finger on it.

"How did you find out about this place?" Jake asked as we tried to decide what drinks to order.

"One of the women in the surfing community is a professional mermaid. She came into the café and we got talking, so I followed her on Instagram and she posted that she's working here tonight." I glanced at the tank again, but there was no sign of Mariah. I had to imagine the mermaids rotated in and out over the course of the night. That would be a *long* time to be swimming, otherwise.

"How do they even see underwater?" Jake said, shaking his head as we watched them undulate and turn, hair floating around them and the sparkles on their skin glistening under the special lighting. "They must train themselves to open their eyes, because I can't even handle getting a few drops in there when I'm in the shower."

I buried my head in the menu because I did *not* need to imagine Jake naked in the shower.

"Hmm, the Jungle Bird sounds tasty. Campari, rum, pineapple juice and lime." I glanced over the menu. The bar had an extensive list of cocktails with fun names like Zombie, Drunken Mermaid, Shipwreck, Tropical Storm and more. "Maybe I'll go with that."

"Be careful with those tiki drinks," he said with a wry smile. "They taste sweet but they pack a punch."

"I'll go slowly," I promised.

Glancing around the bar I saw some familiar faces, including a few people from the surfing competition today. They'd probably come along to support Mariah. Then I saw one person who I wasn't expecting to see.

"Oh my *god*, Chloe. Fancy seeing you here." Starr Bright swanned over. Her long platinum-blond hair was curled and threaded with glittering strands of a tinsel-like material. A seashell clip held her hair back on one side, and she was dressed in a skimpy top with a mesh overlay that had gleaming pearls and pretty shells dotted all over it.

"I can see you dressed up for the theme," I said, gesturing to her outfit. "Very mermaidcore. I like it."

"I wanted to be Ariel when I was a little girl," she said with a wistful sigh. "But red hair is so not my thing. Like, *where* are the blond mermaids, Disney? I should start a petition. Justice for blond mermaids."

There was a lot to unpack there and, frankly, I hadn't drunk enough for that.

"Being a mermaid seems overrated. I can't imagine the shell bras would be too comfortable," I quipped.

"True." She shook her head. "Anyway, I see you're on a date. Are you going to introduce me?"

She stuck her hand out toward Jake and fluttered her fake eyelashes—which also had something sparkly on them. Starr knew how to pay attention to the details. She was also as subtle as a twelve thousand–pound wrecking ball and when I glanced at Jake, he looked slightly like a deer in headlights. Clearly, he had not ventured into Sprout before.

"Starr, this is Jake," I said, biting back my amusement. "He moved to Azalea Bay a few months ago."

"A new resident I didn't know about." She gasped dramatically. "Like, that's *impossible*."

"I guess it's not." He let out a nervous laugh.

"You're not, like, a hermit, are you?" She narrowed her eyes at him. Clearly, hermits were on her "distrust" list. "I mean, clearly you haven't been into my café so have you even lived? I can't be sure."

Something told me that Jake wouldn't go for the crystal-charged smoothie bowls and anything that promised to clear the vaguely ascribed "toxins" ravaging his body. I swear, one time I saw her selling a salad that was supposed to fight free radicals.

What was wrong with eating something simply for the taste? Why did my salad need to prevent wrinkles?

"I've clearly missed out on something, so I'll make sure I rectify that as soon as possible." He shot her a charming smile, though his eyes darted to me as if to say *send help*.

"As you should." Starr sniffed. "I run the best café in town."

If Sabrina was here, she would have kicked me under the table to prevent me from saying anything snarky. But I didn't need it tonight. I was going to be Teflon to Starr's jabs. Her shade would *not* dull my sunshine.

"Have you been here before?" I asked her. "This is our first time."

"Oh yeah, I come here all the time with my girlfriends." She gestured to another high table a few feet away from us, which featured a group of women in their forties.

They were all carbon copies of Starr with bare tanned limbs, long beachy hair and a vast collection of salon treatments between them. They'd also dressed up for the theme with lots of sparkly hair clips, mesh fabrics and seashell details, and one of the women even had a mermaid tattoo on her calf.

I was starting to wish I'd put something sparkly in my hair. It looked cute.

"Any recommendations from the drinks menu?" I asked, drawing my eyes back to Starr. "I'm having trouble picking."

"Oh yes." Her expression turned all business. I got the impression that she took giving a recommendation quite seriously. "Pass on the Zombie unless you can really hold your liquor. Trish had a few of those last week and it was, like, Goodnight Irene. The Drunken Mermaid is okay, but it's very sweet. Personally, my favorite is the Jungle Bird. It's really tasty and refreshing."

"That's what I was going to order!" I laughed.

"Then you have good taste. Stick with your instincts." She nodded. "And watch your drink, because I heard there was some creep around here slipping nasty crap into girls' drinks a few weeks back."

"Really?" My blood ran cold. "Here?"

"That's what I heard. I mean, you should be careful at all bars and clubs, because creepers are everywhere." She glanced at Jake and narrowed her eyes slightly. "I know you're not all like that but, seriously, your gender has a lot to answer for."

Jake blinked and didn't say anything. Probably a wise move.

"Anyway, be safe, okay?" For a moment, I got a sense of genuine care from Starr and it warmed me inside. Maybe under all that bleach and schadenfreude, there was some goodness.

"You too," I said, meaning every word of it. "And your friends."

Starr winked and waggled her fingers at Jake before heading back to her table.

"I don't know what to make of that entire interaction," he admitted, looking utterly bewildered.

"Probably best not to analyze it."

He shook his head. "I'll go order our drinks at the bar. You still going with the Jungle Bird?"

"Yes, please."

"And don't worry, I'll watch it like a hawk."

As Jake walked away, I couldn't help but think about what Starr had said. There was some creeper slipping stuff into drinks a few weeks back. It immediately made me think of the drawing in Aaron's diary and my suspicions about a drink-spiking incident.

Celina hadn't wanted to part with the page itself, understandably, since now it was one of the few things she had left of Aaron. And I think my reluctance to see the photos of Aaron and Kaila as evidence of cheating had shaken her confidence in that theory. But she'd let me take some photos of the drawings, from both sides, so I could show Ethan.

I pulled out my phone and opened up the photo. And that's when I noticed something.

Originally, I'd been fixated on the pill bottle and the martini glass. But underneath the glass was a napkin. I'd noted that it had a logo on it, but it hadn't meant anything to me at the time. It was a cute flamingo cocktail glass—where the leg was the stem and the body was the glass and then a long neck extended up from one side, with the signature curved beak holding an olive.

It was the logo for Salty's Flamingo Shack.

That seemed like *way* too much of a coincidence.

But before I could think about it in too much depth, the lights suddenly dimmed and the music lowered. A voice came over the speakers.

"Welcome, everyone, to Salty's Flamingo Shack. Tonight we have a special treat for you, a show of mystical proportions featuring three of our wonderful in-house mermaids and a very special guest. You may know Mariah the Mermaid from her fantastic social media posts, where she spreads important information about ocean conservation and helps to destigmatize the toothiest beasts under the sea. Tonight she is here for your entertainment, so please put your hands together and give her a warm, Flamingo welcome!"

The audience clapped and the lighting shifted to highlight the huge tank on the far wall. We had a great view from our table and Jake returned with our drinks right as things were getting started. Music began to play through the speakers and Mariah swam into view, looking every bit a real mermaid. She was wearing a spectacular tail that was aqua blue at her waist and slowly graduated into a gleaming almost iridescent gold, with fins that were gossamer thin, rippling behind her with each undulating movement.

Her long blond hair streamed behind her and she wore a sparkly shell bra on top, complete with an orange starfish on one strap and tendrils of a gold iridescent material that shimmered like underwater treasure. She waved and then brought her hand to her lips, blowing a kiss that released a flurry of bubbles around her.

What happened over the next few minutes was an impressive feat of athleticism, underwater gymnastics and total showmanship. Mariah seemed to dance, if that was even possible with her legs bound in a silicone tube, her arms graceful like those of a ballerina, as she used the whole tank to move and interact with the other mermaids who joined her. They even wheeled in a large martini glass from the side of the tank, where there must be a section that was not visible to patrons and Mariah splashed around, playing with a large olive and a stuffed clownfish.

The mermaids tossed the olive back and forth, like they were playing an underwater game of catch, and then they swam together, creating shapes and formations that had the audience enraptured. At the end, the mermaids all swam to the front of the glass, pressed one hand to it and the other to their lips, blowing bubble kisses and waving while the crowd whooped and cheered.

As the mermaids disappeared off the side of the tank, the music lowered once more. "Don't be sad, folks. Our mermaids will be back again soon. In the meantime, we've got specials . . ."

I tuned out the announcer's voice and turned to Jake. "That was amazing!"

"I don't think people understand how hard that stuff is." Jake nodded. "I lived next door to a girl who was a synchronized swimmer training for the Olympics. People used to tease her that it wasn't a real sport, but she trained eight hours a day. Six in the pool and another two doing ballet, Pilates and cross-training."

"Eight hours a day!" I gaped at him. "I would *not* cope."

"*And*," he continued, "it's common for them to have head injuries. They do this type of kick called the 'eggbeater' which helps them stay upright, but it's such a powerful kick that when the swimmers are close together some of them get kicked in the head and end up with a concussion."

I reached for my drink. "That's fascinating."

"It's such a weird sport, but I loved hearing all her stories." Jake nodded. "I'm that person who always wants to know the strange and wacky personal details. I don't care what sports they like or what kind of car they drive. I want to know about the hobbies they love to nerd out over, and if they have any weird collections or an unusual former job."

"Well, why don't we cheers to that." I raised my glass. "To getting to know each other, including all the funny extra bits we would never put in our online bios."

"Hear, hear." Jake laughed and touched his glass to mine across the table. "On that note, I feel like we need to share something quirky about ourselves."

I sipped my drink. Starr was right, it *was* refreshing and tasty! A nice balance of warmth from the rum, sweetness from

the pineapple juice, bitterness from the Campari and tart fresh-
ness from the lime.

"Hmm, something quirky . . ." It occurred to me then that I
was, perhaps, the opposite of quirky. A type A, high-achieving
teacher's pet who was always too scared to put a foot wrong.
Didn't make for a lot of interesting personal facts. "I once
forced my family and my entire school class to call me Anais
for a whole year after I discovered that my name wasn't actually French in origin. I was eleven and devastated, because all
I'd ever wanted was to move to Paris and wear berets and cycle
around the city with a baguette in the basket on my bike."

Jake chuckled. "Where did Anais come from?"

"I saw it written on a perfume bottle in my grandmother's
bathroom." I wrinkled my nose. "Don't even say anything, I
know how cringe that is. Peak emo preteen behavior, right
there. Now, your turn."

"Okay, well if we're going more with *cringe* than quirky, I
once wrote a valentine poem for a girl I had a crush on. Except
instead of actually writing anything myself, I just wrote out the
lyrics to a My Chemical Romance song and she totally called
me on it."

"No," I gasped, hiding behind my hands.

"In the middle of an assembly with the entire year level
there."

"No!" I shrank even further into my hands, a giggle bubbling up in the back of my throat. "Oh, the secondhand em-
barrassment is real."

"Yeah, so you want to play Who Is the Cringiest? I would
think twice about it, because I'll whip you good."

I laughed so heartily tears sprang to my eyes. "I mean this
in the nicest possible way, but you are the *exact* opposite of
my ex."

"Oh, he was French, right? Probably bought you roses and
kissed you in the rain and had all the moves?" Jake was flush-

ing now, and cursing himself a little. But I loved every second of it.

As far as I was concerned, cringe was real. Red roses and "moves" were not.

"Yeah, he did. But he also took himself so seriously I felt like I had to book a third seat at dinner for his ego." I rolled my eyes. "Being around someone who can laugh at themselves is incredibly refreshing."

"I *do* have that going for me." Jake's eyes met mine over the table and my heart skipped a beat. "I had a boss tell me once that I needed to be more serious at work, because people wouldn't respect me if I was always making jokes."

"That's some BS." I frowned. "What did you say back to him?"

"That heart attacks and cancer and surgery were serious, and our work of making the rich richer was little more than a blip in the universe so if we couldn't laugh at it, we'd massively overinflated how important it was." Jake bobbed his head.

"Oof." I shook my head. "I wish I could have said something cool like that to all the mean bosses I had over the years."

"I didn't have a boss too much longer after that." He took a sip of his drink. "He told me to get out of his office and I wrote my resignation letter half-drunk that evening after deciding to move out here."

"I admire that so much. You took control of your life rather than waiting for someone else to do it for you."

"I had to get out. Wall Street was killing me." His tone was anything but sad or regretful. In fact, the way he looked at me across the table made me feel like he was talking about the best thing that ever happened to him. Maybe he was. "I'm grateful every day for that boss telling me not to laugh. Because it made me realize just how important it is *to* laugh. And that led me here . . . to you."

"Then I'm grateful for your boss, too," I said, my heart thudding unsteadily in my chest.

Before we could continue the conversation, however, a server turned up at our table and apologized for making us wait so long. We'd just ordered our food when the lights suddenly went dim again.

"Have you been missing the mermaids? Well, get ready for the Salty's Flamingo Shack Beauties! Our regular mermaids, Cassie, Eliza, Jade and Harmony are here to take you on an underwater journey . . ."

I glanced around the room. Everyone was riveted to the large aquatic tank and waiting for the next part of the show to begin. It sounded like Mariah wasn't in this section, so this could be my chance to catch her alone. I might not have much time, so there was no point overthinking it.

"I'll be back," I said to Jake as I slipped off my stool and went in search of a mermaid.

CHAPTER 20

I wound my way through the crowded room to a section that said STAFF ONLY. With the lights down low and everyone's attention on the mermaid tank, nobody noticed me slip down the hallway. There were several closed doors, marked with titles like SUPPLIES and STOCKROOM and MANAGEMENT OFFICE. There was a sign pointing left down another hallway that said TANK ENTRANCE. Further down, light spilled from the crack under a closed door and I heard tinkling laughter.

Mariah.

I hurried down toward the door, but before I knocked I tried to listen to what was going on inside. It was difficult to hear too much, except muffled voices. I pressed my ear to the door and that's when the words became clearer. There were two people talking, Mariah and someone else. A young male.

"In all seriousness, you're going to get yourself in trouble," she said. "You can't be pulling stunts like this, okay? It's a crime. I know things are hard right now, but don't throw away your future. He wouldn't want that."

Sucking in a breath and painting on my brightest smile, I rapped my knuckles against the door. The voices quietened and a second later there were footsteps.

I was surprised when Mariah opened the door herself, legs free of their beautiful silicone prison for the moment. But she was still in full mermaid makeup, with sparkles dancing across her skin, artfully painted scales on her cheekbones and thick black liner to make her eyes stand out. It was truly a work of cosmetic art.

"Chloe." Mariah's expression brightened. "It's so nice to see you. Did you come along for the show?"

"I did. You're absolutely magnificent," I gushed, meaning every word of it. "I don't think I've ever seen anything like that before!"

"You're too kind." She lowered her eyes in modesty.

"Is there any chance I could come in for a moment? I just . . . this might sound strange, but I have a few questions for you, woman to woman."

Her brow rose in interest, but I sensed a hesitation in the air around her. She was probably preparing for her next part of the show.

I put on my most pleading smile. "It'll only take a minute, I promise."

"Okay, sure."

She stepped back and opened the door, revealing a modest dressing room with big mirrors and lots of lights. There was a clothing rack on one side, from which hung a selection of mermaid costume elements—bras, arm and wrist adornments, even a gauzy shawl that looked white but had an iridescent sheen to it. There was makeup scattered across the counter under the mirror, except for the spot where a teenage boy sat, his eyes locked on mine.

He was dressed in all black—definitely the guy I'd seen her talking to at the beach. Only now he wasn't wearing the black baseball cap and a shock of ginger-red hair stuck out in all directions. His cheekbones were sharp and his eyes looked warily in my direction.

"This is Cooper, Aaron's younger brother." Mariah gestured to the teen, who didn't make any attempt to wave or say hello.

When Ethan had mentioned Aaron's "younger brother," for some reason I'd pictured a boy of eight or ten, but Cooper was at least thirteen or fourteen. Maybe a little older. It was hard to tell. Like Aaron, he was slight in build but there was a lankiness to him that hinted he was due a major growth spurt, almost as if he needed the rest of his body to catch up with his longer arms. His nails were bitten to their quicks and there were heavy circles under his eyes.

"Coops, this is Chloe. She's . . ." Mariah stalled for a second. "A baker."

"Hi," I said. "I'm really sorry about your brother."

Cooper didn't reply.

"Can you give us a minute?" she asked him. "And don't go into the bar area. You're not allowed in there."

Rolling his eyes, the teen pushed himself off the counter where he'd been sitting and landed graceful and silent, before stalking out of the room. I glanced at Mariah and she let out a big sigh as the door slammed behind him.

"He's devastated, obviously." Her eyes brimmed with compassion. "They were so close, those two. Aaron would have done anything for him, including finally getting his shit together."

The pain in her voice was like a knife—sharp-edged, glinting.

"You miss him a lot." It wasn't a question.

She looked up at me with tears in her eyes. "I have loved Aaron ever since I was a little girl. But I messed it all up, and I made some mistakes. Too many mistakes. But I was still happy to have him as a friend, you know? Because something is better than nothing."

She didn't kill him. I could feel it deep in my gut—the emotion in her voice, the shaking in her hands, the tears in her eyes. She loved him. As for the money . . . Well, maybe there was part of her that expected never to get it back. And didn't we all make foolish decisions when we were in love?

"And now Cooper turns up." She rubbed at her temples. "Stole his aunt's credit card and bought a plane ticket to California because he wants to speak to the police. I told him he's going to get himself in huge trouble if he keeps pulling stunts like that."

Ah, so that's what I'd heard them talking about when I'd eavesdropped before I came inside. "Sounds like you two are close."

"I feel responsible for him, you know? I've known him ever since he was born. He's like a little brother to me, too." She shook her head.

"That poor kid." I wasn't sure what else to say, especially not whether I should mention that I thought Aaron had been murdered.

"Anyway, what did you want to ask me about?" She shook herself and whisked away the tears clinging to her lashes. Thankfully, with all that waterproof makeup, not a single smudge occurred. "I have to get into my LED tail for the next part of the show. I don't usually do costume changes because the tails are such a pain to get in and out of, but they're paying me well and I've got tuition bills to cover."

"What do you know about girls in the surfing community having their drinks spiked?" I asked, deciding there was no time to beat around the bush.

Mariah's expression was very telling—there wasn't an ounce of surprise on her face. "I've heard things."

"Like?"

"Like there was a party after one of the competitions a while back and one girl woke up on her friend's couch, having no idea how she got there. He said she went off to go to the bathroom at some point in the evening and didn't come back out for a while, so he went looking for her. Found her passed out on the floor and there was a creep hanging around outside the women's bathroom." She shook her head. "He thinks he might have saved her from something terrible happening. And this girl had only had two drinks—not enough to get blind drunk. They think one was spiked."

"When was that?" I asked.

"I can't remember, exactly. Maybe after the Huntington Beach women's series. It was a month or two ago, at least." She frowned, her eyes fixed on something I couldn't see, like she was flicking through things in her memory. "And Kaila ended up leaving early the last time we were all out together. There was a party for a surf brand and we were all networking, so we were drinking a little but not too much. Got to be professional, you know?"

I nodded.

"Anyway, I saw her in the restroom and she was looking rough. Sweaty, slurring her words. At the time I thought she was drunk and I told her to go home before she made a bad impression on the sponsors." Mariah looked at me with guilt in her eyes. "I might have been a little harsh."

"You don't like Kaila?" I cocked my head.

"I don't like that Aaron has always been gaga over her," she admitted. "I was jealous. Kaila is so beautiful and funny and I felt like I could never compete with her. So I made it clear I thought she was a mess for drinking too much. And I didn't stay with her when she was like that. I left her alone in the restroom."

The guilt in her voice was heavy. It was a cardinal rule she'd broken—never leave a sister in a dangerous position.

"But you think it was possible her drink was spiked, too?" I asked.

She shrugged. "I mean, I *know* Kaila isn't a big drinker. She and Makani are two peas in a pod with all their yoga classes and smoothie bowls and Instagram "fitspo life" image. She cares about her figure and public image too much to drink regularly."

"When did this all happen?" I asked.

"A couple weeks back." She bobbed her head. "It's how I got this gig, actually?"

"What do you mean? You were all here, in Salty's Flamingo Shack?" I thought back to the drawing of the pill bottle and the martini glass sitting atop the napkin with the flamingo cocktail glass logo on it.

"Yeah." She nodded. "I got chatting with the owner and showed him my socials. Then he booked me for this gig tonight."

"Interesting."

"Now that I think about it, Aaron said to me recently that I should watch my drink more closely. I met him at that bar down by the beach the night we both got in. He said I was oblivious to the dangers in the world and I laughed it off, but he got really upset. He took my drink and tossed it onto a plant. I thought he was being a jerk and I told him to get lost." She blinked tears from her eyes. "That was the last thing I said to him."

"You didn't know what was going to happen," I said, shaking my head. "You can't hold guilt over that. Do you have any idea who was spiking people's drinks?"

She shook her head. "No, not a clue. Do you think Aaron knew something?"

Out of the corner of my eye I saw a shadow flicker at the bottom of the door to the changing room. Cooper was probably listening in, so I would have to be careful about what I said. I didn't want to upset the poor kid any more than he already was. Losing a loved one so young. . . . I couldn't even imagine how painful it must be.

"I think he might have," I said keeping my voice down, hoping Cooper wouldn't be able to hear. "I think he knew, at the very least, who drugged Kaila and how they did it. And I think it got him killed."

"I knew the suicide theory was wrong." She shook her head vehemently. "Aaron would never leave Coops like that."

"What about the time he was on the roof of his house threatening to jump?" I asked.

Mariah frowned. "That was a big misunderstanding."

"His aunt told the police she had to talk him down."

She shook her head. "Cooper told me all about it. Aaron and his aunt had a tense relationship at times. Aaron was . . . difficult and his aunt was very high-strung. They had a huge fight one day and he climbed up there to get away from things. She freaked out, thinking he was going to jump. She lost a close friend to suicide when she was young, so she was terrified of it happening again."

"But you don't think he would have jumped?"

"No way. Aaron had *severe* abandonment issues after his parents left him and Coops—it's why he was seeing a therapist. He would never do that same thing to his brother. *Never.*"

Mariah's response made me realize how improbable the story of Aaron jumping off the roof was. After all, if he already had access to sleeping pills, then why would he do something as potentially traumatizing to his younger brother by jumping off a roof where Cooper might see it happen or find him after. It didn't add up.

"I won't keep you any longer," I said. "I know you have to perform. Thanks for talking with me."

Mariah nodded, but her eyes were faraway. I headed out of the changing room and into the dimly lit hallway, expecting to find Cooper. But there was no one around. Music thumped from the bar and I glanced down to where the tables were, guilty I'd abandoned Jake on our date. But something was brewing. I needed to make a quick phone call to Detective Alvarez and then I would give Jake all my attention for the rest of the evening to make up for leaving him stranded.

But I needed to make the call outside. The music was too loud here.

I walked further down the hallway toward an exit sign, where I found a door. Peeking my head outside, I could see it led out to a small staff parking lot behind the venue. Reaching down, I grabbed a loose brick and used it to stop the door from closing, because I wasn't sure if it was one of those types that locked automatically. The last thing I wanted was to be locked outside at night in an unfamiliar area.

I grabbed my phone out of my purse and navigated through my contacts until I found Detective Alvarez's number. Then I hit dial. The call rang a few times before her voicemail cut in.

"You've reached Detective Adriana Alvarez of the Azalea Bay Police Department. If this is an emergency, please hang up and dial 911 immediately. Otherwise, leave a message after the beep."

"Hi Detective," I said, walking a little farther into the parking lot to get away from the bass rattling behind me. "This is Chloe Barnes. I'm calling regarding the death of Aaron Gill—"

My words were cut short when a leather-gloved hand clamped over my mouth from behind me and another strong arm wrapped around my waist, pinning my arm to my side. My phone clattered to the ground and I tried to scream, but the sound was muffled against the leather. I wriggled and tried to break free, thrashing my head back and forth but my attacker held me fast.

"You nosy little bitch." The words were hissed into my ear and the grip tightened around my waist. It felt like my heart was going to punch its way out of my chest, that's how hard it was beating. "But actions have consequences."

The person was speaking low, but I was sure it was a man. He was taller than me, stronger than me, and I had no idea how I was going to get out of this. Out of the corner of my eye, I saw a flash of white as something was brought up over my face. At first, I smelled something sweet, almost citrus-like, and then I got a whiff of an acetone smell. I felt my body sway, as the floor suddenly tilted beneath my feet.

Or did it? Maybe I was the one who tilted?

I suddenly felt very dizzy and my eyelids drooped, panic slicing through me like a hot-tipped spear. No. No! Then there was a loud bang behind me and a cry, I saw a body go sprawling across the floor and caught a flash of red hair before the ground came rushing up to me. I registered pain as my body hit the asphalt, a skinned palm and the crunch of my knee. Sharply tilting earth that caused my stomach to lurch.

Then pounding footsteps. I tried to lift my head, but it felt as though it weighed too much. I caught sight of black boots darting away from me in the direction of the street.

"Are you okay?" A young voice. Cooper. He groaned as he pushed himself up. "That guy grabbed you . . . It didn't look good."

"It wasn't." I let myself slump down so the world would stop spinning. "It wasn't good at all."

Five minutes later I was seated in the management office of Salty's Flamingo Shack, several worried faces looking over me. The bar's night manager heard the loud bang from when Cooper tripped over the brick I'd used to prop the door open, knocking it out of place and causing the heavy door to slam shut. He and Cooper had helped me up and half carried me into the management office, so they could get me some water and find out what had happened.

Then Jake had come looking because I'd been gone for too long. Now he was sitting next to me, his eyebrows knitted in concern and a dark look on his face.

"Don't look at me like that," I said, feeling very tender—both of head and of soul.

"It's not anger at you," he said through gritted teeth. "It's at whatever jerk tried to abduct you!"

"Did you get a look at him?" The night manager was a big barrel of a man with a long, gray-flecked beard and a shaved head. He looked like he could take just about anyone in a fight and I was glad he was in the room with us. "Either of you."

Cooper had a graze on his cheek from where he'd fallen and he kept his head hanging slightly forward, so his shaggy ginger hair partially covered it. "All I saw was some guy in black grab her. He put a rag over her face and she went all woozy. I tried to stop him but . . ."

The guilt in his voice made me want to hug him.

"You scared him away," I said. "That's the best possible outcome. And no, I didn't see him. I was on the phone and he came at me from behind."

"I'll ask the boss to check the cameras tomorrow," the bar manager said. "I don't know how to do all that tech stuff, but if he was in here then we should have him on screen. It is possible he was already outside or he came down the street, though."

"I appreciate you trying," I said.

"We should get you home." Jake touched my shoulder. "Your grandma is going to be pissed at me."

"It's not your job to protect me, Jake," I said quietly. "But I appreciate that you care."

He looked at me, a hint of warmth breaking through his ice-cold worry. "I really do, Chloe. I care a lot."

I let Jake help me out to the car, with the bar manager and Cooper following us out there to make sure we got off safely.

"Thanks again," I said to Cooper as Jake opened the door for me on his car. "If you hadn't come running outside . . ."

I didn't even want to think about what might have happened.

"It was nothing." Cooper looked at the ground.

It certainly wasn't nothing, but something told me the teen

wouldn't respond to my insisting otherwise. He'd pulled the zipper down on his hoodie to reveal a band T-shirt for some emo group with pale skin and scowling faces. Turns out his all-black outfit at the beach was nothing more than a teen rebelling against social norms and *not* the uniform of a killer.

Would we ever figure out what happened to Aaron?

Hopefully there would be evidence of my attacker on-screen. I was at a dead end otherwise. I knew what had happened to Kaila and the other female surfer and I knew that Aaron was onto the perpetrator. I even knew *where* some of the incidents had happened: right here in this very bar. What I didn't know the most important piece of information of all: *who* did it.

But unfortunately for me, now the killer knew I was onto them.

CHAPTER 21

That night I couldn't sleep.

Or rather, I couldn't *stay* asleep. Every time I drifted off, I'd have strange dreams about cocktails and pill bottles and faceless men wearing black leather gloves and photos fluttering in the air before being torn to shreds. By seven thirty a.m., when I'd woken up in a cold sweat for what felt like the hundredth time, I finally gave up and got out of bed.

After Jake had returned me home last night finding Aunt Dawn on the couch dog-sitting, she'd made the call that we wouldn't open Baked by Chloe today. It was probably safer for me to stay in the house, at least until I heard back from the detective and the day manager from the bar with news about the security cameras. I was disappointed to lose a day of trade, especially with so many tourists in town, but given we'd surpassed my wildest expectations already, it wasn't the worst idea.

Jake, Dawn and I had sat up until Grandma Rose got home from her date, where Jake had spilled the beans about what had happened and I'd gotten an earful all over again. But how was I supposed to sit by while awful things happened to innocent people? While girls were targeted in bars and the person who'd tried to help had likely been killed for it? How could I

sleep at night if I simply said, "Oh well, that's not *my* problem," and went about my life, selfish and uncaring?

Neither Grandma Rose nor Aunt Dawn had been able to
come up with a satisfactory answer to those questions. Jake
hadn't even tried. Before he'd gone back to his house, he'd
pulled me in tight for a hug and told me to be safe.

For a moment there, I thought he might kiss me. His eyes
had lingered on mine and something fluttery and desperate
had stirred in my stomach. But instead he'd touched my cheek
and then he was gone. It wasn't the right moment for it, I knew
that. Yet it hadn't stopped me wanting it to happen.

Now I was here, without work to keep me busy and without
sleep to keep me oblivious for a few more hours. It wasn't cold,
but I felt chilled to my bones, so I grabbed the fluffy pink robe
hanging on the back of my bedroom door and cocooned myself in it, dropping my phone into one of the deep pockets.
Grandma Rose always had a floral-scented laundry detergent
and the smell was comforting because it reminded me of my
childhood.

I crept quietly along the hallway and started down the stairs,
being careful to skip the step that creaked loudly so as not to
wake Grandma Rose. When I approached the bottom step,
however, I saw a shadowy little figure waiting for me, two lu-
minescent brown eyes begging for my attention.

"Why are you awake so early?" I whispered, bending down
to scoop Antonio into my arms. He nestled into the crook of
my elbow and stuck his little snout in there, so that only his
giant ears stuck out. I snorted. "Well, maybe awake is a bit of a
stretch."

I flicked on a lamp and settled on the couch with him in my
lap, stroking his velvety ears. Outside, a streetlamp illuminated
the sidewalk and road, both of which were unsurprisingly deserted. What other people were up at this ungodly hour besides me when there was no reason for it? Today was my first
day off in what felt like forever.

I was exhausted. And I knew from working for other passionate business owners that downtime was just as important as work time. Next week I would get the ball rolling on hiring a staff member to help me in the kitchen, at least for over the summer. Then when things slowed down in the off-season, I could either scale back or work a little less.

Antonio nudged at the flap on my dressing gown and I chuckled softly, loosening the belt so that he could crawl inside the gown. I pulled the fluffy fabric around him and, satisfied, he promptly fell back to sleep. For a moment I simply sat, letting my mind whir like a machine, unable to do anything to slow it down.

Then I heard a creak on the stairs. Crap.

"What are you doing up? You should be sleeping in," Grandma Rose said as she came down the stairs, wrapped in a robe similar to mine, only in a deeper fuchsia shade. "Oh, there's my sweet boy."

I stroked Antonio's ears. "I couldn't sleep."

"How about a cup of tea, then?"

I smiled for her sake, even though I didn't feel like it and nodded. "That sounds great."

I followed Grandma Rose into the kitchen where she filled the kettle and set it on to boil. Then she fetched two proper china teacups from the cupboard which, of course, had roses printed on them. One cup was yellow and the other was a soft peach, and the roses on both were a crisp white. A fine gold rim decorated each cup and Grandma Rose filled two infusers with loose-leaf Earl Grey tea.

"I know you'll always be the kind of person who sticks up for others, Chloe," she said, turning to face me while we waited for the water to boil. "And I know that is partially because I instilled such values in you."

"You did." I wasn't going to say it was hypocritical for her to raise me that way and then be annoyed when I acted in accordance with the values she'd provided me, but I'd certainly thought it in a moment of frustration last night.

"I just want you to be safe," she said, interlacing her hands. She wasn't wearing a scarf or a wig since she'd only just woken up, and I could see how fine and patchy her hair had become. Her scalp showed through clearly now, the shape of her head visible as the light hit what remained of her hair. At this point it might be easier to shave it all off, but I knew it was a troubling side effect of the treatment for her and, therefore, a sensitive topic, so I hadn't said anything. She was preparing for another round of chemotherapy soon, so there might not be much left to shave off soon anyway.

"I want other people to be safe, too," I said. "The world would be a lot better if we all looked out for one another."

Grandma Rose sighed. "I can't argue with that, now, can I?"

"Nope." This time when I smiled it was genuine. "Because I know you believe it, too. And unfortunately values aren't really values if we only stick to them when it's easy."

She narrowed her eyes at me. "Sometimes I don't like how wise you've become."

"You've only got yourself to blame."

She chuckled and came over to pull me into a hug. I let my head rest against her, sucking in the scent of the faded perfume on her robe and the softness of the fabric against my cheek. She stroked my head and for a moment I was a little girl again, seeking support in the arms of the only mother I'd ever really had.

Cold hard fear gripped my heart like a fist. I couldn't lose her.

"So let's figure this out, then," she said, releasing me as the kettle whistled. She walked to the counter to finish making the tea and I shook the worry from my mind. Stressing endlessly about her health didn't help anything. "Because everyone will clear out this afternoon once the competition is over."

I hung my head. "I know."

Last night I'd gotten Grandma Rose and Aunt Dawn up to speed, right up to my conversation with Mariah.

"At least one of the times there was a drink tampered with, it was at the place where you were last night, right?" she asked.

"Yep."

"Have they had any reports about such behavior in the past?"

"That's a good question." I nodded. "I'll ask when they call me today about the security footage."

"And that poor girl hasn't come out of her coma yet?" Grandma Rose's forehead wrinkled deeply in concern.

"Not that I've heard." My stomach twisted just thinking about it. I really hoped Kaila would be okay.

"I wonder if we can find out *who* was at the party where it happened," Grandma Rose mused. "Maybe that might point to some suspects."

"Good idea. We could check Kaila's social media accounts!"

I didn't have Kaila's Instagram handle but when I looked up Ethan's account on my phone, I soon found a photo of him with a group of familiar faces, including Kaila, who'd been tagged. Clicking through led me to her page. But a quick scroll through her photos showed no mention of a party. Mostly it was glamorous shots of Kaila wearing perfectly coordinated yoga sets, doing poses that showed off her flexibility and the occasional selfie with a friend or her brothers. I managed to find Makani's profile, but his didn't mention a party, either. Nor did Ethan's.

Drumming my fingers on the tabletop, I tried to think of where else we could look.

"I wonder if Celina was there taking photos," I said. It seemed like surf photography was her main gig, but she *had* been at the mansion party with her camera so it was possible. She'd also mentioned always keeping her smaller camera on her for "happy snaps."

I Googled Celina Sato Photography and found her Instagram account easily. Most of the photos were of surfers doing their thing out on the ocean and they were *beautiful*. Every single photo was a work of art—the angles, the lighting, the way she managed to capture movement in a still picture. Wow. Casual photos were sparse, but I found one of her and Aaron at some beach, and they both smiled like neither one of them had a care in the world. After more scrolling—she posted *a lot*—I found what I was looking for.

"This is the place!" I showed the post to Grandma Rose.

It featured Celina and Aaron, their arms around each other with the Salty's Flamingo Shack mermaid tank in the background. I swiped to see the other photos nested in the post. There was one of a mermaid waving from the tank. Another shot of some fancy-looking cocktails. And the final one featured Celina and another young woman with strawberry-blond hair holding up martini glasses to the camera, their bodies encased in very tight sparkly dresses. It looked like quite a party.

The last photo seemed different from the others. There was a watermark on the bottom of the photo that had the Salty's Flamingo Shack logo on it. The bar's account was tagged and when I clicked through I found even more photos from that night. Clearly, there had been a photographer at the event, and Celina had been there as a guest by the look of things.

The post's caption stated that the party was a PR event for a surf brand named Riptide and the date indicated it took place a few weeks back. There was also a note saying more photos could be found on the bar's website and it linked to the photographer, a guy named Mike Schmidt. I Googled the website and the event was mentioned on the home page, with a whole album of professional PR photos.

I immediately saw some familiar faces—Makani and the man I assumed to be his father, Greg, because they had the same jaw and lips, even though the older man was fair-haired and lighter in skin color. So Makani *was* there, he just hadn't shared the photos on his social media. That wasn't suspicious, necessarily, because party photos didn't really fit with his wholesome yoga-health image.

There was a picture of Aaron and Ethan that struck me hard in the chest. The two men looked so happy and full of life. Ethan's hair was as wild and curly as always, a shock of blond next to Aaron's vibrant ginger mop and toothy smile. I wonder if Ethan had a copy of this photo. I took a screenshot of it with the plan to forward it to him.

"What's going on there?" Grandma Rose looked over my shoulder and pointed to something in the background of the photo. "Can you zoom in more? I can't see properly."

I pinched my fingers on the screen and then spread them apart to zoom. The photo was shadowy behind the boys, but I could just make out an outline of a man and a woman. He was holding a martini glass out to her.

Was that . . . ? Oh my god, it was Kaila.

"It's her! The girl who's in the hospital." I gasped. "And the guy is holding out a martini glass to her, just like in the drawing in Aaron's journal."

I'd wondered if the martini glass in his drawing had simply been because the bar's logo had a flamingo-shaped martini glass, but perhaps the drawing was more literal than that.

"Oh dear," Grandma Rose said. "Are they in the background of the other photos?"

We clicked through the next few and zoomed in to the same spot in the background. It was too hard to see the man's face in them, but there were dozens more photos and they appeared to have been uploaded in chronological order. Kaila was taking the martini and smiling. She seemed relaxed. Then she was holding the martini. Then drinking it.

But I still couldn't see the man.

He was wearing dark clothing and long sleeves. Kaila was

drinking and talking to him. Still, I couldn't see his face. I kept flicking through the photos—desperately zooming in to each one to see if there was anything else we could glean. Just as I was beginning to wonder if we would find anything, I saw something. The man in the background had pushed his sleeves up.

He had a full sleeve of surfing and ocean-themed tattoos on one arm. Orcas, waves, tropical flowers, the sun, shells and a surfboard. I'd seen them before.

"Oh my god. It's Aaron and Ethan's surfing agent." My blood ran completely cold, but I couldn't stop flicking through the photos. "Bryce Whitten."

The man who'd stood before a crowd and lauded Aaron's talents in a memorial and conducted a moment of silence. The man who'd comforted Ethan at the party after Aaron's death. The man who'd seemed genuinely saddened by the loss of his young client. Could *he* be the killer?

I thought about Aaron's suicide note.

I can't do this anymore. Whatever I thought this life would be, it's not this. I need to be released.

"The suicide note was written in bullet points. But what if it wasn't a suicide note at all? What if they were *talking* points?" I put my phone down, my mind whirring. "And what if the words 'I need to be released' weren't about dying, but about exiting out of a contract? An *agency* contract?"

"You did mention that Ethan said Aaron had trouble using his words. Maybe he was preparing to break up with his agent," Grandma Rose said, nodding. "It's something a lot of people do. They write their thoughts down so they feel clear *before* having a big conversation."

Then something else hit me. The night of the party when I met Bryce for the first time, he talked about his trouble sleeping. *You know I don't sleep well in the best of circumstances and I didn't get a wink after you texted about Aaron last night, even with some assistance.*

"Bryce also takes sleeping pills," I said.

A cold, hard feeling gripped my stomach. I would bet every cent in my bank account that the assistance he was referring to were the same type of pills that Aaron was taking.

"What if he used those pills to spike Kaila's drink and then he used those *same* pills to murder Aaron and make it look like suicide?" I pressed a palm to my forehead. "Just because it was the same type of medication Aaron took, doesn't mean they were *his* pills. Bryce could have used his own pills and then emptied out Aaron's bottle after he was dead to stage the scene. *And* Bryce would know that you shouldn't mix the pills with grapefruit juice!"

It was a perfectly despicable solution—kill the man with his own type of medication and use his mental health struggles against him. Then he went after Kaila and now she couldn't speak out against him, either.

I didn't know how Bryce could sleep at night.

"You need to call Ethan and warn him," Grandma Rose said gravely. "And then we call the police."

CHAPTER 22

I tried Ethan's phone for the third time, frantic. But it went to voicemail yet again. I'd already tried calling Matt, but he wasn't picking up, either. Grandma Rose was on hold with the police station, trying to get in touch with the detective. But it was the grand final for the surf competition and I knew the police would be busy wrangling the crowds and keeping people safe while the town almost burst at the seams.

This was Azalea Bay's busiest day of the year, bar none.

I hung up the call when I heard *"Hi, you've reached Ethan—"* for the third time. Then, not knowing what else to do, I called Ben.

He picked up on the second ring. "Hey, Chloe. What's up?"

"Are you home right now? Are Ethan and Matt with you?" I tried to keep the sheer panic out of my voice because I didn't want to freak Ben out, but I wasn't sure that I'd done a very good job.

"No, I'm at the airport. I'm flying to Vegas for a tech conference." He let out a sigh. "I told Matt that I should cancel and stay home with them, but he wouldn't have it. Practically shoved me out of the door. My plane leaves in fifteen minutes."

Crap on a cracker.

When I didn't immediately respond, there was an intake of breath on the other end of the line. "What's going on, Chloe?"

"Oh, I . . ." What was the point of worrying Ben when he was about to get on a flight? I would only put him in a position where he felt stressed and helpless. "I wanted to make sure I didn't miss Ethan before he headed home, that's all."

I crossed my fingers behind my back as I lied, guilt settling uncomfortably in my gut. I hated lying to my friends.

"Aww, aren't you sweet." All the worry eased out of his voice. "Ethan said he was going to stay a bit longer, since we've got plenty of room for him. Matt's at the gym, so if you tried to call him and he didn't pick up that would be why. He always leaves his phone in his locker when he's doing weights."

"Do you know where Ethan was headed this morning?"

"He's gone to settle the bill at the hotel and officially check out."

Oh no.

"Sorry, Chloe, they're calling for us to board. I'll have to let you go."

I wished him a good trip and pressed the end call button on my phone, my blood running ice cold. If Ethan was at the hotel by himself . . .

What if Bryce went there to confront him? After all, if Bryce knew that *I* was on the cusp of figuring out who was behind the spiked drinks and Aaron's murder, then maybe he assumed I'd told Ethan.

Only I hadn't.

Ethan didn't know about the incident in the bar last night. He also didn't know what I'd found out just now, but Bryce might be wanting to cover his tracks anyway.

I looked over to Grandma Rose and she shook her head, tutting in frustration to indicate that she was still on hold. I took my cell phone upstairs in case either Matt or Ethan called me back, and got changed into jeans and a T-shirt. My phone stayed frustratingly silent the entire time.

I jogged back downstairs and Grandma Rose was finally talking to someone.

"Well, this *could* be an emergency," she said, concern creating an edge in her voice. "We're not exactly sure."

I located my purse and slung it over one shoulder.

"What do you mean the detective is too busy to take calls?" She huffed. "This is important."

She paused.

"Yes, well I know the police are extremely busy this weekend . . . yes, I know I said we're not exactly sure that it's an emergency, but we're *somewhat* sure." She glanced at her phone, her mouth tightening. Then she glanced over to me. "She put me on hold again."

"I can't just sit here and do nothing," I said, rifling around in my purse for the keys to the Jellybean. "I'm going to the hotel to see if Ethan is okay."

"Chloe, no." Grandma Rose came forward but I stopped her in her tracks with a serious look.

"If something happened to him because I stayed in my house, I would never forgive myself," I said and Grandma Rose sighed.

She wasn't going to give me her blessing, but she wasn't going to stop me, either.

"I'll leave Matt's number here for you," I said, grabbing a pen from the kitchen countertop and scribbling his cell number down on a Post-it. "Keep trying to get ahold of him and stay on the phone with the police. If you don't hear from me within half an hour, tell them it *is* an emergency."

I raced out of the house, leaving my grandmother looking very worried. But there was no time to ease either of our worries—I *had* to get to Ethan.

* * *

The drive to the hotel was excruciatingly slow. Every road in Azalea Bay was clogged to the teeth, bumper to bumper with cars, the sidewalks heaving with beach-going pedestrians. I sat in a trailing line, my impatience bubbling like a witch's cauldron.

I tried Ethan again. This time I got a text back.

ETHAN: Sorry busy. Talk later.

How did I know he was the one who'd sent the message, however? What if Bryce had him knocked out with whatever stuff he'd tried to use on me last night? What if he'd killed Ethan, too, and was simply buying time? I wanted to write back but I couldn't be sure who I was talking to and I didn't want to risk tipping Bryce off.

I banged my palm against my steering wheel and cursed our town for being such a tourist trap. Eventually I was able to make the turnoff toward the hotel and I planted my foot, accelerating to a more normal speed than the crawl I'd been doing a few moments ago, until the hotel came into view.

I saw Matt's car immediately in the short-term parking out in front of the hotel and I pulled my car into the spot next to it. The parking lot was empty. Jumping out of the Jellybean, I closed the door behind me and locked it before hurrying inside the hotel.

The place seemed even creepier today, in light of everything that was going on. It felt like all the stuffed mounts were watching me, their beady lifeless eyes following my every step toward the front desk. It wasn't the same gum-snapping girl who'd been working there before, however. Now there was an older man with silvery hair and dull brown eyes, who looked even more bored than the girl had.

Who knew that was possible?

"Hello?" I waved to get his attention and he dragged his eyes up to mine with a reluctance that seemed bone-deep. "Hi there. I'm wondering if Ethan Wilson has checked out yet?"

I supplied the room number, but the man made no move to check for me.

"I can't give out personal information of guests at the hotel," he replied. His voice had the robotic tone of someone who'd said those exact words a thousand times before.

"I'm not asking for personal information," I said, trying to keep my cool. Being rude to this guy wouldn't help, but I wanted to reach over the reception desk and shake him. "I already know what room he's in. I just need to know if he's checked out yet."

"I can't give out personal information of guests at the hotel," he repeated.

I turned around with a huff, about to walk to the stairwell when I almost stepped smack bang into someone. It was Jake.

"What the heck are you doing here?" I asked, blinking like he might be a mirage.

"Your grandmother called me in a panic and said you'd taken off by yourself to confront a killer." He folded his arms across his chest. "You really *are* a glutton for punishment."

"Grandma Rose is . . ." I couldn't even say anything bad about her, because she was only trying to protect me while I tried to protect Ethan. "Follow me."

I grabbed Jake's hand and hauled him outside, away from the reception desk attendant.

"I think Ethan is in his hotel room and I'm worried Bryce is there with him," I said. "He could be in danger."

"Based on . . ."

"My gut feeling," I replied honestly. "But I'm convinced Bryce is the one who drugged Kaila and then he killed Aaron for figuring it out. If he's killed someone before, he could do it again. Look what happened last night."

"Exactly. You almost got hurt." Jake scrubbed a hand over

his face. "But I said when it comes to you, I know to be ready for anything, so . . ."

My heart lit up with hope. "You'll help me?"

"What else am I supposed to do?" He gave me a crooked grin that made the dimple appear in his cheek. "Wimp out while you charge into battle? No way. We go in together."

I grabbed his face and, before either of us could think about it, I planted a swift kiss on his lips. It felt so right in the moment, but I didn't have time to linger. "Come on. This way."

We scurried around the side of the hotel, right to where the balcony of Ethan and Aaron's hotel room was overhead. The sliding door was ajar, like it had been last time. Two voices floated out.

"No one will *ever* believe this." It was Ethan and he sounded furious, but also scared. "I would never kill my best friend."

"Everyone loves to see a wholesome guy turn out to be a monster, Ethan. They'll eat it up."

I clamped a hand over my mouth so I wouldn't gasp and draw attention to us. Instead, I pointed up to the hotel room and mouthed, "It's him. The killer."

And my suspicions were correct—he had Ethan. We had to do something!

I pulled Jake toward me, yanking him down to my level so I could whisper in his ear. "I'm going to climb up onto the balcony and you go around to the front of the hotel room and knock on the door to distract them. But don't let Bryce get you inside, okay? I just need him looking away from the balcony."

Jake shook his head, eyes wide. "No way. *I'll* climb up."

"It won't work." I pleaded with my eyes. "If he opens the door and sees me, I'm toast."

Besides, Jake had a good several inches on Bryce and was strong from all the work he did restoring his grandfather's car and going running along the beach. So if Bryce tried to grab him, he'd have a fighting chance of resisting.

"Do you trust me?" I asked.

Jake closed his eyes for a moment, but he nodded.

"Help me move this table."

As quietly as we could, we lifted the table from the court yard of the room on the ground floor and gently placed it next to the slatted divider that provided privacy from the next room's courtyard. I could climb onto the table and then get a foothold in one of the slats to hoist myself up onto the balcony. Ethan and Matt had been able to do it, so I knew it was possible.

Glancing up, I gulped.

If I was being honest this *did* feel a little beyond my physical skill set. Yoga had barely taught me to balance on one foot, let alone scale a second-floor balcony. But I needed the element of surprise.

Jake disappeared back around the corner of the hotel and I counted to sixty before I started to climb up. The first bit— getting onto the table—was easy. But my sneakers didn't want to find purchase between the wood slats on the courtyard divider because the rubber sole was too bulky. I also lacked the upper-body strength to simply grab the lip of the balcony and haul myself up.

I'd never completed a chin-up in my life, so why did I think I would be able to do one now?

"Just sign it." Bryce's usually lazy voice was filled with prickling agitation. "You're delaying the inevitable."

"I won't admit to something I haven't done." Ethan sounded surprisingly calm. "I won't let you frame me."

Trying not to panic, I planted my feet flat against the wood and used the high-grip rubber soles to help me stabilize. Then I inched my way up, jamming my fingers between the slats and doing the most awkward climb up in existence.

"Why are you doing this?" Ethan sounded desperate. I *had* to get him out of there.

"Because Aaron was sticking his nose in my business, just like you and that nosy blond woman have been doing."

My fingers tightened on the next run of slats.

"Your business being drugging women so you can hurt them." Ethan's voice was filled with acid. "You deserve to be locked up."

"Don't act so high and mighty, Ethan," Bryce said in a dismissive tone. "Those women are always flaunting themselves if they think it will get them what they want. Why is this any different?"

I had to stop myself from screaming out loud. Bryce was a real piece of work.

I hoisted myself up another rung.

"You'll have to force those pills down my throat," Ethan said. "I'm not going to help you get away with *any* of this."

"I did it before, I'll do it again," Bryce snarled.

There it is. Bryce killed Aaron, no doubt about it.

I finally got high enough that I could reach out for the ironwork on the balcony. It had an intricate design, which provided several places to hold on to, and I curled my fingers tight around one of the rails. Then I shimmied myself into a position where I was standing on the top edge of the courtyard divider, hopefully out of sight of the window.

But if anyone came outside . . .

My cover would be well and truly blown and there would be nowhere to go but down.

A single plant sat on the balcony in a heavy-looking terracotta pot. I'd noticed it here previously. It wasn't a great weapon, but a crack over the head should slow Bryce down enough for us to get Ethan out of the room.

"You didn't have to kill him," Ethan said, his voice dripping with disgust. "You *chose* to kill him because you're a terrible human being."

"You should be grateful I took someone out of your way. You'll never measure up otherwise. You lack the drive to *hunt*, Ethan." There was a yelp inside and I cringed, praying that

Jake was almost at the front door. "You don't have that killer instinct Makani and Aaron have."

"Aaron *had*," Ethan corrected him, his voice raw.

Knock, knock, knock.

The room went silent. This was my moment. I heard a muffled voice, which must have been Jake on the other side of the hotel door. Holding my breath, I swung one leg over the balcony railing and pushed off from the divider. Suppressing a squeak as I—stupidly—looked down, I got myself onto the balcony with as soft a landing as I could manage.

Through the glass, I could see where Ethan was on the bed, restrained with what looked to be the belt of a fluffy bathrobe holding his hands behind his back. Bryce was at the door, peering through the peephole. He had a large knife in his hand.

Be careful, Jake.

The knocking continued.

"Ethan?" Jake called out. "I know you're in there."

Bryce swore and I went to grab the pot. Only . . .

I couldn't pick it up. The damn thing weighed as much as the Jellybean! I heaved and it wouldn't budge. Ethan glanced over at me with wide eyes.

I was now without my planned weapon. Bryce was still at the door, his back to the balcony, but I only had seconds before he turned and saw me. Ethan nodded his head to the side, and I looked into the room to where he was indicating. There was a glass bottle of grapefruit juice sitting on the bedside table.

It wouldn't be enough to knock Bryce out. But short of jumping straight off this balcony and possibly breaking both my legs, what other choice did I have? I slipped into the room and grabbed the juice, just as Bryce turned around and saw me.

"You!" He lunged straight for me with the knife and I screamed, swinging the glass bottle at his head.

But he brought his arm up to deflect the blow and the slippery glass flew straight out of my hand and bounced onto the carpet at my feet. Thankfully, it also knocked the knife out of his hands. But then Bryce had both my wrists in his hands, squeezing me tightly, his eyes wild as his plans spun out of control. He looked down at the knife, but Ethan jumped up and kicked it under one of the beds, out of anyone's reach.

"The police are on their way," I shouted to no one in particular. At least, I hoped Grandma Rose had been able to get through. How much time had passed? I had no idea. Panic fluttered in my chest. "You're done, Bryce. They know everything."

"You're bluffing."

I sensed the hesitation in his voice. "Are you going to kill me, too? How will you explain that away? You can't give everyone the same pills without them figuring out what you've done."

His eyes darted back and forth, and I saw him looking at the balcony door. He was going to make a run for it. Behind us, Ethan hobbled over to the front door with his hands still behind his back. He tried to knock the chain out of place with his shoulder so he could let Jake in.

At the sound of the chain dangling, Bryce looked back. He was outnumbered.

He shoved me away from him so hard I stumbled, my calves hitting one of the beds and my knees buckling, causing me to fall onto my back.

"No! Stop him!"

As I was trying to right myself, I saw the door burst open and Jake bolt in, tackling Bryce to the ground right as he made it to the balcony door. Bryce might be good at climbing things, but Jake was miles faster.

"Help me." Ethan was at my side, facing away and shoving his bound hands in my direction. As soon as he was untied, he piled on with Jake, pinning the squirming Bryce to the floor.

And that's when we heard sirens in the distance.

*   *   *

It took a good half an hour for the police to collect all the evidence, including Bryce himself. Detective Alvarez was on the scene—tan pants and shiny black shoes ready to do justice now that she finally admitted there was justice to be served. She talked in hushed tones to some of the officers helping out at the scene, all business.

The police recovered a typed "confession note" that Bryce was trying to make Ethan sign, which outlined how Aaron had been killed and laid claim to the attack on Kaila as well. Plus they took the bottle of pills that Bryce hadn't been able to remove the label from yet, the grapefruit juice, and his satchel, which contained Aaron's missing journal—more "evidence" Bryce had been hoping to plant in framing Ethan for his own crimes.

After the police had taken statements from Ethan, Jake and me, we were released. Now we'd gathered at home, where Matt met us, after Grandma Rose called him to explain what had happened. When I walked through the door, she flung herself into my arms and berated me with such ferocity I thought she might never forgive me. I owed her. Big-time.

Soon we were seated, with cups of tea and leftover blondies I'd baked and frozen a while ago. They were cannabis free, but I found myself wishing for something from the café to help calm my nerves. In fact, as soon as we were done I was going to set up in the kitchen and whip up something with the Christmas Morning sample Niki had given me. Then I would crash. I'd never needed sleep so bad in my entire life. I was *not* fit enough to be climbing onto balconies and wrestling with killers. My once-a-week yoga class just didn't cut it for that.

"Thank you for believing me," Ethan said, his quiet tone cutting into the contemplative silence. He raked a hand through his curly blond hair and Matt looked on with a furrowed brow and lips flattened into a line.

I was sandwiched between Grandma Rose and Jake on the big couch. Jake held my hand on one side and Grandma Rose cradled Antonio, whose tail wagged as he looked around the room, blissfully unaware of what the day had held for us all. He was such a sweet little thing.

"Bryce might have gone on hurting people if not for you listening to me," he continued. "Hell, he might have killed me. I'm forever in your debt."

"We both are," Matt said, his eyes misty as he slung an arm around his younger half brother's shoulders. "If anything happened to Ethan, I would *never* have forgiven myself."

"The police have what they need to put Bryce behind bars," I said, hoping I sounded a lot more grounded than I felt. Things could have gone sideways in a very bad way today. I knew that.

But I also knew I had a group of people around me who had my back. Always.

I glanced at Jake. "I feel like I need to thank you for being ready for anything."

He squeezed my hand. "Maybe next time 'anything' could be more of the spontaneous road trip variety than the 'tackling a killer' variety. Just a thought."

"I'll take it under advisement." I flushed.

Right now, a spontaneous road trip sounded amazing.

"I can't believe it was Bryce all along." Ethan shook his head, a haunted look making his eyes appear distant. "We've worked with him for years. He was a surfer, one of us."

"There are bad eggs in every community," Grandma Rose said sagely.

"I had no idea what happened to Kaila. Aaron never told me, but Bryce thought I knew everything," Ethan said, the shock still making his voice sound hollow. "There was one other girl whose drink he spiked, but he got interrupted before he could take things further. He was muttering about that today."

"She must be the person Mariah mentioned last night." I nodded. "So it was her and Kaila."

I was grateful that we'd stopped Bryce before he could do this to anyone else. Nobody deserved to have drugs foisted on them against their will. Nobody deserved to feel unsafe when they were out with friends. Nobody deserved to be preyed upon. And that was it—Bryce was a predator, through and through.

I would keep Kaila in my thoughts every day until she woke up, and I hoped that she would be able to recover from all this, mentally as well as physically. My heart squeezed thinking about what she'd been through.

"Why would he *do* something like that?" Ethan's lip curled in disgust. "Drugging people's drinks, *murdering* someone. I don't understand it. I tried to get an answer out of him but all he could say was that they had it coming. What kind of an answer is that?"

"Why do any bad people do *anything*?" Matt asked, shaking his head. "They think the rules don't apply to them. They think morals don't matter. They're entitled."

We sat in silence for a moment, contemplating. It was a hard pill to swallow—no pun intended—that no matter how hard we all strived to be good people, there would be others in our midst who didn't.

"Let's be grateful there are still good people in this world like you all." Grandma Rose patted my knee as if reading my thoughts. "And although you're determined to give your old gran a heart attack, Chloe, I'm proud of your tenacity and strong moral compass, anyway."

"Thanks to you, a terrible person is getting the outcome they deserve," Matt said, nodding. "Kaila and the other woman he drugged will receive justice and Aaron's family will know what really happened."

I couldn't take the pain away from Bryce's victims, but I

hoped at least they might have some closure. I made a mental note to call our local florist, Heavy Petal, and have some flowers sent to Kaila's hospital room. It felt paltry in the scheme of what she'd experienced, but I hoped at least that when she woke up to news of Bryce's arrest, she would feel safe again.

"Speaking of which, Aaron's brother Cooper is in town," I said, remembering that I still hadn't filled Ethan in on all the details from Salty's Flamingo Shack yet. "Maybe we could have dinner tonight. We could invite him and Mariah to join us. Make it a celebration of Aaron's life."

"That's a great idea." Ethan's face lit up. "I'll go call them now."

"I'll head out and get some supplies," Matt said, standing up and dusting himself off. "Like wine. Lots of wine."

"I'll come." I jumped up to join him.

"And you can help me chop some vegetables," Grandma Rose said to Jake, her tone inviting no possible argument.

"I would love to," Jake replied graciously.

And with that, the five of us got to work planning a dinner that would celebrate life and the people who tried to do good in the world. It felt fitting for what I knew of Aaron, someone who lived in the moment and tried to keep his eyes on the future.

Something told me he would have been thrilled to see everyone working together.

CHAPTER 23

One week later . . .

Grandma Rose and I turned off the main strip and walked toward Azalea Bay's premiere nail salon, Nailed It. Cute name, right? I loved this little salon. Everything was white with a touch of sparkle—from the quilted leather chairs studded with shimmering gems, to the pearlescent reception desk just inside the front door, to the elaborate mirrors hanging on the walls. It allowed the impressive display of polish colors to stand out and gave the space a calming feel. There were pedicure chairs along one wall and little stations for manicures along the other side.

After the intense business of the surfing competition week, all my mental hoop jumping around Jake *and* the stress of trying to solve my second murder, it was nice to have a day off to do nothing more than have a little self-care and hang out with my favorite ladies.

I spotted Aunt Dawn waiting outside the salon. When she saw us approaching, she lifted her hand up in a wave, which caused a hefty stack of bangles to slide down her arm and jingle with the motion.

"This was such a good idea," Grandma Rose said, her arm tucked into mine. She was wearing her wig out today and seemed to be getting used to it. She'd even thought about getting a second one that had a slightly curlier style to mix things up. It was great to see her finding her confidence again. I'm sure the fact that she and Lawrence had another dinner on the calendar had something to do with it and, whatever the reason, I was thrilled to see her so happy. "Nothing better than a girls' pampering day, I say."

"I agree."

"Hello, you two," Aunt Dawn said as she reached in for a hug. Her hair tickled my cheek and I caught a whiff of her perfume, which never failed to put a smile on my face. "It's so good to see you in one piece, girlie."

I laughed. "It takes more than one killer to knock me down. Or I guess now that should be it takes more than *two* killers to knock me down."

"You shouldn't joke about that," Grandma Rose admonished. "You could have been seriously hurt."

"I know," I said, nodding my head solemnly. "But now Bryce Whitten is behind bars and that's one less creep on the streets. And it's justice for Aaron's family and for Kaila, too."

Earlier in the week, Ethan had texted me to let me know that Kaila had come out of her medically induced coma. Apparently, they'd completed all the necessary tests and determined that they'd avoided the risk of severe brain swelling after her head injury. She'd woken up to find her family all around her, and had confessed what happened to her the night of the party at Salty's Flamingo Shack.

Bryce had bought her a drink, which he'd spiked, and then he'd tried to corner her in the women's bathroom, just like he had done the first time. Kaila had managed to fight him off when another woman came into the bathroom and startled him, but the experience had left her deeply shaken. Given

Bryce's prominence and standing in the community, Kaila hadn't been sure anyone would believe her. But Aaron had.

Now word of Bryce's deeds was slowly spreading through the community and everyone knew the truth. Kaila and her family were heading back home to Hawaii, where I hoped she would be able to heal. I'd written a letter and asked Ethan to pass it on, letting her know that I was so sorry for what she had been through and that anytime she was in town, she could come to Baked by Chloe. Lunch was on me.

"You're braver than most," Aunt Dawn said, wrapping an arm around my shoulder. "For better or worse."

"I think it's for better," I said. Yes, my tendency to have a bleeding heart and my desire to always stick up for the people who needed help might get me into sticky situations. But wasn't that better than standing on the sidelines letting bad things happen and not doing anything about it? "I want to be the kind of person who helps those around her. You both taught me to be like that. You could have easily dusted your hands off and said 'not my problem' when Mom skipped town. You could have let me end up in the system."

"Never," Grandma Rose said fiercely. "Family is more important than anything."

"Exactly. And now Aaron's and Kaila's families can sleep better at night knowing Bryce is where he belongs." I knew in my heart I'd done the right thing. Dangerous as it might have been.

"You're a stubborn girl," Grandma Rose said, her eyes twinkling. "You get that from me."

Over on the road I noticed a white truck pull up and I caught a glimpse of Maisey through the window. My head snapped toward Aunt Dawn, who suddenly looked a little squeamish. "I hope you both don't mind, but I invited Maisey along to our girls' day."

Excitement and happiness fizzed in my chest. "You want me to meet her *officially*."

"Please don't make a big deal out of this," Aunt Dawn pleaded and suddenly I felt like the aunt and she like the niece. Her cheeks were flushed pink and she glanced nervously over to the car. "I thought this might be a nice way for you to get to know her."

"I promise I will be on my best behavior." I grinned. "I won't put a foot out of line. Just you see! I'll be perfect."

Grandma Rose and Aunt Dawn exchanged looks that told me they doubted it, but I would prove them wrong.

"However," Aunt Dawn continued, a cheeky sparkle decorating her eyes. "I would like the favor to be returned."

"What do you mean?" I frowned.

"I want to meet Jake. *Officially.*" She looked rather smug, since she knew that I would feel obligated to return the favor now that Maisey was joining us at the salon.

"That's a really low move," I grumbled. "You know I can't say no now."

"By the time you get to my age you know how to play dirty." She lifted one shoulder into an unapologetic shrug.

Maisey headed over to us, a nervous smile playing on her lips. Her blond hair was cut shorter than it had been when I'd seen her last and she looked tanned, as though she'd been spending more time outdoors. Her tall frame was dressed in a pair of neat blue jeans, a white linen shirt and a pair of designer pointed-toe flats. Style-wise, she was the antithesis to my aunt. Maisey looked like she belonged in a country club and Aunt Dawn looked like she belonged . . . well, in a weed café.

"It's nice to meet you officially, Maisey," I said, sticking my hand out. I wasn't going to bring up the whole thing about me having her as a murder suspect not too long ago. That wasn't really a good early getting-to-know-you topic of conversation.

"Likewise," she replied, shaking my hand. "Thanks for letting me crash your girls' day."

"You're not crashing, dear." Grandma Rose patted her arm. "We're very happy to have you with us."

I saw Maisey's shoulders relax a little and her smile become easier. Her impending divorce had been a hot topic around town, especially once people found out that Maisey had booted her husband out of her family's company for siphoning money out of their business accounts. I'd heard Starr gossiping about it just the other day. It was one reason Maisey and my aunt were taking things slow with their relationship—better to keep a low profile until all the legal matters were resolved.

And as much as I loved Azalea Bay, there were still some closed-minded people who thought it strange for two women to be together. Ben and Matt sometimes encountered the same thing. As far as I was concerned, the only thing that mattered was whether those two people loved each other and treated each other right. And I had a feeling that Maisey and my aunt were doing exactly that.

"Shall we?" I said, motioning toward the salon. "I don't know about you, but I'm feeling some bright colors today!"

"Maybe hot pink?" Grandma Rose suggested.

"Of course you would suggest pink," I replied with a laugh. "Ooh! Or lime green? Or purple! It seems like a day for something loud and fun, right?"

"I know exactly what you mean." Maisey smiled and I saw her slip her hand into my aunt's as we all entered the salon.

I, for one, was thrilled that my family unit was growing in size. Maisey was joining our day out and Lawrence was coming over for dinner tonight. I wondered if maybe I should invite Jake along, too. He'd stood by me twice now in the face of bad things, and it hadn't seemed to shake his desire to get close to me. In fact, I'd awoken that morning to a text from him.

JAKE: Hope you slept well. Azalea Bay is safer today because of you. Remember that.

As Grandma Rose, Aunt Dawn, Maisey and I were all seated in our fancy quilted chairs and presented with a seemingly endless supply of nail polish colors, I decided that I *would* invite Jake to come for dinner tonight, so long as Grandma Rose was okay with it.

After all, I could hardly encourage my grandmother and aunt to embrace love and discard their insecurities if I couldn't do that myself.

Later that day I was sitting on the couch in the front room of the house, with Antonio tucked into my side and sleeping like the sweet little bean he was. I extended my leg and admired the pretty sparkly violet polish on my toes. The silver and pink glitter particles winked in the light. The pampering had been wonderful and the cheerful color had been putting a smile on my face all afternoon.

As I was sitting there, my phone pinged with an alert to say I had a new email in the Baked by Chloe inbox. There had been quite a few today—including an interview request for a popular foodie podcast, someone asking about gluten-free menu options, and a farm owner inquiring about a potential partnership. This new email had a subject line that told me it wasn't going to be about business, however.

It probably wasn't something I wanted to read at all.

HOW DARE YOU BRING SIN TO OUR TOWN

The all-caps shouted at me from my phone screen and I debated whether I should simply trash the email without opening it. But something in my gut told me to read it. I opened the email with one eye squinted shut.

> Chloe,
> You are a disgrace. I thought you would have been raised better than to open such a foul business in our wonderful town. Your drug café is not welcome here. I suggest you close your business or else face the wrath of

the people who want this town to remain clean and
wholesome.
   We know where you live.

My blood boiled. Baked by Chloe had been open almost a month and I had probably received about four or five such emails.

Not everyone believed that weed should be legal. This was despite all the research that pointed to its benefits, such as the positive impact on the economy and employment opportunities, *and* the fact that having production be regulated protected people who chose to use it, like Grandma Rose and some of the other patients at the cancer clinic.

Rather than simply choosing to exercise their right not to patronize my café, however, these people came into my inbox and threatened me. Everything about my business was aboveboard and ethical: I had an accountant to ensure I paid the right taxes, I paid Erica much higher than minimum wage, and I sourced my ingredients from local farms. Heck, I even furnished the café with secondhand furniture salvaged from charity shops and garage sales up and down the coast. It was sustainable AF!

I was about to delete the email without responding, but something in my gut told me it would be wise to keep the nasty communication saved in my inbox. I'm not sure why. I hadn't kept the others, but there was a niggling little voice in the back of my mind that told me this wouldn't be the last I'd hear about this.

I turned off the screen of my phone and tossed the device onto the other side of the couch. I was *not* going to let some anonymous, narrow-minded, pitchfork-wielding internet troll ruin my evening. Today had been full of laughter and great company and *wholesome* vibes.

"Sometimes humans are the worst," I said to Antonio, who

cracked one eye open as though he felt obligated to listen to me complain, but would much rather keep on sleeping. "Be thankful you're a dog."

At that moment, as if to prove that the world wasn't full of bad eggs, there was a knock at the door and I saw both Lawrence and Jake standing there. Lawrence looked dapper as ever in a pair of gray trousers, a sports coat and one of those fancy silk hankies in his chest pocket. Jake was dressed more casually, but still looked handsome in dark wash jeans, tan leather shoes and a navy-and-white–checked shirt with the sleeves rolled up. The two men were chatting animatedly about something and Jake laughed so loud I could hear him through the door.

I paused, listening to the two men getting to know each other as I felt my heart swell. There might be some nasty folks out there, but I was surrounded by the good ones. The people who jumped in to help, who loved to tell stories and make connections. The ones who wanted to bring positivity and goodness to the world, to uplift others and support their dreams and who loved to laugh and listen and care.

They were the people whose opinions I cared about.

I wrapped my hand around the handle to the front door and just as I was about to open it for our guests, I looked back and saw Grandma Rose standing at the bottom of the stairs, her face lit up like New Year's Eve fireworks. Cancer hadn't dulled her shine. If anything it had given her permission to live more fully than ever.

I decided I would put the nasty email out of my mind and focus on the good things that were happening right here and right now. Family, friendship, and love . . . I might just be able to have it all.

Recipes

Cannabis-Infused Butter (aka Cannabutter)

Infused butter is the backbone of many cannabis baked goods and you can substitute it for a 1:1 ratio for regular butter in any recipe. Beginners can reduce the amount of cannabutter by supplementing regular butter to make up the correct quantity.

Ingredients
  1 oz. high-quality cannabis flowers
  2 cups unsalted butter

Note: these ratios are only a guide. How much cannabis you use will depend on the particular strain you're using, how experienced you are with using cannabis and your personal tolerance levels. If unsure, use less.

Directions
Begin by decarboxylating your weed to make it psychoactive (the process which allows you to experience a high from consuming it):

1. Preheat your oven to 245 degrees F / 120 degrees C with a rack in the middle of the oven.
2. Line a baking sheet with parchment paper.
3. Break up the cannabis flower into smaller pieces to allow it to bake evenly.
4. Now, you have two options. You can either

    A. arrange them evenly across the baking sheet and create a pouch with the parchment paper, or:

    B. place them into an oven/turkey bag. This option might require buying some bags, but it will better help to avoid making your kitchen smell while this process is happening than option A.

5. Bake for 30 minutes. The cannabis should now be a brownish color.

6. Remove from the oven and allow to cool in the bag or parchment pouch.

7. Store in a cool dark place if not using immediately. It's recommended to use within three months.

Now it's time to infuse the butter. This recipe uses a slow cooker, but it's just one of *many* ways to infuse butter. Experiment with the different methods to find the one that suits you best!

1. Grind your decarboxylated cannabis flower to a coarse consistency (think ground coffee). Don't grind it too fine, as it will make it harder to strain your butter later on.

2. Set your slow cooker to low (around 160 degrees F / 70 degrees C, but no more than 200 degrees F / 90 degrees C).

3. Add butter.

4. When the butter is starting to melt, add your decarbed and ground cannabis flowers.

5. Cook for a minimum of three hours, up to eight hours. The longer it cooks, the more potent the flavor of the butter.

6. Once you have cooked for your desired amount of time, turn the slow cooker off and allow butter to cool.

7. Using a fine mesh strainer or a piece of cheesecloth set into a funnel, strain the butter to remove all the plant

matter, which can then be discarded. Be patient, this process can take some time.

8. Store butter in an airtight container in the refrigerator.

Everything But the Kitchen Sink Cookies

These have been a staple in Chloe and Grandma Rose's baking repertoire for years! What a great way to use up all the leftover baking bits and pieces into one yummy snack. Make with canna-butter to give your cookies a higher purpose, or substitute with regular butter in a 1:1 ratio for cookies the whole family can enjoy.

A note on mix-ins: this is where you can let your creativity go wild! Chloe loves to use chocolate chips, pretzels, walnuts and toffee chips. But try anything you like. Crushed up potato chips for a salty crunch, your favorite breakfast cereal, different types of chocolate chips (like white or dark or semisweet), dried fruit, other types of nuts, sprinkles, M&Ms, chopped up brittle or candy bar, marshmallows . . . or anything else your heart desires.

Yield: 12–24 depending on your desired size and dosage. To get the dosage, take the total THC content used in the ¾ cup of cannabutter and divide by number of cookies.

Ingredients
    2 cups of all-purpose flour
    ¾ cup softened cannabutter
    ½ cup packed brown sugar
    ¼ cup granulated sugar
    1 large egg

1 teaspoon of high-quality vanilla extract
1 teaspoon baking soda
½ teaspoon salt
2 cups of mix-ins (see note above)

Directions

1. Add cannabutter and both types of sugar to a medium-sized bowl and use an electric mixer to beat at medium speed until creamy. Alternatively, you can mix in a stand mixer, if you prefer.
2. Beat egg and vanilla into butter mixture.
3. Add dry ingredients (minus mix-ins) to a smaller bowl and stir to combine.
4. Gradually add dry ingredients into wet ingredients until just combined.
5. Add mix-ins and stir to combine.
6. Cover bowl and chill in refrigerator, ideally overnight but at least for a minimum of 3–4 hours.
7. Preheat your oven to 350 degrees F / 180 degrees C.
8. Use a cookie scoop or tablespoon to place dough onto baking sheets lined with parchment paper.
9. Bake for nine minutes and then begin checking for golden exterior. Total bake time will depend on the size of the cookies, but could be up to fourteen minutes.
10. Remove from oven and cool completely (minimum of twenty minutes).

Sparkling Canna-Gria

Aunt Dawn loves sangria, and what better way to take this fruity drink to a higher level than by adding some cannabis and fizz! Perfect for a party or summer barbecue, you can customize to your taste by switching up the fruit with something local and seasonal. Chloe loves a sparkling rosé for a pretty pink touch, but you can substitute for any nonalcoholic sparkling wine.

Yield: 1 pitcher

Ingredients
- 1 lemon, sliced into rounds
- 1 orange, sliced into rounds
- 1 apple, cubed (skin on)
- ½ cup strawberries, halved (you can also switch this out for other seasonal/local fruits like blueberries, blackberries, raspberries, peaches etc.)
- ½ cup cranberry juice
- ½ cup orange juice
- ½ cup lemon juice
- 1 bottle nonalcoholic sparkling wine of choice
- Cannabis tincture of choice (you can use either THC or CBD for this recipe)

Note: Chloe recommends dosing each drink individually rather than dosing the whole jug. This way you can ensure that each drink contains the correct dose and dosages can be adjusted for each individual person. This also helps to avoid overconsumption, as subsequent drinks may be consumed without any THC/CBD product, if required.

Directions
1. Add lemon, orange, apple and strawberry (or any substituted fruits) to your pitcher and muddle lightly.
2. Add cranberry, orange and lemon juice to pitcher. Stir to combine. Seal and refrigerate for at least 1-2 hours, minimum.

3. When ready to serve, pour in sparkling nonalcoholic wine and gently stir.
4. Add ice to serving glass and use ladle to scoop out some fruit. Then top with sangria liquid.
5. Add the desired dose of THC or CBD tincture (follow package instructions) and stir gently to combine.

Acknowledgments

The power of story is its ability to whisk us away from the difficult things we face in our lives. I have known this as a reader for a long time, but I recently learned that this is also true for us authors as well. This book was written and revised while my husband was dealing with some serious medical issues, and being able to feel Grandma Rose's warm embrace, Chloe's tenacity and Aunt Dawn's cheeky smile was something I needed more than I could put into words.

I first must thank the incredible team of EMTs, nurses, doctors, and surgeons at St. Joseph's Hospital here in Toronto, as well as the gastroenterology unit at St. Michael's. You are all angels on earth.

Thank you to my family, who didn't let the fourteen thousand–odd kilometers distance stop them from supporting me in every way they could. Special thanks to my mum, who is easily the strongest person I know and who can always set me on the right path emotionally. To my dad, who knows nothing cheers me up more than a video of the dogs doing silly things. To my sister and Albie, who are both bright sparks of positivity.

Thank you to our friends, who were so ready and willing to

help. To Luke, Jill, Myrna, Shiloh, Keith, Janette, Tammy, Madura, Becca, Erik, Lorne and Calita for being there for us both.

Thank you to my agent, Jill Marsal, my editor, Elizabeth Trout, and the rest of the team at Kensington for your immense patience while I tried (struggled) to juggle everything. Thank you for being patient and kind and not complaining when I took far too long to answer emails.

Most of all, thank you to my amazing husband, Justin. You are a fighter. It would have been understandable if you crumbled, but you fought like a lion. Not only that, but you did it while making friends with everyone who came by your hospital bed, even if they were giving you injections. I love you more than anything.

And to the readers who all took a chance on Chloe and Azalea Bay the first time around, you have my eternal thanks. I couldn't do this without you.

Visit our website at
KensingtonBooks.com
to sign up for our newsletters, read
more from your favorite authors, see
books by series, view reading group
guides, and more!

BOOK CLUB
BETWEEN THE CHAPTERS

Become a Part of Our
Between the Chapters Book Club
Community and Join the Conversation

Betweenthechapters.net

Submit your book review for a chance to win exclusive
Between the Chapters swag you can't get anywhere else!
https://www.kensingtonbooks.com/pages/review/